# JAIL BAIT

*On the street, survival comes at a price...*

Daisy Lane's nightclub is bringing in money, helped by her connections to notorious gangster Roy Kemp. Roy's presence gives Daisy's club an air of glamour, but when he leaves for London the punters disappear, and Daisy's fortunes take a spectacular fall. She takes comfort in her son Eddie, who is growing up as courageous and spirited as his father, but his younger brother Jamie couldn't be more different – deeply disturbed, he is capable of the most brutal violence. Meanwhile there's a killer at work in Gosport. Daisy spots him and takes it upon herself to have him apprehended – with devastating consequences.

This book is dedicated to the specialists, doctors, nurses and staff of Russells Hall Hospital, Dudley, West Midlands. Thank you for giving me back my life.

# JAIL BAIT

*by*

June Hampson

**Magna Large Print Books**
Long Preston, North Yorkshire,
BD23 4ND, England.

British Library Cataloguing in Publication Data.

Hampson, June
Jail bait.

A catalogue record of this book is
available from the British Library

ISBN 978-0-7505-3375-1

First published in Great Britain in 2010 by Orion Books
an imprint of The Orion Publishing Group Ltd.

Copyright © June Hampson 2010

Cover illustration © Ilona Wellman by arrangement with
Arcangel Images

The moral right of June Hampson to be identified as the author of this
work has been asserted by her in accordance with the Copyright,
Designs and Patents Act, 1988

Published in Large Print 2011 by arrangement with
Orion Publishing Group

Magna Large Print is an imprint of Library Magna Books Ltd.

Printed and bound in Great Britain by
T.J. (International) Ltd., Cornwall, PL28 8RW

There is no wealth but life

JOHN RUSKIN

# Acknowledgements

Grateful thanks to my loyal readers. God bless you all. And as always, Orion's brilliant team who are like a family to me. And Juliet Burton, a very special agent.

# CHAPTER 1

Lol, eyes closed, stretched her neck up so she wouldn't have to see his face. He was holding her arms, his spit dribbling from his grunting mouth as he ripped into her.

'You fuckin' love it!' The others were yelling and laughing, watching and waiting as she continued to struggle, the gravel cutting into her flesh. Tears were running down her face. God, how it hurt.

'Lemme go, you fuckin' bastard!' Amazingly, he lifted himself from her back and rolled off. For a moment he lay on his side.

Her body raw, Lol moaned, opening her eyes, and made to rise from the dirt. The smell of his sweaty flesh and the horror of what had been done to her forced her to puke, and she tried in vain to wipe her long hair away from the vomit.

'Help me,' she whispered, looking up at them. But now the man was standing and Lol could do no more than watch as he bent and grabbed her by what remained of her skirt and blouse, lifted her, and swung his other arm in a stiff arc, hitting her mouth with his clenched fist.

'Anyone else want a go?' he growled before throwing Lol down again as though she was a rag doll.

Someone slapped the man on the back and he laughed then staggered away from her. Lol closed her eyes. No one, nothing could help her now.

She lay there, afraid even to moan. From some-where came the muted sounds of Abba.

'You're cute.' A second man was bending to-wards her now, licking his lips. He mumbled something and shoved a red froth of lace in her broken face. Her panties. The laughter grew. 'You certainly know how to get a bloke all of a quiver, you do.'

'Ma! Come 'ere!'

But Eddie Lane didn't wait for his mother. He could see what looked like a woman struggling with a man in the near darkness of the alley near the tobacconist's shop. He turned from the win-dow and elbowed his way through the drunken crowd celebrating Red Rum's third Aintree Grand National win. Out through Daisychains' brass and wood door, and then he was quickly across the road towards the ferry, narrowly missing being hit by a car and running straight into the small crowd of young thugs.

'Get off 'er!' He yanked at the clothing of a bare-arsed bloke about to give his all to the girl face down on the ground. While the man clutched at his genitals, Eddie hit him – a well aimed punch that lifted the bloke off his feet and sent him staggering back into his group of mates.

Eddie stepped back, his hand sliding to the breast pocket of his leather jacket. He withdrew his knife and pressed the button that locked the blade in the open position. The silence was now palpable.

'Which of you fuckers want this?' Eddie was breathing hard. He was also aware that at nearly

12

seventeen he was probably younger than at least three of the men but he was banking on the blade scaring the shit out of them. He thanked God he was tall, well built, and had had the advantage of growing up on Gosport's tough streets. He stood his ground.

A voice yelled, 'The fucker wouldn't dare...'

'I ain't takin' the bleedin' chance,' said another.

He noted it took less than a blink of an eyelid for the group to clear and for the coward adjusting his clothing to yell back at him from the safe distance of Rennie's Boatyard's entrance along Beach Street.

'Fuckin' freak!'

Eddie breathed a sigh of relief. His heart was beating like a fucking hammer drill. Despite his practised skill with the blade he hadn't had the faintest idea what he would do if the group had called his bluff. He put away the knife and bent down to the girl.

At first she screamed, 'Get off me!' then fell back, rolling on her side, crying and groaning. He stared at the blood in her blonde hair and the cuts on her skin from the sharp gravel. He put out a hand and stroked the side of her face. She flinched as his fingers made contact and struck out at him, sobbing.

'No more!'

Eddie grabbed at both her flailing hands, noticing that several of her long painted nails had been torn away.

'Relax,' he said. Her small heartshaped face was streaked with mascara and she'd lost one false eyelash. His heart went out to her; his Auntie

13

Vera was always having trouble with her false eyelashes and his mum was forever fixing them. 'I'm not going to hurt you,' he said.

She tried to yank her hands free.

'Relax,' he said again. And then she opened her lids and looked pleadingly up at him with frightened eyes: violet eyes, swimming with tears, pitifully searched his face. He stared at her, past her straight nose below which a very kissable mouth trembled, despite a top lip split in two places, while blood was fast drying into the heavy puffiness already covering one side of her face.

'They've gone,' Eddie said, letting go of her wrists, which felt small and fragile, almost birdlike.

The girl's eyes went right through him as if he was naked. He squirmed beneath her gaze and then he was pushed aside.

'Come out the way, let the dog see the bleedin' rabbit!'

He stepped back and the fierce small woman hunkered down in front of the girl – no mean feat, for Vera was wearing a tight skirt and four-inch heels. A waft of her heavy perfume flew into his nostrils.

'How bad is she hurt, Vera?'

'How the fuck do I know when I ain't looked at 'er yet. Let's get her back to the safety of Daisychains,' she said. 'People are beginning to gawp.'

'If it had been darker you'd not have noticed the bastards as did this,' said Daisy, his mother, who had followed Vera out of the club. She put her hand on her son's arm. 'Wouldn't you 'ave thought that at least someone else would have stepped in and stopped this before it got ugly?'

'People are scared of gettin' involved, Daisy. It was lucky for 'er Eddie looked out the window.'

His mother didn't answer Vera, but smoothed back the hair that had fallen across the girl's face. 'You're safe now,' she said, and there was no mistaking the compassion in her voice. Then to Eddie, 'Give us your coat to cover her with, son.'

He slipped out of his leather jacket and handed it to Daisy, who said, 'You'll be getting a reputation like your father 'ad for flashin' that fucking knife about. You know I don't like that thing, even though it served its purpose this time.' She looked down at the girl. 'C'mon, sweetheart, let's get you sorted out.' They pulled the girl gently back into a sitting position and slipped Eddie's jacket around her.

'I ... I'll be ... I'll be all right.'

She was struggling to gather her torn clothing around herself when there was a gasp from Vera, who was helping her. 'Fuck me!'

'Oh!' Daisy whispered. She turned her head and stared up at Eddie.

'What's the matter, Mum? She's going to be all right, ain't she?'

He couldn't explain but it suddenly mattered very much to him that the girl would be safe and sound.

'We'll do our very best, son. You probably saved her life. Carry her over to Daisychains.' He could determine nothing from his mother's steady gaze until she whispered, 'Only this little girl ain't a she, he's a he!'

# CHAPTER 2

'We're losing money every fuckin' day.' Daisy waved the small wad of notes she'd just removed from the till beneath Vera's nose.

'Calm yourself, Dais, you'll give yourself an 'eart attack!' Vera pushed Daisy's hand away and continued leaning on the bar top. 'What d'yer expect?' She waved a scarlet-nailed hand around Daisychains' near empty bar. 'You wants this place run squeaky clean, so without the pull of drugs the punters goes elsewhere. You can't bloody blame 'em.'

Daisy sighed, folded the notes, and slammed the till drawer shut. She put the notes in her pocket. 'We're goin' under, Vera. Can't afford decent wages no more for top line girls so we have to make do with scrubbers.' Vera opened her mouth but Daisy stopped her. 'Let me finish. I'd like to smarten the club up a bit, a lick of paint 'ere and there. Maybe that'd liven things up.' She took a deep breath, and smelled only polish and air freshener. At this time of night the club should be reeking of fags and men and the leathery smell of their plump wallets, she thought.

'The outside do look shabby, Dais...' Vera walked to a table and picked up a lone fag packet that she brought back to the bar and placed on an empty ash tray.

Daisy stared at Vera's trim small body in her

tight black skirt and red frilled silk blouse, wafting her trademark perfume about her.

'There just ain't the cash, Vera.' Daisy pointed across the room to where a good looking man in jeans and flowered shirt was rubbing a table with a yellow duster. 'Even Alec gives us a couple of hours' work a day for free.' Daisy gazed at the man who, feeling her eyes upon him, looked up with a smile that transformed his sad face.

'Only because the school's closed, Daisy, an' he don't 'ave to get up in the mornin's. He can't teach when there ain't no kids there, can he? Thank God teachers get paid during the 'olidays so he don't mind workin' for nothing.' Vera leant forward and whispered, 'He only comes in because he likes you, Dais, an' I reckon he needs a bit of company. Lately he's seemed more depressed than usual...' Vera's eyes fixed on Alec and Daisy could see she was deep in thought, then Vera straightened up and said, 'But if we can't afford to pay staff we certainly can't afford no tins of bleedin' paint.'

'Shut up about the fuckin' paint. And an alcoholic workin' in a pub is enough to make anyone depressed,' said Daisy. She remembered when Alec had been a defeated man, hunched on his patch opposite the club outside the men's urinals. People travelling by bus and ferry boat to Portsmouth chucked coins into a tin for him, if he was lucky. He was a pavement artist of the highest calibre but a drunk as well. He'd had long matted hair and he'd stunk to high heaven.

She and Vera had got him into a special detox programme over in Portsmouth and he'd been clean ever since. More than clean. He'd embraced life and gone back to teaching, but there were times like today when Daisy could almost reach out and touch his loneliness.

Daisy saw Vera's eyes take in the four male customers huddled over their dregs of beer. David Soul was singing 'Don't Give Up On Us Baby' and Daisy wished with all her heart that she wouldn't have to give up on the club she'd fought so hard to keep running. 'I sent the croupiers home, Vera. There's no punters at the gaming tables.'

'But it's not even midnight, Dais.'

Daisy shrugged. 'We used to 'ave such a lot of fun in 'ere, didn't we?' She looked at the clock and her voice was wistful as she added, 'Remember when the Kray twins brought that gangster film star George Raft in 'ere? All our girls were over 'im like a bleedin' rash.'

She saw Vera smile. 'Customers was fallin' over themselves to get in then, but you can't live in the past. Roy was around a lot in them days an' he brought a sort of swagger to the place.'

'What you're sayin', Vera, is the place 'as gone downhill since I made Roy opt out of this club an take his bleedin' drug deals with 'im.'

Vera shrugged.

'So, it's me own fault, is it? Don't you understand I didn't want my boys, Eddie and Jamie, brought up in a bloody druggie's paradise?'

Vera held her gaze steady.

'You could let me put some money in, Dais?'

'Don't you fuckin' patronise me!' Daisy snapped. She tapped her fingers angrily on the bar top, but she knew that without help of some kind

18

there was no way she could pay the pile of household bills and club invoices she'd hidden at home in a drawer. It had got to the stage where she didn't even open the envelopes any more, just dumped them in the kitchen cabinet to join the others as soon as the postman delivered them.

But pride wouldn't let her accept Vera's money. Her outburst had caused her friend's face to crumple in on itself like a screwed up paper bag. Daisy knew the offer was genuine but she also knew the high street massage parlour Vera owned was going through a slump.

Birth control pills had taken away the fear of unwanted pregnancies and women were giving sex away like sweets from a bag. Only the regular johns went to Vera's shop, Heavenly Bodies, now. Nevertheless, Daisy knew she shouldn't have snapped at her friend.

And no way was she going to worry her further by telling her she suspected some bloke was spying on herself – or on the goings-on in the club. Twice Daisy thought she'd caught a glimpse of the same dark-haired man peeping through the smoked glass windows of Daisychains, but he'd melted away into the shadows before she'd copped a better look at him. It wasn't worth worrying about, she told herself.

'I'm sorry,' she said, with a deep sigh that shook her body.

Vera took out a silk handkerchief and dabbed at her eyes. 'It's all right. I knows you're upset. You're findin' it difficult to cope lookin' after everyone at home.' Daisy put her head to one side and shrugged. It was her duty to look after her two

19

boys, Eddie and Jamie, as well as Susie and young Joy, wasn't it? Susie had lived with Daisy for years and was a damn good friend to her and Joy, Susie's daughter, was a lovely little dot of a girl. Vera wasn't finished talking, though. 'And then you willingly takes on the burden of Lol.'

Daisy thought of her large house in Alverstoke. A roof over everyone's head was one thing, feeding them and paying the bills was another. But they were *her* family, weren't they? She'd manage somehow. Hadn't she always until now? She certainly wasn't afraid of hard work, and it wasn't as though her boy Eddie and friend Susie didn't contribute when they could. And she was always finding five-pound notes tucked in her purse that she knew Vera had put there. Daisy put her arm around Vera's shoulder. Vera was just letting off a bit of steam. She knew Vera liked Lol as much as she did.

'Lol's all right. I likes the way she keeps an eye on your bleedin' false eyelashes for me. She straightens 'em better'n I do!' In all the years Daisy had known Vera she'd never seen her put her false eyelashes on straight.

'She knows loads about fashion an' make-up,' said Vera, giving a sniff into her handkerchief.

'I wonder why she's called Lol?'

'Lol, short for Lolly. Her real name's Laurence.'

Daisy knew she was blushing. 'Oh! I'm a bit of a dimwit, ain't I?' She poked Vera in the arm and grinned. 'Anyway, I like 'avin' her around.' Daisy giggled. 'You remember that other trannie you 'ad workin' for you? Marie looked like a bleedin' 'orse an' was as big as one an' all. My Eddie was only a little dot then, but I remember 'ow he used to gaze at 'er. I'll say one thing, Vera, at least me boys get to see the real side of life. And Lol? I knows she'll pull 'er weight when she gets over that fuckin' dreadful experience...'

'Lol don't show her feelin's on the outside, Dais. She knows a lot about all sorts of things, you know, 'ighbrow stuff like good books an' antiques. I reckon she went to some posh school. An' she wasn't brought up in no backstreet, neither. She can talk to anybody, Dais. She gets on well with me girls, especially Samantha.'

'Everyone gets on well with your girls, they're the most proficient prossies in Gosport.'

'Don't mean everyone likes 'em, Dais.' Vera looked thoughtful and fiddled with her black curls. Her words came out in a rush as she groped for the tall stool behind her and hoisted herself up on it. ''Ere, Sam's asked me for 'er savin's again, and she's been heard muttering words in some foreign language, Spanish or Italian, like.'

Samantha had worked for Heavenly Bodies since she'd been a teenager. Surely she wasn't about to leave Vera in the lurch?

Daisy said, 'Not like 'er to leave a sinkin' ship, is it? Perhaps she's takin' a foreign 'oliday and wants to learn a bit of the lingo. But it is her money. Has she said what she wants it for?'

'I never asked. She's such a silly bitch with cash. I ain't got over the fuss she caused when she bought into that Lee-on-the-Solent caff an' it went tits over arse before it started, 'cos they stole 'er money and scarpered.'

Daisy sniffed and pushed her black roll-neck

21

jumper's sleeves further up her arms. 'I remember the police was about as useful as a chocolate bucket about that.'

'Your Vinnie should have sorted that little scam out, Dais. Poor Sam.'

Daisy snapped. 'How many times do I 'ave to say he ain't my Vinnie!'

Daisy knew Vera wouldn't leave the argument there. When she got something to chew on she was like a dog with a bleedin' bone.

'DCI Vinnie Endersby might be living in a posh 'ouse in the country all hunky-dory with his wife, but you got his son an' if you needed 'im he'd be down 'ere back to Gosport faster than a cork from a pop gun,' said Vera.

Daisy glared at her. 'You might be right. But all that with Samantha happened a while ago an' she ain't bothered about it now, is she?'

Vera shook her head and used a finger to trace a pattern in a puddle of beer on the counter.

'Roy then, he should 'ave sorted it out...' Vera slid off the stool and stood back from the bar with her hands on her hips determined to have the last word, but Daisy wouldn't let her.

'Will you stop it? You know I 'ardly see Roy nowadays, and anyway, he's busy up in the Smoke.'

'Not so busy that he ain't got time for a bit on the side!'

Vera was about to walk out of the bar. Daisy was well used to Vera's 'parting shots' as she called them, but she didn't want to be reminded that Roy was paying a great deal of attention to a blonde called Eve. Stupid name for a woman, Daisy thought. Small and skinny she was, and

Daisy was reminded of herself when she was ten years younger. 'A man can't live on bread alone,' Daisy muttered.

'He's got a bit of cake there, though, ain't he?'

'Shut up!'

'If you'd paid 'im a bit more attention things might 'ave been different,' said Vera. She edged back to Daisy and stood watching for her reaction.

'Anyway,' said Daisy, who knew the words Vera flung at her were the truth, 'he's got problems.'

'Oh, yeah?'

Daisy decided the only way to get Vera to stop nagging at her was to tell her what she knew. It wasn't as if they usually kept secrets from each other. She took a deep breath.

'Sit down again, you silly tart.' Vera wriggled herself back on the high stool. 'There's this snout, Bertie Smalls. He's been givin' Roy grief getting in on this supergrass act. And another bastard, Maurie Nelson, is tryin' to put Roy out of business 'cos he's working with the coppers as well. He wants to take over Roy's empire.' Vera let out a gasp of breath. Daisy continued, 'It's like every bleedin' thing that Roy does the coppers know before he does it!'

'What d'you mean?' Vera had put her elbows on the bar and her chin in her hands.

'Well, Nelson's an informer, an ex-robber who's got the fuckin' rozzers in the palm of his hand.' Daisy could see Vera was puzzled. 'They've given 'im police immunity as long as he informs on the underworld.'

'That's not nice, Dais. I thought there was some unwritten law about honour among thieves?'

23

'Not any more. It seems that fat little git Smalls is doin' some whisperin' about jobs what Roy's been involved in. An' Nelson reckons now the Krays is banged up, Roy should be back in the nick as well.'

'But Roy's always given backhanders to the cops to turn a blind eye to his businesses. Ain't he got that Drury bloke, you know, 'im from the Flyin' Squad, on his payroll?'

'It's all fallin' apart, Vera. The Sweeney's under suspicion. Since that new bloke Mark got to be commissioner he's been doin' his 'ardest to cut corruption. And that ain't all...'

'What?' Vera sat back, a frown on her face.

'Roy's mate, Teddy Baird...'

'Who's that?'

Daisy sighed deeply. She really thought Vera would have remembered Biffo Baird.

'The bleedin' actor bloke what can stand six pint glasses on his hard-on–'

'Daisy Lane, you should wash your mouth out with soap!'

'You remember him now, don't you?' Daisy saw Vera's eyes were twinkling.

'He's that big bloke, all cuddly, always ready for a laugh.'

'That's 'im. Princess Margaret found him cuddly as well, so the story goes. Not that I believe it. And Biffo don't say a dicky bird,' smiled Daisy.

'Hush your mouth, that's our Royalty you're speakin' about. Anyway, I know he's been Roy's oppo for years, an' even you've known 'im for ages, Dais.'

Daisy nodded. She turned and poured herself

and Vera a couple of inches of orange juice into two clean glasses and then filled them with water from a jug on the bar. She pushed one across to Vera. She thought back to the first time she'd met Teddy Baird, way back in the sixties.

She'd gone to Roy's house in London and found him sitting upstairs in the meeting room with the Krays and the Richardsons along with Roy. Roy's mother had pressed her to take up a tray of tea and freshly baked scones.

'Call me Biffo,' he'd said, standing up and offering her a hand the size of a dinner plate. His handshake was warm and firm and Daisy liked him, instantly.

At the time she'd thought the name had stuck because he was a cuddly bear of a bloke. Roy had soon put her right. 'Cross 'im an' he'll biff you one,' he'd said.

'Wasn't he in that film with Carol White? *Poor Cow.*' Vera didn't wait for Daisy's answer. 'I loved that film. What's Biffo up to now?' She took a swallow of the orange drink.

'He's just got back from America where he was supposed to be lookin' out for that rock group, Led Zeppelin. 'Cept he caused bother over there an' they got rid of 'im. Now he's back 'ere givin' Roy grief because he ain't got no money.'

'I thought he was doin' all right.' Vera pursed her lips.

'He is, or was. A bit of television, some films as well, but the tax man's after 'im an' he likes to drink an' take a few other recreational pleasures.'

'An' 'ow the bleedin' 'ell do you know all this, Daisy Lane?'

Daisy tapped the side of her nose. 'Roy and Biffo look after each other. A bit like Roy an' me lookin' after each other. Just because Roy's got a bit on the side don't mean Roy an' me ain't still good friends. Besides, Roy's got my Eddie workin' for 'im sometimes, ain't he?'

Daisy didn't really like it that her Eddie, her firstborn son, dark and good looking, the image of his late father, also Eddie Lane, was involved with Roy's nefarious businesses. But she also knew Roy loved him like he was his own and he'd die sooner than let anyone harm him.

'Roy Kemp might be a gangster but he's got a bleedin' 'eart of gold as long as you don't ruffle 'is feathers.'

'Ain't that exactly what them informers is doin'?'

'Too right, Vera. With Nelson and Smalls doin' 'im down he needs eyes up his arse. But like I said, Teddy Baird's a good mate.'

Vera shrugged. 'Your Eddie's a good boy as well.' A shadow crossed her face and she spoke now in a low voice. 'A different kettle of fish to your other boy, Jamie—'

'Don't start!'

But Daisy's heart plummeted. She wondered where her life was heading with a club that was going broke, bills she couldn't pay and two sons she adored but had no control over.

# CHAPTER 3

She was never again going back to Vera's massage parlour in the High Street. At long last she had a future! It wasn't as though she was unhappy there with the rest of the girls but she wanted something more out of life. Despite the murky darkness, Samantha caught a glimpse of herself in a shop window; she straightened herself to her full height of five foot three and continued striding purposefully.

It'd worked for Kirsty, Samantha thought. She'd got out of Heavenly Bodies and now she was married to one of *her* customers, living in Australia *and* expecting his baby. And Kirsty had been working for Vera just as long as Samantha had, which had to be ... what was it? Fifteen years at least!

'Shit!' One of Samantha's high heels slid on the cobbles, turning her ankle. She stopped in the night mist that clouded the lonely street to Tragedy Bank and checked her nylons weren't laddered. She didn't want to be less than perfect when she met Bruno.

Everything was good. She rubbed her foot and then hugged her black plastic handbag to her ample body. Inside it held all her savings, earned from fucking Vera's customers.

Vera hadn't asked her *why* she'd wanted her savings this time. Last year when Samantha had demanded the nest egg Vera kept safe for her, Vera had kicked up a fuss. Sam had planned on going into business with another of the girls, a redhead who'd recently joined Heavenly Bodies. The tea shop in Lee-on-the-Solent was run down but Sam was persuaded it would soon become a going concern. The day after Sam had handed over her money the girl never turned up for work. It was then she realised she'd been well and truly conned.

Samantha loved Vera for not prying this time, and she felt bad she hadn't been able to share her good fortune with her friend and mentor.

But Bruno wanted their special love kept secret and she'd been persuaded to agree with him. Anyway she didn't want anyone letting on to him about *her* secret, did she? It would be awful if he found out she normally worked in a massage parlour. He'd leave her for sure, and she loved him so much. Especially the way he talked with his English all mixed up with Italian. Though normally he didn't say very much. When he did speak, his main conversation was how wonderful his country was and how clever his fellow Italians were. Sometimes she wondered why he'd bothered to come to England.

'English people don't really like the Italians,' he'd confided. 'They reckon we got no backbone. It was the war, you see?'

Samantha didn't know what he was on about and didn't care, though she knew the other girls would tease her about going around with a 'fuckin' Eyetie'.

Her father wouldn't have minded. He was Polish. Paul Kowalski had come along at just the right time for her mother, who was living with her sadness after losing her husband in the war. The Pole, who was younger than her mother, took on her child and then fathered another one who was Samantha. Her father was dark-eyed and full of fun and she'd never got over it when a gas explosion took the lives of her brother and her parents. It would have taken her as well if she hadn't been on a school trip to London for the day.

She'd grown up in a children's home because every potential foster parent only seemed to want babies. As to adoptive parents, that was where the babies won out *every* time. Samantha hadn't been allowed to grow up like most children though. She thought about the church in the home's grounds, recalling its smell of burnt candles and damp. She remembered Father's coarse black cassock beneath her bare legs as he'd bade her sit on his lap. She remembered the hardness that had grown beneath it.

'Can you feel me, child?' he'd asked. Her heart had been pounding but she'd been too scared to get off and run away so she said dutifully, 'Yes, Father.'

'You know what to do, don't you?'

And so she'd wriggled around on the hardness like he wanted her to, and all the while he grunted and his knobbly Adam's apple tried to free itself from his white dog collar until he groaned like he was dying, then flopped back on the pew. Samantha was allowed to go, then. To climb off the sticky stuff which had seeped through his black gown and join the other children as they played in the quadrangle.

The Father came to her at night as well. He

29

would lie on the scratchy blankets making her do things to him that made her feel sick. Samantha would breathe a sigh of relief when his footsteps stopped before they got to her dormitory bed. Of course she was sad for the girl who was going to be the Holy Father's partner for the night but at least *she* had a reprieve.

Samantha ran away from the home when she was nearly thirteen and soon realised that selling her body could pay for food and somewhere to sleep. She found she could get money by trading what the priest had taken for nothing. But then a nosy parker of a bloke had told this brass that Sam had been kipping on the Gosport ferry boats and flaunting her fanny. Samantha sailed to Portsmouth and the Guildhall steps and stayed for a couple of years, finding solace with the sailors.

So she was fifteen when she met Vera by her pitch down near Gosport ferry's taxi rank.

Vera was her saviour, even if she had marched down the pontoon yelling, 'Come off that boat, you little cow. Don't you know somethin' bad could 'appen to you?'

Vera looked out for her, got her a room in Bert's Caff. Not that Bert allowed her to take men up to her room. No, he was too straight for that. But when Vera bought the premises in the High Street that she turned into Heavenly Bodies, her beloved massage parlour, Samantha went with her to work there.

And now she was going to be married!

It hurt her that she couldn't share her good news with her oldest friend but she so wanted to please the man who loved her.

Only he didn't really *know* what she did for a living, did he? That was *her* secret.

Bruno believed she was a barmaid in Daisy-chains, Daisy Lane's place opposite the Gosport ferry. That's where they'd met. Of course he hadn't been a customer buying a drink, he'd been waiting outside in the shadows. Said he'd spotted her through the window and fallen in love with her. Love at first sight! Samantha had been filling in for Emm who was off sick. But when she looked into Bruno's long-lashed brown eyes she felt as though she was being sucked into heaven.

God, but her legs ached. Tonight she'd been run off her feet in the bar. An American cruiser had moored in the Dockyard and all the sailors were after fanny and ale. Vera and Daisy had rubbed their hands together with happiness. It had been a long while since the bar had been so full.

Bruno didn't approve of women who worked in clubs and bars.

'Bad women,' he'd said. 'These women go with men. You must leave.'

Samantha liked the idea that he might be jealous.

Then he'd told her of an Italian married woman who had been stoned to death for taking a lover! Samantha decided she'd never let on about her past.

Bruno had even quizzed her about the man's ring she wore on her left thumb. He swore it belonged to a past love – which, in a way, it had. It had belonged to her father.

Two days after the gas explosion, Samantha walked out to Clayhall from the Portsmouth

31

Children's Home and steeled herself to look at the gap in the houses that had been her home in Waterloo Road.

Blackened bricks, broken slates and smashed glass filled the spot where number nineteen had stood. She poked around in the ruins, hoping to find a memory or two that hadn't already been scavenged, but the waterlogged mess was simply that, a waterlogged mess that stank of grease.

Samantha sat on a pile of bricks and cried. When she had finished crying she took her fists away from her eyes and saw a glitter of green sparkling near her right shoe: her father's ring. After she had dug out the silver band with the green stone set in it she didn't even bother to clean it but slipped it on each finger in turn. Her thumb was the only digit from which it didn't fall. And there it stayed to this day.

She turned her hand to look at the ring's now polished brightness. Never had she seen another ring like it.

'It belonged to my father and his father before him.' Samantha remembered her father's words as though he spoke them only yesterday.

Maybe she would pass the ring on to her firstborn son!

Bruno had promised to take her back to his family in Italy! She'd seen a photograph of his stern-faced Mamma, clothed in black. Only a head and shoulders print but he carried it in his wallet next to a photograph of the Pope.

They'd be married in Pettorano Sul Gisio, a tiny village in the hills near Rome, he'd told her. There, the sun shone, the olive trees provided fat juicy fruit to be harvested, and the very air smelled of sweetness.

She'd be Signora Bruno Pace: his surname meant peace in Italian. They would live together in a big house with his sisters and their husbands and children, many children. She'd like that, she thought, to be part of a large loving family.

Not that Vera and the girls weren't a sort of family; they were. A family of caring whores.

*'Non ti scordar di me,'* he'd whisper. She knew it meant she was his little forget-me-not.

Samantha didn't know much Italian but it didn't matter. Words didn't seem to matter when she *knew* he loved her.

*'Andiamo via,'* he'd said. 'Let's go away.' And her heart had risen like a bird in flight. It was one thing having a bloke banging away at you with his cock and no feelings except wanting to come inside you. It was another matter for a handsome man to be telling you he wanted you to run away with him.

And he was *so* bloody good-looking. He wasn't tall, barely her height, but with that dark soft curly hair and those deep pools for eyes who cared? Anyway, they fitted together exactly right when they went to bed in his lodgings in South Street. She sometimes wondered if the secrecy thing didn't go too far for he always took her into the house through the alleyway and the back scullery door.

But since that first time two weeks ago she'd been with him almost every night after her shift ended at Daisychains.

And he wanted to know all about her life

behind the bar, about Daisy, about the gangster Roy Kemp who had made it possible for Daisy and Vera to open the club in the first place. Bruno had said didn't that prove how much Roy Kemp loved Daisy? Enough to spend plenty of money on her at any rate!

Samantha had felt a momentary pain in her heart. For the Italian never had any money to spend on her. It was all tied up in the family olive business and he was awaiting a large cheque to be sent to his bank.

'You don't have to worry about money,' she'd told him. 'I have enough for both of us and I know when we get to Italy everything will be just fine.'

'Roy Kemp. He gets his money from drugs. I no like this gangster. Bad man to run club. Bad man with plenty money.'

Fair enough, Samantha had thought. His English was good enough for her to understand he didn't like Roy Kemp and he seemed to know what a gangster was. Only she couldn't be bothered to go through the rigmarole of explaining that Daisychains didn't belong to Roy Kemp any more but to Daisy Lane and Vera. In fact Roy hardly ever showed his face in the place.

She passed the iron railings that divided the road from the moat below the hill that was Tragedy Bank and looked across the stretch of water separating Gosport from Portsmouth. It was too dark to see the actual ships and boats moored there, but the smell of the water and the sounds from the sea were all about her.

Samantha strained her eyes to peer through the darkness.

There he was!

His shortie raincoat tightly belted, he was standing near the dull light of the solitary lamp post. His hands were thrust deep into his pockets as he moved impatiently from one foot to the other. Excitement coursed through her and her tiredness was forgotten as she ran lightly across the cobbles to meet him.

He came towards her, opening his arms so she could slide into them. So what if he was younger than her? What did it matter? They were in love, weren't they?

'You here?' he said in his lovely broken English.

'I'm here,' she said and allowed herself to be pulled through the broken railing to climb the slope to the top of the bank where the trees would hide them and they'd lie beneath the twinkling stars.

Tragedy Bank, so named for the girls who'd conceived unwanted pregnancies there. But for Samantha the bank with its bushes that hid them from prying eyes was a magical place.

'You bring money? All your money?' He took off his raincoat and folded it. They never lay on it. She dropped down beside him on the damp grass.

'Yes.' She ruffled his hair and he immediately started to undress her. First her coat, then her dress, pulling it over her head. She shivered but snuggled into his warmth, breathing in his male scent.

He kissed her for a long time while removing her stockings and pushing his hand through her suspender belt and panties and searching for her wetness.

Little quakes ran up and down her body and Samantha was filled with loving for this wonderful man who was going to liberate her. He wedged his fingers inside her and she felt his cock, big and hard against her skin, searching for its way into her folds. Samantha wriggled to make it easier for him, trying to ignore a stone beneath her back that was cutting into her flesh. And then he slid down her body kissing every part and his lips were on her cunt as he sucked at her with his soft mouth. Samantha thought she would explode with the gloriousness of it all as he wildly moved his tongue around her.

Then he entered her, holding one hand beneath her bottom, pulling her into him. It was violent and desperate and Samantha grasped at him never wanting to let this man, her man, go. He pumped into her flesh, faster and faster, then gasped as his cum flowed.

Almost immediately he rolled off her and lay on his back, gasping. Samantha stroked his soft hair and whispered, 'I love you so much.'

He gazed up at her and she bent her head down and kissed him on his nose. He grinned at her then moved to refasten his clothes. Then he scrambled to his feet and bending down picked up her dress and handed it to her.

'You put on,' he said. Overhead the stars were glittering like diamonds.

Slipping it over her head, she thought at first she'd caught her neck in the dress's folds as she couldn't wriggle free from its tightness. Out of the corner of her eye she thought she saw the foot of her nylon stocking dangling in front of her eyeline. How ridiculous was that? And then she realised Bruno must have slipped something around her neck and he was pulling it tighter.

And then her arms and legs were flying in all directions as she tried to disentangle the thing from her neck that was stopping her from breathing properly. Without breath her senses were slowing down and her struggling was growing weaker.

Her chest was bursting with the desire to breathe. She tried to scream but her mouth was suddenly stretched to its utmost and she could neither close it nor cry out. Bruno had put something in her mouth!

The glittering stars were closer now, but they seemed to be inside her eyes and brighter than anything she had ever seen before. And then she sensed she was sliding along on the grass and then being hoisted up and the tightness around her neck meant she didn't have to breathe at all.

The colours were so beautiful, orange, red, green, yellow, like fireworks in November, and they were taking ... the pain ... away...

# CHAPTER 4

'That's a glorious sight for so early in the morning!'

'Who the fuck!' Eddie, naked, whipped round at the sound of her voice. The gentle scent of her flowered perfume flowed over him, sharpening his sleepy senses.

'Even better now I can see exactly what you're made of,' said Lol.

Eddie – flustered – glared, made a grab for his genitals and ran for the bathroom's open door.

'You need two hands to cover that lot, Ducky.' Eddie kicked the door shut behind him but it didn't close out her voice, 'Lovely arse as well.'

Fuck! He let his urine stream into the bowl, watching the steam rise. Relieved, he shook himself and then moved over to the mirror above the sink. He ran a hand through the dark wavy hair that his mother never stopped telling him was so like his father's and stared into his own green eyes. He muttered at his reflection, 'If a bloke can't even get up in the early hours to take a piss in his own home...'

'There are others waiting,' came the small voice, accompanied by a gentle tapping on the door.

'Jesus Christ!' Eddie said softly. He'd spent two weeks in London thinking about Summer, the girl he loved, and how he could get her interested in him. And here was Lol, all over him like a fucking rash first thing in the morning when normal people should be asleep.

Actually, he remembered, Lol hadn't been the first inhabitant of Western Way to greet him. Vera's cat, Kibbles, had done the honours and asked to be let out as soon as Eddie had opened the front door. He smiled to himself; he loved that old fleabag.

He whipped a towel from the rail and tucked it round his midriff, flushing the bowl before opening the door. He sighed. 'I suppose if I was to say I was goin' downstairs to make tea you'd want a cup?' He gazed into the well-scrubbed face that still bore traces of bruising but was as smooth looking as his mother's skin, then looked away. Of course he liked Lol. That she was a bloke didn't faze him at all. She was pretty – no, beautiful – daintily formed, and not at all like Marie, his first encounter with a transvestite. She'd been six feet tall and built like a shithouse, with a voice that rivalled a foghorn. But much as he'd accepted Marie and got on well with her, he didn't fancy Lol. There was no spark there, not on his side anyway, even though she was lovely.

But Tyrone, his mate, was hooked! Only the poor sod was too shy to do anything about it.

Now he'd slip on some 501s and a teeshirt and go down to the kitchen. Maybe by then the rest of the household would be awake. After breakfast he'd go and meet Tyrone. He didn't want to spend the morning hiding from Lol and her innuendos.

'If you're brewing?' Lol grinned at him then her gaze fell to the towel. 'Pity you've covered up,' she said.

Eddie narrowed his eyes. Why did this ... this ... *person* always have to make even the simplest questions and answers sound like some kind of invitation?

Lol was wearing a pair of his Auntie Susie's cotton pyjamas and they swamped her. Eddie knew he was colouring up as she pushed past him into the bathroom and he again caught the tempting smell of her perfume. He coughed to hide his embarrassment, and went back into his bedroom.

Minutes later as he descended the stairs he noticed the light that was always left on in his mother's room. She was scared of the dark after a horrific experience when he was a toddler. She didn't like talking about her experience of being kept prisoner in a locked room by the boxer, Valentine Waite, but Eddie knew her fears ran deep.

He looked at his watch: six o'clock.

If Susie were at home she would have been up and about ages ago. She was never one to lie in bed, especially of a school day when she had to get her daughter, Joy, ready. They were in Littlehampton for a week, so his mother had told him on the phone. Apparently Susie was being very coy about who she'd gone with.

Vera was an early riser as well. She called his mother all manner of things for lying in bed but his mum reckoned a lovely way to spend a wet day was to stay curled up with a good book, a cup of tea and Auntie Vera's cat Kibbles sprawled on the bed beside her.

Poor Vera. She was practically out of her mind with worry about the murder of her favourite girl, Samantha. She'd closed down her massage parlour, Heavenly Bodies, for a whole week as a mark of respect.

'You've got to 'elp me find out who killed my girl, Daisy,' had been Vera's heartfelt plea to his mother. Samantha'd been a great favourite with the punters and Vera had loved the girl as though she was her daughter.

In the kitchen he switched on the kettle and while he was waiting for it to boil he got out mugs and rinsed the teapot. Why his mother didn't use teabags like the rest of the country he couldn't fathom. Vera said it was because she didn't trust teabags to make a proper cup of tea. His mum liked her tea as strong as treacle.

A scratching at the window was followed by strident meows, and Eddie gave the old tabby a big grin as he leaned across the sink and let him in.

'Where you been, boy?' He tickled the cat in the exact spot the animal liked, behind one ear, and was rewarded by a loud purring that filled the kitchen. Then he put some milk in a saucer and was given a few friendly head butts as a thank you.

'You love that cat, don't you?'

'Jesus, do you always have to creep up on people?' Eddie hadn't heard her come down the stairs. She'd brushed her long hair and he could smell fresh toothpaste.

'You was miles away talkin' to that ol' cat.'

'Why not? He's been with me all me life,' said Eddie.

'Wise cat,' said Lol with a grin.

'Is everything a joke to you?'

'I wasn't laughing when I got gang-banged a fortnight ago, was I? And where you been since then?'

Shit, he'd put his foot in it again. He guessed her life never had been easy, looking as she did, all delicate like. People could be cruel bastards, especially men, wanting to dominate folks they never understood.

Eddie picked up the kettle and filled the teapot.

'Roy wanted me in London. He's opened a new nightclub in Bermondsey. He hasn't been himself lately. His boy Michael, practically the same age as me, died recently. Throwin' himself into new ventures gives Roy less time to grieve.' Lol

41

nodded, pulled out a kitchen chair and sat down.

Eddie had known quite a few so-called Nancy boys and trannies. He got on really well with Robin who worked for Vera down at Heavenly Bodies. He knew Robin had a partner called Henry who was a lot older than him and was always buying him presents. Only Lol wasn't really a Nancy boy, was she? And he kept forgetting she was a trannie. She was more like a fuckin' girl than most of the Gosport girls!

Roy Kemp, the face who owned more brothels in England than the Queen owned country houses, and Vera, an ex Gosport prostitute, had added to Eddie's education in more ways than one.

Eddie had had his first woman before he was fourteen, a fresh young prostitute Roy had provided for him. Since then he'd had his pick of girls, some a lot older than him. They'd come back for more because he knew exactly how to please them – and himself. He knew he wasn't lacking in knowledge in that department.

What he didn't understand was one day, quite out of the blue, he'd looked at Summer, and he'd felt something tighten up inside his heart.

And yet him and Summer had practically grown up together. She was his cousin on his father's side. Her mother had been some sort of traveller who liked drugs better than she liked Summer, and Bri, his uncle, had brought Summer up after her mother had died of an overdose. In his mind's eye he could see Summer, her flame hair framing a small heartshaped freckled face. And her temper – God, when she got wound up she was like a coiled spring!

Lol coughed and Eddie's thoughts came back to the present. He watched as she pushed her long hair back from her face then crossed her shapely legs.

'Roy's been like a dad to me.' Eddie shrugged. He wasn't going to tell her how much he cared about the man who'd been a part of him all his life.

'You got a brother, ain't you?' Lol smiled a white-toothed smile. 'Where's he?' She pointed to a photograph on the window ledge showing his mother, himself and his blond-haired brother.

'Jamie's with his father. Visiting.'

Lol nodded. 'He's pretty.' Something inside Eddie's gut tightened. Jamie, young as he was, was trouble.

'I really like your mum,' Lol said.

'Just as well, as it seems she's providing a home for you, ain't she?' Eddie busied himself pouring tea into mugs.

'She's a diamond. Not many would have taken me in and looked after me...'

Eddie turned at the sadness in her voice and saw her eyes cloud over and her mouth close to a thin line. Lol had secrets, he could tell. She'd explain everything when the time was right, he was sure of that. You couldn't push people to talk about themselves.

'Mum and Vera are understanding women ... that's if you 'aven't already opened up to them.'

'Where's that tea?' Lol said, quickly changing the subject. 'I'm gaspin'.'

'Did I 'ear that magic word, tea?' His mother's voice intruded. Eddie was relieved, but Daisy looked tired. She wasn't sleeping well lately and he knew there were money worries. He also knew it was more than his life was worth to go behind her back and discuss her finances with Roy. Roy would hand out cash to his mother immediately, and she would throw it back in his face and tell him she wouldn't be beholden to him. Eddie resorted to the same trick he knew his Auntie Vera was doing, slipping a few notes into her purse when she wasn't looking.

'Mornin', Ma,' said Eddie, taking down another mug. After pouring the tea he took two cups over to the kitchen table and set them down. He smiled at Daisy. Her hair was sticking up after her restless night and despite her old off-white dressing gown tied tightly at the waist giving her hardly any shape at all, she looked like a girl.

Eddie had to admit his mother was a good-looking woman. He'd noticed the men's eyes following her. Especially Alec, the bloke who normally did sketches for the club's customers and helped around the bar in his spare time. He was a teacher at St John's School down in Forton Road. Bit of an anomaly really, thought Eddie, who had noticed Alec a few times just standing, staring into space with a sad look on his face. Come to think of it, he seemed more down than usual lately. Alec didn't seem the type to want to spend his weekends in a strip joint. He certainly didn't have much to do with the scrubbers there and Eddie suspected he only worked there because he idolised Daisy. He was always staring after her. Eddie knew Alec had a drink problem but he never let the liquor past his lips now. 'One day at a time,' was Alec's mantra. It was probably a good thing for him to help out at Daisychains. At least there he was among people and not at home on his own, brooding.

'Mornin', you two,' said Daisy, coming over to him and kissing him on the cheek then looking longingly at the tea. 'Nice to 'ave you back again, son. I heard you come 'ome last night. Roy okay?' Eddie nodded. 'Pour out another mugful,' she said. 'I heard Vera stirring an' I thought I just saw that bleedin' moggie slink into 'er room. A cuppa in bed might do 'er a bit of good instead of 'er getting up an' frettin' about Samantha an' what she can't change.'

'Was you with her when she got the news? Please don't say Vera was on her own when Vinnie Endersby told her Samantha's body had been found?'

Daisy's eyes filled with tears. 'I was there, Eddie, in Heavenly Bodies, and wishing what I was hearing wasn't true. Vinnie told her to sit down as he had something to tell her. "I'm all right standing, come on, spit it out," she said to 'im. '"Your Samantha has been found dead on Tragedy Bank," he says in that soft way he 'as of speakin'. Then him an' me grabbed hold of Vera before she fell. "I got to sit down," she says. But it was her face, Eddie. Underneath all that make-up it was putty grey. Nobody spoke for a long while. It was as though we was waitin' for Vera to take the lead.' Daisy brushed her hair with her fingers, smoothing it back off her face. 'Samantha was the daughter Vera never 'ad. Vera was shakin' then, like she 'ad no control of 'erself. "What you means, Detective Vinnie Endersby, is that my girl 'as been murdered?" and he could do no more than nod. Afterwards he asked if one of us would go down the morgue to formally identify Samantha. Vera just looked up at him from the depths of her blue leather sofa and said in a tiny voice, 'Never you mind, I'll come an' see my girl.'

Eddie went over to Daisy and pulled her into his arms. He knew the pain of Samantha's death was gnawing at her and she was trying to be brave. And Vera? She liked to pretend she was strong, but not where family was concerned, and Samantha *was* family. He released his mother and stood back from her.

He said, 'Any news about who did it?'

His mother gave him a look that could kill. 'Don't be bleedin' stupid. D'you think the rozzers are bothered about a prostitute? It won't stop me trying to find out who killed her, though I'm sure I've no idea how to go about it.'

Eddie poured out another mugful of tea and Daisy trickled in sterilised milk from the long-necked bottle. Eddie saw her give Lol a big smile as she moved past the girl on her way upstairs. 'Put the radio on, Eddie, it's like a dead an' alive hole when there ain't no music.' Manfred Mann's Earth Band were singing 'Blinded By The Light'.

'Done good, our local band, ain't they?' shouted Daisy.

And then the music was interrupted by an announcement.

'Am I hearin' right?' Daisy stumbled back into the kitchen, her tea slopping on the floor. 'Elvis is dead?' Eddie saw her face had lost all its colour. He felt sick at the news and the unemotional

46

tone of the male announcer's voice. 'The King of rock and roll gone?'

Eddie nodded.

His mother, standing with Vera's mug of steaming tea clutched in her hand, was frowning.

'How?'

'They didn't say,' Eddie replied.

'Well, they wouldn't, would they? But I'm willin' to bet everyone takes his death more seriously than poor Samantha's.' She swept out with a grim look on her face, again slopping the tea on the parquet flooring.

Lol sighed. 'She won't 'ave any tea left in that mug by the time she gets to Vera's room.' A thoughtful look washed over her face. 'You all really care about each other,' she said. 'Yet except for you an' your mum an' your brother, none of you is related.'

'What's wrong with that?'

'Nothin'.' Lol shrugged her thin shoulders and took a gulp of tea. 'I just find it unusual. Quite touching. It wasn't like this when I was a kid.'

'You must 'ave 'ad a bleedin' 'orrible life if you ain't never seen no love.' The words had slipped from his lips before he could stop them. Too late he saw the flash of tears before she turned her head away from him.

'I'm sorry, Lol. I didn't mean... Oh, shit! I'm always puttin' me foot in me bleedin' mouth!' His heart was beating furiously.

'It's okay,' said Lol. 'When I gets to know you better I'll tell you things. That's if I'm allowed to stay 'ere.'

'Why? Where you thinkin' of goin' then?' Daisy

paused in the kitchen doorway. It was obvious on her return downstairs she'd picked up on the last of their conversation.

'I don't want to outstay me welcome,' said Lol. Her eyes were damp.

Daisy put her arm around Lol's shoulder. 'Me an' Vera'd soon tell you if you was, Girly.'

# CHAPTER 5

Vera couldn't stop thinking about Samantha.

DCI Vinnie Endersby had come to Daisychains and collected her for the formal identification.

The morgue was behind Clarence Road Church. The disinfectant smell hit her as soon as they were led inside. The body was lying, covered, on a large metal table. Vinnie gently pulled back the sheet from Samantha's face. He was careful not to expose Samantha's choke-marked neck and Vera was touched by his consideration. She sat down miserably on the chair next to the table, then she leaned across and put her face next to Samantha's. Someone had thoughtfully closed Samantha's eyes. Her hair was brushed severely back behind her ears and it made her look different. Vera was used to seeing the fall of her hair loose over one cheek.

From behind her Vinnie Endersby asked, 'Is it her?'

'Of course it's my fuckin' Samantha. You think I don't know me mate?'

Vinnie came and stood in front of her, partly obscuring her view of the body. 'I have to ask. You know that.'

'Piss off an' let me say goodbye to 'er.' Vera glared, defying him to oppose her. She noticed that the white wall tiles around her were clean and shiny. Even the terracotta floor was spotless.

Vinnie moved from Vera's view and, impulsively, she loosened Samantha's hair. 'There you are, love, you ain't never 'ad your 'air pulled back like that, 'ave you? That's better now, isn't it?'

It was strange to see the young woman so pale and still. It was as though all the colour had been wrung from her.

Vera was holding herself rigid, scared that her body might betray her. Scared that the great scream she was keeping back might be wrenched out of her.

'Your life 'as been cut short, girl...' And then Vera's voice petered out and she thought how much she hated the man who had done this.

Vera's hands, clenched together, were trembling. She realised how cold the room was, how white and starched the sheet covering Samantha. How it flowed from Samantha's feet in a straight line until it reached the mounds of her breasts. Even in death, thought Vera, her Samantha had glorious breasts.

Fifteen years old Samantha had been when Vera took her in, gave her a room so she didn't have to sleep on the ferry boats, and made sure she ate properly. She watched Samantha blossom into the kind of woman who should have had children and a husband to love her. Now, Vera

49

thought, here she lay, mouth slightly open, like a young girl dreaming of her lover. But he'd never come, not now.

Vera stroked the dead girl's brow. It was cold and smooth, as though life had not touched her. And in that moment she realised how precious living was. How the wheels were turning and she and Daisy, and Roy, too, were hanging on to an existence that could be taken from them as easily as a candle was snuffed out.

She bent and kissed Samantha then, lifting her head, she wanted to cry out, to tell Samantha that she wouldn't let her go. But instead she turned away and bit her lips and rose from the chair. Her eyes sought Vinnie's face.

'Are you all right?' Vera saw his different-coloured eyes were watching her intently.

'I don't want to talk any more now about how she died.' She paused. 'But Samantha had a lot of money on her an' I don' suppose it was still with her when she was found?'

Vinnie shook his head. 'Later I'll need to take a proper statement, will that be a problem?'

'No.' Vera was surprised at the calmness of her voice. She stepped from one foot to the other, wanting to go, but loth to abandon Samantha. 'I need to...'

'You need to be with Daisy. I understand. D'you want a lift back to Daisychains?'

'No.'

Vera left the morgue then. Glad to be in the fresh air. Glad to be walking through the back streets, past Blundell's furniture store, past the pet shop, past Murphy's hardware emporium.

And she wondered whether Daisy might be upset that she'd gone on her own to say goodbye to Samantha. Don't be fuckin' stupid, she told herself, Daisy would understand. Daisy always understood.

Vera wiped a stray tear from her cheek, then she began to run, as fast as her four-inch heels would let her.

Needing to be with Daisy.

Eddie pushed open the door to the secondhand bookshop. The bell jangled, and Bri looked up from the novel he was reading.

''Allo, son. What can I get you?'

'Just popped in to see if you was all right, Uncle Bri.' Eddie liked his father's brother. He was tall and broad and had the reddest hair he'd ever seen on a bloke. And he'd passed on his colouring to his daughter, Summer. 'I also wanted to see if you got any true crime books.'

Eddie liked to lie in bed at night and read, with Kibbles curled up beside him on the pillow, purring away. Eddie felt lost if he didn't have a substantial pile of reading matter on the bedside table so he could pick and choose.

Breathing deeply of the shop's papery air he thought what a comforting smell it was.

It *was* true he'd entered the shop in North Street for books, but more than anything he'd come in for a glimpse of his cousin and his heart dropped when he saw she wasn't there.

'Got some good detective stuff, only came in earlier this morning, but they're novels. I got *The Andromeda Strain* an' I don't reckon you read that Michael Crichton one.'

'No I ain't,' said Eddie. 'I've been after that book.'

Bri got up from his stool to show Eddie where the books could be found. Bri was wearing some kind of piney smelling cologne and it reminded Eddie of walks in the New Forest. Bri took down a book from a shelf and handed it to Eddie. For a couple of seconds Eddie glanced through the pages, liking what he was reading. Before long he had four novels that he'd piled beside the till.

'I'll take these–' His words were interrupted by Summer's voice proclaiming, 'Move them off the counter before I spills tea all over them.'

Eddie's heart leapt and began beating so loudly he was sure Bri and Summer could hear it. He immediately scooped up the books and the girl set down an overflowing mug on the formica top.

''Ere you are, Dad,' she said. Her long hair was damp, as though she'd just washed it or come from the shower, and her face was shiny and bereft of make-up. She smelled like peaches, thought Eddie. He tried to joke with her.

'Where's my cuppa, then?'

'If you wants tea, Eddie Lane, you can make it yourself. If you don't know where our kitchen is now, you never will.' She made a face at him.

'You'll stay like that,' said Eddie.

Her dad let out a belly laugh. 'Go on up, Eddie.' And he added, 'Thanks for the tea, Summer.'

She treated her father to a broad smile. Eddie wished she'd smile at him like that. But then Summer was barely sixteen and didn't even know Eddie Lane was on this planet.

The long legged girl in her tight jeans and skimpy top flounced back up the stairs to the flat above the shop.

'Eddie...' Eddie turned to Bri and saw that his face was creased with worry. The man waited until Summer was no longer within hearing distance. 'I needs a few words with you. A favour, like.'

'Anything,' Eddie agreed without hesitation. Bri moved closer and said in a hushed voice:

'I'm a bit worried about some of the yobs Summer brings home.'

A needle passed through Eddie's heart.

'What d'you mean?'

'I knows girls grow up quicker in Gosport but half her boyfriends got long hair, longer than yours.' Eddie felt as though he was being given marks out of ten for his haircut. 'An' some of 'em look like they ain't ever seen a bleedin' bath...'

Eddie's thoughts jumbled themselves into a sort of order. 'But Summer *does* bring 'em home?'

Bri shrugged. 'Yeah.'

'Then I don't think you got much to worry about. Time to fret is when she don't bring her boyfriends 'ome. They'd be the blokes who are trouble.' Eddie saw Bri's face relax.

'Never thought of it like that,' he said. 'I suppose I worry too much. It'd be different if she 'ad a mother to advise her.'

'They'd probably fight like cat and dog. You should hear my mum go. Seriously, all the time Summer's open about who she's 'angin' about with I don't reckon you got much to be concerned about.'

Eddie uttered the words, but he was thinking

that if anyone ever harmed a hair of that little spitfire's head...

'You're older than her. Bloody amazing what sense an extra couple of years brings. Still, your dad was a smart bugger an' all. You know, I don't know why she can't meet a nice bloke like you. Still, I suppose she's got some growin' up an' living to do yet.'

Eddie smiled at him. He wanted to be gone upstairs now to talk to Summer. He didn't want to think of her with other blokes.

'Eddie.' Eddie paused, one foot on the bottom stair. The door-bell jangled, announcing a customer. 'When you're out an' about, if you sees her, look after her for me, will you?'

'Of course,' Eddie said. 'But I ain't playing gooseberry. She'd hate me for that.'

He took the carpeted stairs two at a time. She was in the kitchen, the heel of one bare foot on the table. A pot of bright red nail varnish sat on the tablecloth and her body practically bent in two as she leaned across applying the sharp smelling colour. Her concentration showed in the tip of her tongue protruding childishly through her teeth.

'Kettle's over there,' she said, without looking up. Eddie slipped off his jacket and threw it across a chair then lifted the kettle, weighing it for water before plugging the lead in the socket. Pretty soon the comfortable sound of water starting to heat began.

'You want me to finish paintin' them for you?' He noticed she'd smudged a couple of nails and smears of red clung to her toes.

'I'm nearly done,' she said. ''Sides, you'd prob-

54

ably make a worse mess than me.' She looked up and Eddie caught the full blast of a smile, with her green eyes twinkling away like jewels.

He grinned back at her but she never noticed for she'd gone back to the serious job of nail painting. He felt somehow momentarily lost.

The kettle started to wail and Eddie asked, 'You want a drink?'

'Nah,' she said. 'I need to do me hair. Me an' Val are goin' to the pictures.'

His heart dropped again. That meant she wouldn't have time for a proper conversation with him. *And* he'd have to make himself a cup of tea and drink it, otherwise he'd look stupid for being in the flat in the first place.

He noticed a thin book, its pages face down on the table, like she'd been reading it before she'd made her dad a drink and decided to paint her toenails. He picked it up.

'Don't lose me place.'

'I wasn't goin' to,' he said. 'Just lookin' to see what you're readin'.'

'It's a Mills and Boon.'

'A lovey-dovey story,' he laughed.

She looked up and glared at him. 'I don't suppose a good-lookin' bloke like you who can 'ave any girl 'e fancies believes in *true* love.'

If only you knew, he thought, but he said, 'My mum really loved my dad. I'm the proof of that.'

'My mum done the dirty on my dad time an' time again. I'm lucky he *is* me dad.' Her face had gone hard, her mouth two straight lines.

Eddie said, reaching out to touch her wrist, 'She was a hippy. She lived her life the way she

55

wanted. Don't think bad of your mum for that.' He didn't like to see Summer upset. There was the glitter of tears in her eyes.

'She cared only for drugs 'n' drink 'n' blokes who'd give her the money to get 'em. She never wanted me.' Summer pushed her long hair away from her face and sat back on the chair, her nails finished. She screwed the brush back into the small bottle. 'She OD'd in one of the bedrooms in your house and I was shut in a wardrobe. But you know all about that, Eddie Lane, same as you knows your mother 'as been more like a mum to me than my own ever was.'

And I'm nothing more than an older brother to you, he thought miserably.

He bent down and put his arms around her. Her shoulders were thin.

'You are *so* loved,' he said.

And now her voice was shrill. 'You think I don't know that, Eddie Lane? Sometimes I feel like I'm suffocated with all the love. It's like everyone 'as got to make it up to me for me bad beginnin'. I *got* to find out what real life's like in me *own* way.'

Eddie let his arms drop to his sides. She was a complex baggage. Sometimes he didn't understand her. He picked up his black leather jacket and turned to go.

'No tea?'

He smiled at her. 'Nah, can't be bothered,' he said. At the doorway, he turned. 'Just you be careful, Summer, it's a jungle of a world out there.'

# CHAPTER 6

Daisy pricked up her ears at the sudden sound. It was as if something had been sloshed against a wall.

She tried to pacify herself. 'Don't be so bloody stupid, girl. There's only you in 'ere.' Taking a gulp of her almost cold tea, she went back to poring over the Daisychains bank statement. She sighed and picked up the invoice from Brickwood's brewery. Her head leaning into her hand, her elbow on the table, she closed her eyes – knowing when she opened them there still wouldn't be enough money to pay last month's account. She was damned lucky the draymen had delivered ale today, and *that* was probably only because Vera had met them on the street, stood chatting away to them and had insisted she pull both the blokes a pint before they went on to their next delivery.

Wondering if the bank manager would consider giving her another mortgage on her house, she swigged back the last of the tea. Then she thought about the payments she'd missed. Another mortgage would be right out of the question.

Damn, she'd have to hide behind the curtains when the Provi man came. She thought of the brand new BMX bike she'd bought with the Provident cheque.

Jamie had been on about this particular model for ages and it had been worth every penny to see his eyes light up when he'd come home from his father Vinnie's house in the country. He'd behaved himself there, too. Apart from pulling up Clare's newly planted rock garden and throwing bricks at the greenhouse. Daisy sighed. Jamie was what Vera called 'very highly strung'. Wrinkling her nose, she sniffed. Burning ... she could smell something cooking.

'The worry's makin' you daft, silly cow,' she told herself. But she could hear the sound of crackling and the frying smell was getting stronger. Bit like Vera's burned breakfasts, she thought.

Daisy rose from her desk and opened the office door. The moment she stepped into the bar the stench and smoke from burning paint and upholstery knocked her back.

'Fuckin' 'ell!' The curtains were blazing! All she could think of was thank God the few customers they'd had in tonight had left. Then she saw the brass-handled heavy oak front doors were smouldering. The fire began whooshing through the bar and she suddenly realised that she couldn't get out. Her heart was pounding and the heat, or fear, was making her sweat. Rivers of perspiration caused her underwear to cling to her body. 'Don't panic,' she thought. 'Phone for help, yes, that's it. Phone for help and run like fuck for the rear door.'

Back in the office she picked up the phone. It was dead. 'Bastard,' she cried. 'Bastard, bastard, bastard.'

There was no way she could contain the fire by herself. Escape was the answer. Running, staggering and choking, she made it to the back door of the club.

58

Daisy slid the heavy bolts back and pushed against the door. Nothing. It seemed to want to open but there was something stopping it. The padlock! The outside padlock had been snapped shut, securing the door.

A violent coughing fit had her bent double. She wiped her hands across her stinging, streaming eyes. It was difficult to see now. Her head was swimming and she could feel the heat spreading closer. Hot, she was so hot. And from the bar came the sound of windows breaking.

Daisy sat down on the floor. She tried to think but it was so so difficult. She wanted to feel cool. The cellar! She must get to the cellar.

She heaved herself to a standing position and then stumbled towards the kitchen. Why had she insisted on burglar bars on all the windows? She yanked open the cellar door and practically fell down the stone steps.

Cool. It was cool here. She gulped shallow breaths of the cold air, which smelled of beery hops and yeast. Her chest hurt so much she seemed to have lost the ability to take a deep breath. It was then she realised she was caught in a raging fire with no escape route. *She could be burned alive.*

*She wouldn't see her beloved boys ever again.*

*She was about to die!*

Daisy looked around the whitewashed room containing boxes of spirits and mixers. Peanuts in cellophane packets, fastened on cards to hang behind the bar, were lying on top of boxes of crisps. Then she stared at the new barrels delivered that morning – and at the trapdoor where the barrels had been rolled down the cement slope to be hauled into place in the cellar.

The trapdoor!

'I ain't goin' without a fuckin' fight,' she said.

She crawled up the slope, the cement drawing blood from her knees. She pulled back the bolts and pushed upwards. The wood moved. From the small slit fresh air rushed in.

'Yes!' Daisy was elated.

Then the heavy doors fell back into place.

Anger poured through her body as she sank to the floor again. She had a way out but she wasn't strong enough to push up the fuckin' opening.

'No!' Her voice was a roar as she leapt to her feet and with both hands and every last bit of strength and defiance in her, she shoved at the heavy trapdoor. She felt it give. With her knees bent and her back and arms taking the strain, she thrust upwards. Daisy had no idea where her sudden burst of strength came from but the trapdoor flew back and hit the cobbles, and salty air from the harbour poured in.

Daisy scrambled out and was caught in a coughing fit that had her twisted with pain. She was in the alley at the back of the building. She could smell and see flames from her club reaching into the sky.

She fell then. Sank to the cobbles. Her head was swimming, her eyes filled with grit and so sore she could barely open them. She forced herself to crawl along the alley fearing her heart would burst as she panted and painfully tried to take in air.

From the High Street came the clanging of a fire engine.

When Daisy reached the Old Northumberland pub she took a final gasp and collapsed in the doorway.

'Why would someone do this to me, Vera? I could 'ave died in that bleedin' office. If the landlord of the Old Northumberland hadn't found me and took me in...' Daisy tried to shout but her voice was a whisper; thank God at least she could now breathe. Her chest hurt like fuck but she'd think about that later.

She'd really believed her number was up as she'd tried again and again to make herself heard above the pandemonium, the racket from the firemen and their hoses spraying water, and the noise from excited people standing around watching the inferno.

'Well, you didn't fuckin' die, Daisy, an' what the bleedin' 'ell d'you mean we got no insurance?'

Vera grabbed hold of her and swung her around. The heat from the flames made Daisy feel as though she was being roasted. The stench of burning plastic hung in the air and clouds of black smoke were billowing from the building and blowing over them. Daisy felt her tears drying with the extreme heat the moment they fell from her stinging eyes and landed on her cheeks, even though she and Vera were well back from the burning building.

'You don't believe someone was trying to kill me, do you?' Daisy grabbed at Vera's blouse, forcing her friend to look at her. 'This fire didn't fuckin' start itself.'

Vera's eyes were glimmering in the orange light

61

from the blaze that was their club. She shrugged away Daisy's arm.

'Well, fuck you then!' Daisy was hurt that Vera thought she was making up the story about an intruder to cover up the grave mistake she'd made by not paying the yearly insurance premium on Daisychains. She looked at the fire, smelled the choking gases, and felt utterly defeated at the destruction before her.

'Dais, I'm not exactly saying I don't believe you, but I do 'appen to think with all the stress you've been under...'

'I'm not makin' it up! Someone set this fire, someone who knew I was alone in the club!'

'An' you really think people is goin' to believe that when they 'ears how badly Daisychains was doin'?'

'I don't give a flyin' fuck what others think, but it do matter to me that you think I'm makin' it up. I thought you was me best friend. Have I ever lied to you?' Vera's forehead was furrowed. 'Answer me. Do I lie?'

'No. But Dais, who would want to kill you? What you done that would warrant someone settin' fire to Daisychains with you in it?'

Daisy shook her head, she had no answer to that. All the same, she *knew* she'd come close to dying and the feeling was more than scary.

Vera spoke again. 'An' there wasn't no money to renew the insurance?'

Close to tears again Daisy said, 'Not when it was due, no. Then the weeks rolled by an' I forgot about it because I *was* payin' wages an' drinks bills an' trying to make a little bit of cash go a long way.'

There was a moment of silence between them as Vera stared into her friend's eyes. There were smudges of soot all over Vera's face just like huge beauty spots gone wild. Daisy could see the glitter of anger in her eyes, then Vera's anger suddenly turned to fear.

'Do you think the same person who murdered my Samantha set fire to this place and tried to kill you?'

'How the fuckin' hell can you think that! Ain't I scared enough already?'

'I'm sorry, Dais, I know we both put everything we 'ad into this place, and I know despite the club not doin' well, you wouldn't 'ave wanted it to burn down. I'm sorry I was bein' a bitch to you, but you should 'ave told me there wasn't enough money for the fire insurance. I could 'ave raised it somehow.'

Vera pulled her close and stroked her hair. For precious seconds Daisy allowed herself to be comforted, then her eyes were drawn to the inferno once more. Vera's words haunted her. Was the person responsible for the fire the same person who killed Samantha? Would he try to burn down her home in Western Way? Maybe she wouldn't get out of the blaze next time. Maybe her boys... She closed her mind to those thoughts and watched with great sorrow as tall spires of flame lit up the dark sky, refusing to be quenched by the firemen's hoses.

As she clung to Vera, loud bangs told her that more bottles of alcohol were exploding.

A man's voice broke into Daisy's thoughts.

63

'Was there anyone inside?'

'Yeah, me.' Her answer came quickly.

Daisy guessed by his notebook and pen that he was a reporter.

Vera squeezed Daisy's arm and moved closer to her.

The small man in the hat and raincoat with the shiny red notebook tried again. 'I'm from *The Evening News,*' he said.

'How did you find out about the fire?'

'I was doin' some paperwork.' Daisy started crying again. 'Then I went into the bar. There was an explosion an' the curtains was well alight an' I saw that the fire had somehow started near the main door. I got out of there by the skin of me bleedin' teeth.' She suddenly felt incredibly tired. 'Look, I don't want to talk about this now because that's me livelihood goin' up in smoke over there.' Daisy turned and buried herself in Vera's arms again.

A familiar voice soothed her shredded nerves. 'I got this tea from The Dive. Drink it while it's hot.'

Daisy opened her eyes. Eddie, his face streaked, his clothes filthy, held out a flask. Tyrone, his mate, stood next to him with a box of Peek Frean biscuits.

The man was jotting down notes.

'Clear off, mate,' Eddie said. 'We appreciate you're doin' your job but our nerves is in pieces.'

Daisy could see the man weighing up his chances of continuing with his questions against the wrath of six-foot Eddie, then, tipping his hat, he sauntered away into the crowd.

Vera took the heavy cups from Eddie and set them on the wall. 'This tea is gonna hit just the right spot. Did you phone 'ome?'

'Susie and Joy are fine and Jamie's playing cards with Lol. I 'ad to persuade the lot of them they were better staying indoors, not comin' down 'ere. Of course everyone's worried sick.' He ran his hand through his hair but the dark waves fell back immediately on to his forehead again. He sighed then said, 'Alec's been great, taking tea to the firemen an' stuff. You all right, Mum?'

'No. What d'you expect? How did Alec know about the fire? He wasn't workin' tonight.'

'You're right, Daisy,' said Vera after swallowing some hot tea, 'but you know what the jungle drums are like in Gosport.'

'Someone taking my name in vain?' Daisy whirled round at the sound of Alec's cultured voice. His face was sooty and his clothes were just as dirty as Eddie's. He was holding a plate of jam doughnuts, covered with a damp teacloth that he whisked off. He held the plate out to Daisy.

'Take one.' She shook her head, but Vera reached over and helped herself. She took such a large bite that the jam inside the doughnut fell onto her chin.

'Bugger!' she said.

'I drove down here as fast as I could but there wasn't much I could do except help Eddie with the tea,' Alec said. His eyes scoured Daisy's face. 'You sure you're all right?'

Daisy saw the concern in his eyes. 'I'm glad of your support, Alec,' she said. His eyes held hers but she dropped her gaze, embarrassed because she felt drawn to him and suddenly, out of the blue, wondered how it would feel to be in his arms and cry and cry and be comforted by him. For that's what she wanted at this moment: a man's arms around her and a soothing voice telling her everything would be all right.

'Thank God we got just enough money to pay wages for this week. No reason why the staff should suffer as well,' said Daisy, ashamed of her thoughts. 'Then it's the end of our dreams,' she said sadly.

She turned to Eddie. 'I was bankin' on getting a nice nest egg put by out of that place for Jamie – when business picked up again, of course. Only it ain't never gonna 'appen now, is it? He's goin' to be right pissed off when you comes of age an' gets your trust fund money, Eddie.' She thought for a while. 'I don't know, Vera, it's like takin' two steps forward an' one back all the fuckin' time.'

Vera was stirring her tea. 'Trouble was, the trade fell off when you made Daisychains a drug-free zone.'

'You 'ave to grind me down when I'm feelin' bad, don't you?'

'No. I'm tellin' you you're too fuckin' soft to be a business woman, Daisy Lane.'

Eddie handed his mother a cup of tea and she grasped it thankfully. It was obvious to her he was keeping out of their argument. As she sipped the sweet liquid she felt the tears rise again. 'All that 'ard work we put into that place.' She nodded at the blaze. 'It took me ages to pay Roy Kemp back the money we borrowed.'

'Finish your tea, Daisy. And you, Eddie, go an' find out if the firemen know 'ow it was started.' Daisy listened to Vera issuing orders and watched

Eddie walk away. It was hard sometimes to remember he wasn't yet a man. His height and breadth and his manner gave everyone the impression he was much older than he was. She watched with pride as he crossed the road, weaving in and out of the onlookers. His dad, Eddie Lane, the local gangster, would have been proud of his son. Daisy shook herself and took another mouthful of tea; now wasn't the time to be raking over old coals.

'What we goin' to do, Vera?' It was like all the stuffing had been knocked out of her. Tears filled her eyes again.

'You can count on me,' said Alec. He fished around in his jacket pocket and handed Daisy a clean white handkerchief. 'I got a bit of money in the Post Office. You can have it if it'll help.'

'She won't accept help. You should know by now what a contrary cow she is,' Vera said, as though Daisy wasn't there. Daisy was now crying into Alec's handkerchief, but Vera pulled the handkerchief away. 'For a start you can stop that bleedin' nonsense. What's the point of cryin'? And now I'm goin' to tell you somethin' else you ain't goin' to like. Most weeks we didn't even 'ave enough to pay wages so I been subsidising Daisychains from me massage parlour anyway.'

Daisy stopped crying. She wiped her face with the back of her hand and stared at Vera.

'Why ever didn't you tell me?'

'Because I 'oped it was just a passing slump, like bad weeks I've 'ad meself at Heavenly Bodies. Weeks when I paid out more'n I 'ad comin' in, but I survived. I might add though, losing Samantha has taken a toll on me takings.'

'But without a business I can't pay you back, Vera. Everything I 'ad was tied up in that place.' Daisy looked across the road to where the building was still burning fiercely. Another fire engine had arrived, but she knew when the firemen got the fire under control it wouldn't change anything. She was well and truly in the shit. 'I even took out a mortgage on our house, an' I've missed a few of those payments,' she said. A thought struck her. 'I could sell the 'ouse to pay you back, Vera.'

'And where we all goin' to bleedin' live then, you daft cow? Anyway, I don't want me bleedin' money back. An' all the time I got earnin' power we'll be all right. You mark my words.'

'You're always there when I need you, Vera.' Daisy squeezed Vera's hand and peered into the stinking smoke-filled crowd, looking for her son. She *would* survive. And she'd pay back Vera every penny.

'Is that my Eddie over there, talkin' to that bloke in a suit? Can you see 'im, Vera?'

'You rely on that lad too much.'

'Don't 'ave much choice. He's like 'is dad was, takes things out of me hands. Sometimes I forget he's not a man yet.'

Vera gave her an old-fashioned look. 'It ain't years what makes a bloke a man.' Then Daisy heard her mutter, 'Not like the other one.'

Daisy knew she meant Jamie, but decided to let it ride. Now wasn't the time to have an argument about Jamie's shortcomings. Even so, much as she loved her second son, Vera was right. There was a cruel streak in him that frightened her.

Perhaps he'll grow out of it, she thought. He's only a kid yet.

'Eddie loves you,' said Daisy suddenly.

Vera turned and looked at her. Oh, she did look funny with her face and hair all covered with soot and grease, thought Daisy. It made Vera's teeth blindingly white.

'It's my ol' bleedin' cat Kibbles he loves,' said Vera.

'Go on,' said Daisy, nudging her companionably.

Just then Eddie, accompanied by the suited man, came pushing through the crowd.

The man asked, 'You the owners?' Alec inclined his head towards Daisy and Vera and they nodded.

'We've been able at last to control the fire.'

'Thank Christ, an' thank Christ again the fire station's only by St George's barracks an' you was able to get 'ere so prompt. It would 'ave been awful if the places either side 'ad gone up as well,' said Daisy. 'Did any of your men get hurt?'

He shook his head. 'Thanks for asking, there's many that don't.'

Alec asked, 'Do you know how it started?'

'Was petrol stored on the premises?'

Daisy looked at Vera then at Eddie and Alec and saw the confusion on their faces.

'It's a club, not a bleedin' garage!' snapped Vera.

'It could well be arson,' the man said, staring at his clipboard. 'We'll know more later.' He turned to Eddie. 'Thanks, mate, for getting that underground café to make tea for us. Not many people does that, an' we're always gaspin' for a cuppa after the event.'

'Not a problem,' said Eddie. 'Tom didn't mind

getting the urn goin'. He was just pleased that bein' so close like, he only copped a bit of smoke damage.'

'We'll be in touch when we know a bit more,' the bloke said before walking away. Then he turned back and said, 'I'd go home if I was you. Police'll be wantin' a statement. You got transport?'

'Me car's in a side street,' Daisy said.

'Daisy, I'm so sorry that at first I didn't believe you. If you'd died in that ... that...' Daisy saw the tears in Vera's eyes as she looked towards the burned-out husk of the nightclub. 'But you ain't all right to drive. You're shakin' like a leaf an' your eyes is all swollen.'

Eddie jumped in quickly. 'You do look worn out, Mum. You two should go home. Susie'll be worryin' herself sick. I'll 'ang about here a bit longer.'

Vera said, 'Much as I needs to stay with you, Dais, I better go an' sort me girls out at the massage parlour. They'll 'ave 'eard all sorts of rubbish from the johns. Wanna come with me? You shouldn't be on your own, you know.'

Daisy shook her head. Facing the barrage of questions from Vera's girls was the last thing she needed.

Alec jumped in. 'Why not let me take you home, Daisy? Vera's right, you're not fit to drive.'

Daisy saw the kindness in Alec's eyes, and even with the fumes from the fire swirling in the night air, she could smell the clean tang of Imperial Leather soap on him.

'Okay,' she said.

'That's settled then,' Vera said.

'Roy'll get to Western Way soon.'

Daisy swung round on Eddie. 'What d'you mean? Sometimes you takes too bleedin' much on yourself. I never asked you to call Roy Kemp!'

'That's right, Mum, you didn't. But as soon as I heard someone'd deliberately set fire to Daisychains knowin' you was inside, I reckoned he'd want to know. Don't you?'

## CHAPTER 7

Eddie yawned. He really was looking forward to a shower and bed.

'I 'ope to God I never 'ave to witness another fire. Me mum's lost everything. Her life was tied up with that club.'

Tyrone squeezed his shoulder. 'Your mum's a survivor,' he said.

Eddie surveyed the steaming desolation that once was Daisychains. Neither of them spoke and he knew Tyrone sensed he needed a minute to sort out his head.

A lone fox dug his head into the rubbish bin outside the pub before using his front paws to topple it over. Survival, Eddie thought, that's what it's all about. Yes, Tyrone was right. His mother was a survivor. Then, out of the corner of his eye he saw a larger shape. A man broke away from the wall and slipped into the darkness down the alley at the side of the Haslar Tavern.

'Did you recognise that bloke, Tyrone?' His

71

mate peered through the sea mist that had appeared over the town as if by magic.

'I thought that shape was just a shadow.'

Tyrone had long limbs and an easy smile but now his face was full of concern.

'Wasn't no shadow, it was a bloke, an' I got the feelin' I know that sod from somewhere.'

'He's just a tosser come to 'ave a bleedin' gawp at the fire.'

'Why didn't he come up an' make himself known to us then? That's what most people would 'ave done. Maybe he's a firestarter who's been hangin' around to see what damage he's done.'

'You got a vivid imagination, Eddie.'

'Yeah, perhaps I'm tired an' I'm makin' up things. Thanks for comin' down as soon as you 'eard, Tyrone.' Eddie stifled another yawn.

'Bad news always travels faster than good in Gosport. Look, I'm really sorry for your old lady, she's somethin' special is your mum. She still around?'

'Nah,' said Eddie. There were very few sightseers now and the club was a steaming mess of wet muck and eerie shapes that still sent a stink across the taxi rank and ferry gardens. At his feet the tarmac was black with oil and soot and pieces of paper that had escaped in the wind to become trodden in the wet. 'She should be at 'ome by now. Alec's taken her. A rest'll do 'er good.'

The few stragglers were staring at the one remaining fire engine and making comments about the burned-out shell that had been Daisychains. Above the debris the sky was alive with stars, and if Eddie turned his head towards the strip of Solent water where the ferry boats ran passengers to Portsmouth he could smell the mud sludge from the ferry.

'They,' he nodded towards the firemen, 'reckon it wasn't an accident. If I ever find out who did this to me mum I'll kill the fuckin' bastards. She ain't got over Samantha's death yet, an' it's hit Vera real bad an' all.' He stared hard at Tyrone who was giving him a weird look. 'You goin' to give me a lift 'ome, or just stand there like a big prick?'

'I came down to make sure you was okay, didn't I, mate?' Tyrone grinned at him. 'So the fire was deliberate?'

Eddie nodded, then stifled another yawn. His eyes felt full of grit and his limbs had turned to lead; he could even smell his own rank sweat.

'You reckon there was a connection between the fire and Samantha's death?'

Eddie shrugged. 'Don't *you* fuckin' start, Vera asked that question. Who knows?' He stared at Tyrone. 'I really hate it that you got wheels and I ain't.'

Tyrone threw the car keys at him. 'You look and smell like somethin' dug up from a sewer but maybe drivin' my car'll perk you up a bit. It's parked on that spare bit of ground back of Woolworth's. I'm puttin' some paper on the seat afore your dirty arse gets on it.' Tyrone's car was his pride and joy.

As they walked away from the ferry gardens and the bus terminus, an Isle of Wight car ferry ploughed through the Solent waters. Eddie thought he'd never get used to seeing huge ships passing by at the end of the road. It was almost as if he could put out a hand and touch the vessels as they slipped through the narrow strip of water.

He liked Gosport and the people who lived there, but at the moment he wanted to find and kill whoever had taken away his mother's dream. He took a last look at the club's remains as they walked to Beach Street.

'You're only lettin' me drive because you got no bleedin' licence.'

'Neither 'ave you!'

'But I can drive better'n you anyway so there's less likelihood we'll get picked up.'

Round the back of Woolworth's Eddie put the key in the lock of the shiny Mini.

'Nice little motor this.' It was well cared for and Tyrone was always making modifications to it when he had the time and the money. Its chrome gleamed and its interior leather smelled of lemon polish and was slippery where Tyrone was forever cleaning it.

Eddie liked being behind the wheel of a car. His mother wouldn't be too pleased if she knew how many vehicles he'd driven but he just loved cars, especially his mum's red MG that she wouldn't let him touch with a barge pole.

'There's only two better cars than this, me mum's Midget and Vinnie Endersby's MG Roadster.'

Tyrone said, 'Well, you would say that. You spent enough time working on the copper's car when he was livin' down in Alverstoke Village. Meself, I'd go for Roy Kemp's Roller every time.'

'You got big ideas you 'ave, for a bleedin' Gosport bloke,' said Eddie. He took a look at South

Street Police Station as they drove by.

'Shut it!' said Tyrone and Eddie grinned. For a single moment Tyrone had managed to take Eddie's mind off the club's burning and the bloke he'd spotted hanging around. 'Seen Summer lately?'

'Nah,' said Eddie.

'She's a fuckin' prickteaser, that one.'

'Oi! That's my bleedin' family you're puttin' down.'

'All right, keep your 'air on. Just because since you been a kid you been wanting to get into her bleedin' knickers an' she don't even know you exist.'

'She's my cousin, that's all.'

Almost every word Tyrone was uttering was the truth but Eddie wasn't going to let him know that. He wanted Summer with a longing that he'd never known before – but it was more than that. He wanted her for himself, so no one else could have her or ever, ever hurt her.

'Wish I'd a cousin like that, long gold 'air and...'

'Shut your fuckin' trap.'

It hurt Eddie that Summer was the one girl who'd never shown the slightest interest in him. 'She's too young to be thinkin' about getting serious with blokes,' he said.

'She's practically the same age as us!'

'Not quite, and *she's too young.*' Eddie's voice had risen and he felt himself colour up. He was protesting too much. 'Shut the fuck up, Ty, you're givin' me a bleedin' 'eadache an' I got enough on me mind.' He turned the car and began driving up Stoke Road.

Eddie liked Tyrone. He was uncomplicated. They were as different as chalk and cheese but they'd been mates ever since infants' school. He used to invite Tyrone home for tea and his mum and Aunt Susie would put on a show by making loads of cream cakes and green jellies and Instant Whips, especially the butterscotch ones that were Tyrone's favourite. Eddie never got a proper invitation to Tyrone's place but he went all the same.

Tyrone lived in Duke's Road and his dad had buggered off when Ty was small. His mum had a job at the Criterion Picture House as an usherette, working at the cinema afternoons and evenings, so she was never home.

She was pretty in a leggy, frizzy-haired sort of way, and when she did have time off she liked to go out with her boyfriends so Tyrone had the run of the house. It was one of those homes where one day there would be a dozen boxed toasters in the hall that had fallen off the back of a lorry and then, next day, they'd be replaced when another 'uncle' brought home a stolen car and new number plates.

This was how come Tyrone's mum ended up with the Mini. But Tyrone considered it his, especially as it had had a respray to go with its new plates. Ty had put in for his driving test and Eddie reckoned he'd pass if he didn't panic so much at crossroads.

Tyrone grinned at him. 'How you gettin' on with that trannie? I reckon you could 'ave 'im if you wanted.' Tyrone was getting on his nerves now.

Eddie said, 'Her name's Lol. You fancy 'er, don't you?'

'What d'you take me for, a fuckin' shirt lifter?'

'I reckon you're only goin' on about Lol because *you* really want her,' said Eddie. 'Blokes what makes the most noise about bleedin' poofs only does it to take the heat off themselves.'

By Tyrone's lack of answer, Eddie knew he'd hit the nail on the head. But then Tyrone's Uncle George, a hairdresser, was Georgina by night and did a very polished drag act at The White Hart in Stoke Road. Tyrone was fairly comfortable with men dressing as women.

Tyrone was still grumbling good-naturedly when Eddie turned into Jellicoe Avenue. When the Mini slid to a stop outside the house in Western Way, Tyrone, his tongue hanging out at the sight of the Rolls Royce in the drive, said, 'Hey up, the big man's here.'

Eddie caught a glimpse of the curtain moving in Jamie's window.

'Shit,' he said. 'The little bleeder'll tell Mum I been drivin'.'

'Don't worry,' said Ty. 'I'm bettin' she's got more than that to worry her at present.'

'Sometimes I really wish he'd stay at his dad's place an' never come home.' Eddie surprised himself by the fierceness in his words.

He opened the door and got out and Ty slid over into the driver's seat.

'See you,' Eddie said. 'Thanks, mate.' He stood watching as Tyrone drove down Western Way and then pushed against the half open front door and went inside. He saw Roy's velvet-collared coat slung over the stairwell, and could actually smell his expensive cologne in the hall.

Susie was holding court with the tea pot. She smiled as Eddie came into the kitchen. 'I 'eard this one was the hero,' she purred.

He shook his head, but out of the corner of his eye he could see Roy nod with pleasure. Susie poured him a mug of tea. 'You all right?' she asked.

'Of course, Auntie Suze.' His mum had told him Susie had had an unhappy life before meeting up with Vera and her, and the three of them had been pretty much inseparable since. Susie was the one who was the chief cook and bottlewasher in the household. He remembered Si, her husband who'd been killed in a car crash at the time young Joy had been born. He'd liked Si.

At first Susie had taken Si's death badly, but lately she'd started going out a bit more than usual. Vera reckoned she was going to Bingo. Whatever she was doing it had put a sparkle in her eyes. It was great to see his Auntie Susie so happy nowadays. He couldn't see Joy so guessed she was asleep. She had school in the morning.

'Anyone say any more about how it was started?' Lol was perched on a kitchen stool. She looked small and defenceless and frightened.

He said, 'It was deliberate.'

Roy moved along the pine bench. 'We'll get the buggers. You done good, son,' he said.

Eddie looked about the busy kitchen, noticing there wasn't a sign his mother had been there.

'Where's Mum?'

'She ain't come 'ome yet, neither 'as Vera. They might be drownin' their sorrows together,' said Susie.

# CHAPTER 8

'I'm gonna sit in the back; you don't mind, do you, Alec? I want to put me feet up an' relax on the way 'ome.'

He opened the rear door of the Cortina and watched her neat figure climb in. To tell the truth he didn't care where she sat just so long as she was with him.

'And if it's okay, can we go down the bay an' park for a while? A walk along the beach'll get some of this stink out of me lungs an' help me think better before I go 'ome an' that lot starts askin' me questions.'

'If that's what you want, your wish is my command.' Alec closed the door on Daisy then settled himself in the driver's seat.

He was alone with Daisy at last. So what if it had taken a fire that destroyed Daisychains to make his dream come true? An ill wind always blew someone some good. Not that he would ever have told her how he felt about her. Nor for how long he had loved her. No, he was too shy for that. Even now his heart was beating fast and his hands on the steering wheel were clammy.

The nearest he'd ever got to the woman of his dreams was painting likenesses of her and storing them in his front bedroom. Daisy had never posed for him and Alec certainly wouldn't have dreamed of asking her. It didn't matter. He knew every line of her face and body by heart.

Alec stared in the rear view mirror. Daisy was sitting with her knees up to her chin and her head resting on her knees. She hadn't got over Samantha's death and now she'd been hit by the loss of her club.

'Tired?' he asked.

'Worn out,' she replied. The smell of smoke emanating from the pair of them filled the car. Alec wound down a window.

'Does the open window bother you?' he asked, looking back at her again. She lifted her face and he saw the fresh tracks of tears. She shook her head.

'Let's just get away from here,' Daisy said.

Alec drove down South Street, passing Tragedy Bank where the body of Samantha had been discovered. He then took the road by Haslar Hospital out to Stoke's Bay's sea wall. He parked on a grass verge and looked back at Daisy who was bitterly sobbing. His heart went out to her. What could he do to ease her suffering?

Across the vast expanse of dark water, lights from the Isle of Wight twinkled like low-slung stars. The sound of the waves washing against the deserted stone walls was like music. Alec didn't know when he had been so happy nor so confused. It was wonderful being close and alone with his Daisy at last.

He'd begun to lose all hope of ever having a life again. He couldn't say he'd battled with the booze and won because each day was a torment. Once an alcoholic, always an alcoholic, wasn't that the truth? The difference was in being strong enough not to give in and take a drink. He was trying so hard but instead of feeling elated, as he had at first, now his success made him more distraught. In erasing the drink his whole way of life had been obliterated.

When he wasn't working at Daisychains, so he could be near Daisy, there seemed little to look forward to. And the teaching? Some of the little horrors in his class didn't care whether they got an education or not.

Most nights he cried himself to sleep. Yet if someone asked him what the matter was there was no true answer he could have given.

'Don't take on so, Daisy,' he said softly, opening his door and climbing into the back of the car. Daisy budged up so he'd have more room. It was almost as though she was saying, yes, come and sit here, close to me, he thought.

She promptly nestled in to him and sniffed as she said:

'I never expected everything to go bleedin' pear shaped the way it 'as.'

'Everything happens for a reason,' he said. He spoke those words to make her feel better because he certainly didn't believe them himself.

But then, if the fire hadn't been started they wouldn't be together in the back of his car, he thought. He let an arm slip around her. The darkness seemed to have swallowed the car, making them invisible to the night.

He could smell the musk from her body, the remains of lemon shampoo in her smoke-streaked hair. Her face was so close Alec was aware of the salt her tears had left on her soft cheeks.

He kissed her then, his lips tender on her warm mouth, expecting Daisy to move away from him and shout, 'Oh, no, Alec, this isn't what I want.'

But she didn't.

He couldn't believe his good fortune. Here was his Daisy, ready to be caressed by him. He felt the excitement bubbling up inside him, making his penis swell to hardness. His hands roving down into the folds of Daisy's clothes couldn't fail to notice how her nipples had tightened to erect buds inside her black jumper.

Alec then ran his hand gently down her spine. Daisy shivered.

'Do you want me?' His voice was soft, hardly daring to believe she was here with him in the confines of the car and allowing him to touch her.

Running his hands over her belly, he gasped as he felt her fingers searching for the zip on his trousers. Her hands were insistent, soothing him, making him feel that life was, after all, so good.

Slipping off her panties and dropping them on the floor, she wriggled to accommodate him. His fingers felt the warm dampness of her throbbing sex as Daisy moaned with desire. He could sense her wanting to abandon herself to the act of fucking. He plunged inside her, hearing her catch her breath at their unexpected coupling. With deft strokes, desperate with desire, he thrust deep and withdrew, thrust deeper and pulled away, feeling her move with him. He was loving the musky taste and smell of her and, with her arms tight about his body, she was obviously wanting him just as much as he wanted her.

Then when he felt her spasm, he let himself go.

Afterwards as Daisy lay beneath him, her breathing laboured, Alec could hear once more the hectic wave-washed pebbles hitting the fortification that was the sea wall.

He slid from her, pulling her inert body to a sitting position with him.

'I didn't mean...'

'Don't worry,' she said in a shaky voice, 'I got carried away. It's been a long time...'

'Daisy, don't you know how I worship you?'

'I'm sorry if I led you on, Alec.'

Alec felt helpless, caught up in something he didn't understand.

'We did what came naturally to us because we both needed it,' she said. Alec stared at her wordlessly. He watched her fasten her clothing but noticed her hands were shaking. Eventually, he found his voice.

'You can't mean that.'

But he knew she did. Any relationship with Daisy would never be on equal terms. More importantly, the act of love that they'd just shared meant two different things for the pair of them. To him, fucking her meant everything, but Daisy had let him love her because she needed the comfort the act gave her.

He couldn't let Daisy see how upset he was.

'No strings,' he said, trying hard to keep his voice from betraying his feelings of hopelessness.

'No strings,' she replied, and he heard the relief in her voice. His heart was like lead as he opened the rear door and slid into the driver's seat once more.

Neither spoke as he drove down Jellicoe Avenue

and into Western Way. Alec pulled up outside her house and got out to open the door for Daisy. A soft rain was falling as he bent his head and kissed her lightly on the forehead as he had so many times before.

'I'll walk you to the front door,' he said. All the lights were on in her house and he had already spotted Roy Kemp's behemoth of a vehicle in the driveway.

'You coming in?' He knew she asked out of politeness. He shook his head.

He felt more distant from her than ever.

As soon as Daisy's key slid in the lock the oak door was wrenched open and she was pulled inside. He was aware of the noise and warmth coming from the house. The drizzle had turned into cold rain as he made his way back to his car.

Of course there were no lights on in *his* house. Who was there to welcome *him?*

He put his wet jacket over the newel post, switched on the light and went to the cupboard beneath the stairs that smelled of mouse droppings and sawdust. The coil of rope he took to the top of the stairs and threw the end neatly over the black painted beam, securing it.

In his work room he studied his paintings and sketches. Too many were of Daisy. Daisy throwing back her head and laughing like she hadn't a care in the world. Daisy staring pensively through the bar window. Alec allowed his fingers to run over the surface of Daisy's painted likeness. He went over to his brushes, cleaned and standing in pots ready for him. His fingers reached out and

84

caressed the camel hair before his hand moved along the table's surface and he picked up the charcoal. The frisson of excitement he usually felt at creating a new composition was gone.

Alec started to cry. He should never have taken advantage of Daisy's grief. Where she was concerned he'd felt alive when he had hope. But there was no hope now.

He went back on to the landing. His house was chilled and desolate. Its coldness seeped into him. He heard hard rain slashing against the bedroom window. Another sleepless night beckoned and he couldn't face it.

With tears coursing down his face, he fashioned a suitable loop that wouldn't come apart and slipped the noose over his head. The rough feel of the rope was scratchy on his skin. He told himself it wouldn't last long. Then nothing would hurt him any more.

Alec swung himself from the top step and into oblivion.

## CHAPTER 9

As the shower jetted over her, her tears mingled with the spray. What the fuck had she been thinking of to make love with Alec? Now, every time she looked at him, she would be reminded of how stupid she'd been.

A comfort fuck was all it had been for her, but when Alec told her he loved her, she knew it meant so much more for him. Oh, God, what had she done? Opened up a whole new can of worms. But Alec had agreed, hadn't he, no strings attached to their lovemaking? Daisy hoped and prayed he'd forgive her. But could she ever forgive herself?

Before she descended the stairs she looked in on Jamie. Her son was lying on his back with his eyes closed. Daisy listened to his steady breathing and decided he was fast asleep. In repose he looked like an angel with his golden hair and cherubic face. Rain was hitting the windows.

Wrapped in her old dressing gown she finally went downstairs. Roy was the first to greet her.

'Promise me you're all right?'

Enfolding her in his arms, swamping her in expensive cologne that didn't come off the back of a lorry. The concern in his slate-grey eyes gave her reassurance.

'I'm okay,' she said.

'You're still freezing cold,' Roy said. The wave of warmth from the kitchen and her family enveloped her.

'I'll put the kettle on again,' sang out Susie, who was wrapped in her pink dressing gown.

'I've only just got in meself,' grumbled Vera. Her hair was damp. 'Ad to come 'ome by taxi.' She'd obviously taken a shower down at the massage parlour for she looked scrubbed and clean.

Eddie, at the back of the crowded kitchen, winked at Daisy and immediately her spirits lifted. Her family's chattering grew in strength.

The topic was how they would all do their bit to survive the torching of her club.

She knew her eyes were puffy from her tears

86

and Roy asked softly, 'You sure you're all right, girl? I came as soon as I could.' Roy had been her lover on and off for years. Despite living in London she knew Roy didn't need much of an excuse to be near her.

'Thanks,' she whispered, pulling out a kitchen chair and sitting down. Roy reclaimed his seat on the bench that Kibbles had taken, lifting the old cat on to his lap.

'I hear Eddie pulled his weight.' Roy Kemp loved her son. They were easy in each other's company, and only a few weeks ago Roy had asked her if she'd consider allowing Eddie to stay in London permanently. 'Over my fuckin' dead body,' had been her speedy reply.

The room was now suddenly hushed as Roy said, 'I reckon Daisychains was set alight deliberately.'

Vera said, 'That's what the firemen said – arson – only it ain't official yet.'

'Well I never,' exclaimed Susie. The sound of rattling mugs suddenly ceased.

'*I've* had a couple of places torched in this area, and one in London.'

Roy looked sheepish as he shared this information with them. His long legs were stretched out in front of him and Kibbles was now asleep. Daisy knew what it had cost him to confess to the burning down of his clubs. It wouldn't do to broadcast that someone had got one over Roy Kemp.

'But Daisychains don't belong to you, it ain't one of your places!' Vera put her hand to her mouth, realising she'd spoken out of turn. Roy shook his head.

'I know,' he said.

Daisy said, 'If it was money the firestarter was after, he was unlucky. Who could 'ave done this, Roy?' She didn't wait for an answer. 'Why 'ave you had your places set on fire, Roy?'

'That's for me to find out, Daisy.'

'And 'ave you found out who killed our Samantha?'

He shook his head.

'Jesus Christ, am I always goin' to be hurt in some way or another simply because I bloody knows you?' Daisy thought how she had almost died and fear engulfed her. Would the persons responsible try again? Was it only the club Roy's enemies had wanted to destroy, or was it *her*? There was a long silence then Daisy looked Roy straight in the eye and said, 'Will you buy the freehold to Daisychains, Roy?'

Her question had come right out of the blue.

There was a gasp from Susie and when Vera turned to look at her she quickly pulled her dressing gown even more tightly around herself and formed her mouth into a thin line. The clamour in the kitchen had suddenly died to a pregnant silence.

'That's quietened you all down, 'asn't it,' said Daisy. None of them would ever know the courage it had taken her to ask him that favour.

Roy started drumming his fingertips on the kitchen table. 'What makes you think I want it?'

Daisy took a deep breath. 'Years ago I sold you the caff an' you made a handsome profit on that. You could do the same with Daisychains, or what's left of it.'

Still the silence could be cut with a knife, thought Daisy. Her Eddie looked from one person to another. Lol was deeply engrossed in picking at her long fingernails as though they were the most important things on earth. Vera was staring at Daisy with her mouth open, her small white teeth almost glittering in the light. Suze looked as though she wished the kitchen floor would open and swallow her up. Daisy knew she had to front this out. She stood up and put her hands on her hips and stared at Roy.

She was well aware Roy Kemp was the most feared gangster in London today. Him and the Kray twins spoke regularly on the phone, for Ronnie and Reggie needed to know, as Roy'd taken over most of their holdings in the city, that their beloved mother, Violet, was being looked after.

Daisy breathed steadily and evenly. Here was Eddie's hero, the man who looked like an ageing David Essex, and he was staring intently back at her. It was as though the two of them were the only people in the kitchen. She waited, hardly daring to breathe, for his answer. For he *would* give her an answer, she knew that, was gambling on it.

'Twenty thousand pounds,' he said.

'Twenty-five and you settle the outstanding bills on the place?'

'Why so much, Dais?' His slate-grey eyes were calculating.

'Because she needs to clear the mortgage she took out on this place, pay Vera what she owes her, pay the outstanding invoices and sort out our household bills.' This came from Eddie who was sitting with his elbows on the table and his fingers clasped like a miniature steeple. Eddie rocked back on his chair.

'Straight out of the mouth of your son, eh, Dais?' Roy laughed.

He still hadn't agreed and Daisy's heart was thumping so loud she was sure everyone could hear it.

Then, moving the sleeping Kibbles to the bench, Roy stood up and clapped Eddie on the shoulder. 'You got a sharp lad here, Dais. And the boy thinks the world of you. I wish you'd let him come and work for me.'

'He may be sharp but I ain't fuckin' simple.' She looked around the kitchen at her family but her gaze slid back to Roy. 'This Eddie Lane I want alive an' kickin' in his old age, not dead like his father. We got a deal or not?'

Roy walked over to her and put his arms around her, nuzzling into her hair. And suddenly she felt like a deflated balloon as he asked, pulling away from her, 'I suppose this means you ain't got a hope in hell's chance of getting any insurance money for the fire?'

Daisy shook her head. 'Just don't make me tell you why.'

'Well, I never could refuse you anything: it's a deal.' He turned to Eddie and said. 'Your mother's a very special lady, son, and I love her to bits.'

'Thank you,' Daisy whispered. She felt like she'd gone through a mangle.

Eddie was staring at Roy's expensive suit and his gold cufflinks and said, 'You ain't so dusty yourself. But now the negotiations are over I think I could do with a kip.'

Daisy grinned at her son. After the goodnights had been said, he left the kitchen to go upstairs. Daisy followed him, to check on her youngest boy.

They walked in silence up the wooden steps, in single file, Daisy more settled in her mind now she knew she could pull herself out of debt. She'd worry about earning a living later. Anyway, she already had a few thoughts on that score. Then she was smothering a laugh as she heard a soft footfall behind her. Vera's moggie, as usual, was also going to bed, with his beloved Eddie.

Eddie was just about to pass his brother's room when Jamie opened his door and said, 'Bloody blue-eyed boy, ain't you? How come you always get to know what's goin' on?' Daisy pressed herself back against the wall.

Obviously Jamie had no idea she was there.

'Don't be stupid, Jamie. And don't cause a fuss. All this has knocked Mum and Auntie Vera for six. Just be thankful Mum's made it so we can stay in this house...'

'And bleedin' Roy Kemp comes to the rescue again—'

Eddie cut short his words. 'For a thirteen-year-old you can be such a kid at times.' Eddie walked on, opened his bedroom door and disappeared inside, the mackerel cat running ahead of him. He closed the door.

Daisy stood quite still. She heard Jamie's door close. She wanted to go into his bedroom and throttle him. Or at least have it out with him. But then he'd know she had eavesdropped. Alec's

91

face swam before her eyes. Far better she leave things as they were. Hadn't she already made enough bad decisions today?

Back in the kitchen Roy had poured himself a brandy. He got up and fetched another glass as soon as she entered. They were magically alone.

'You making me drive back to London tonight?'

'Is that a way of saying you expect to share me bed?' Daisy could hear voices from the living room and then the sound of the television. She could imagine them squashed on chairs and the sofa and waiting for a fictitious drama to unfold.

'I don't expect anything. I happen to love you, Daisy Lane.'

Daisy sat down on a kitchen chair with a huge sigh, picked up her glass and raised it in salute to Roy before she took a mouthful.

'And what about what's 'er face, Eve?'

He spluttered into his drink. As soon as he had composed himself he said, 'She means nothing to me an' you bloody know it! But I can't be seen without a bit of skirt on me arm just because you won't come up to London when I ask you. What d'you take me for? I'm a fuckin' bloke, Daisy.'

And then she was crying again. He got up, lifted her from her seat, took her in his arms and smoothed back the hair from her face.

'It's been a bugger of a day, Daisy. Sometimes I wonder at the strength of a little thing like you. Let me stay? Let me love you like you need to be loved?'

Daisy sighed. She wouldn't send him home.

# CHAPTER 10

'You don't understand, Vera. It's not like Alec to not pop round or telephone to ask how I am. It's just not like 'im.'

'Go round 'is 'ouse then, Daisy. See what the matter is.'

'I ain't goin' on me own.' After what had happened in the car at the sea wall she was apprehensive about being alone with him again, but she *was* worried about him. After all, his frame of mind was not always stable. Suppose he'd started drinking again...

Vera was sitting at the kitchen table, a square mirror propped against a milk bottle, drawing her scant eyebrows into a thin arched line. She'd just painted her nails bright red so she was using the brow pencil with care. Daisy tried again.

'I ain't goin' on me own.'

Vera slammed the pencil down on the kitchen table and the fine tip broke off.

'Shit! Look what you made me do, Daisy Lane, an' it took me ages to sharpen the bloody thing.'

'I said, I don't want to go–'

'I heard you the first time, and since you won't let me 'ave any peace until I offers to come, I'll be ready as soon as I've put on me lippy.'

'Thank you.' Daisy bent and cuddled Vera's slim shoulders and breathed in her perfume of Californian Poppy. Then she rose and picked up the tea mugs and put them in the sink, running water in them. She went past Vera again and stopped to watch her carefully blot her lipstick with a tissue.

Vera said, 'If you're goin' upstairs to get your coat, will you bring down me red jacket?' Daisy nodded.

Fifteen minutes later Daisy was pulling up at Alec's Elson home. Leaves were swirling around the pavement in the stiff breeze.

'Well, he's been lookin' after the outside of the house,' said Vera, nodding at the front garden while struggling out of Daisy's flame-red MG. Daisy, already out and on the kerb, waited for her to ask why she didn't get a bigger car. That's how any car journey with Vera usually ended. Instead Vera was strangely quiet as she pushed open the gate and strode up the path.

The front garden's lawn looked like it could do with a cut, thought Daisy as she followed Vera, who moved a stone beside the front door with her foot and then bent down and picked up the key.

'How did you know the key was there?'

'Everyone hides their keys in the same places,' said Vera, inserting it into the Yale lock. 'Usually under the mat, or in a hangin' basket or under a stone or sometimes on the top of the door frame. I don't need to be a bleedin' detective, Dais.'

The key turned and the door swung open.

'Shouldn't we knock first?'

'If the poor sod's flat out with the drink, he ain't gonna answer no soddin' door, is he? An' we'll leave the door open, it could do with a bit of an airin' in 'ere.'

94

Daisy said, 'You go in first.' The hall light was on. A couple of bluebottles soared past them.

'He don't need to waste electric, does he?' Vera turned the light off.

'I don't think he's in, it's too quiet,' Daisy said. She thought if Alec arrived home he might be angry at them for invading his space. No telling how he would act after the funny moods he'd been in just lately.

'Cooee!' Vera's voice was loud and made Daisy jump.

'That's enough to waken the dead, your voice is,' said Daisy.

'Well, he ain't in the livin' room.' Vera came out of the front room and began to march down the passage. The kitchen was at the back, the stairs dividing the house. There was a funny earthy sort of smell...

Daisy ran to her and gripped her arm. 'Don't go any further,' she warned.

Vera turned and stared at Daisy. Her eyes were wide. She said, 'We're both thinkin' the same thing, ain't we...'

'Where is the poor bastard, then... Oh my God!'

Daisy huddled closer to Vera, both of them staring up the carpeted stairs. In the breeze that was drifting inside from the front door, Alec's bloated body swung to and fro.

'Why didn't you let me know?' Even after all this time Vinnie's delicious different-coloured eyes had the power to make her knees go weak. Daisy stared at him. Dressed as usual in a suit with a police-issue mac over it, he towered above her.

She could smell his piney cologne.

'What would you 'ave done? Come runnin' from your wife Clare's place in the country an' put the fire out with your bare 'ands? Or perhaps you'd piss on it. You never did like the club.'

'Sarcasm doesn't become you, Daisy Lane.' He ran his fingers through his dark curls. Daisy continued peeling potatoes. Her anger made her dig out the eyes ferociously before she slung them into the aluminium saucepan.

'Yeah, well I don't suppose you'll find out who started the blaze any more than you've found out who killed Samantha.' Daisy flung the words at him but she guessed that, as usual, he wasn't listening to her. 'I won't let this go, Vinnie,' she said.

'I knew nothing until I heard the news from South Street nick, and then from young Jamie. Any idea how that makes me feel?'

'And I had no idea I was under an obligation to tell you everythin'. Nor about Alec committin' suicide neither. Anyway, me an' Vera are sorted without your 'elp.'

'The fire at the club was arson,' Vinnie insisted.

Daisy nodded. 'Tell me somethin' I don't know. Anyway you wouldn't 'ave come running. Not when you found out Roy was 'ere. Not you, with your likin' for a squeaky clean reputation. I just 'appened to think I could do without you, Mr Detective.'

'But you don't mind involving Roy Kemp?'

'I sold 'im the bleedin' freehold! 'Ave you got the dosh to get me and mine out of trouble?' He looked defeated. 'Well, just be thankful that bastard Roy Kemp has. Now I got to do something to get the money rollin' in again.'

'If I can help...' She didn't give him time to finish.

'Like you 'elp with Jamie?'

'He comes to stay–'

'But he don't 'ave the place in your heart that your eldest boy, Jack, does and the poor little bleeder knows it!'

'Don't talk rubbish. And I give you money when you'll *let* me, don't I?'

'It ain't your fuckin' *money* I want. That lad is insecure. Why do you think he suddenly lashes out? Why do you think one minute he's all sweetness and light an' the next he's a bleedin' psycho?'

'That's your own boy you're talking about...' Vinnie's face was as dark as the black dirt on the potatoes.

'At least I'm honest. He ain't like Eddie...'

'Here we go again! Not like the son of the marvellous smalltime Gosport thug. Of course Jamie isn't. I'm not a bloody gangster, though sometimes I wish I was!' He was breathing heavily. Daisy was speechless. She knew she was wrong to have a go at him, but ever since he'd thrown her over to go back with his wife she'd been unable to control her innermost thoughts, especially when Jamie pushed her to her absolute limits.

She could almost reach out and touch the icy silence between them.

He was the first to speak. 'Daisy, I'm sorry,' he said. 'We shouldn't argue.'

He was right. She felt herself soften towards him, but to save face she slammed the saucepan on the top of the gas stove causing the water to spew out in all directions. 'Bugger!' she said. Then, 'No, we shouldn't argue, but I once loved you so much it bleedin' 'urt. And you threw me away so you could get a leg up in your career an' a leg over with your ex-wife. What's next, Detective Chief Inspector Vinnie Endersby? Who d'you tread on next?'

'Stop it, Daisy. I can't help the way I'm made and neither can you. And you do make a great job of bringing up both your boys.'

She sniffed and reached for the cloth to wipe up the spilled water.

'Fair enough,' she said. She knew her temper had run its limit. '*Are* you any further forward in finding out who killed Samantha?'

He shook his head. 'No – and she's not the only woman who's come to a nasty end recently.'

Daisy swallowed. Her fire had well and truly left her now. 'All prossies?'

'No, just ordinary women. A young mother with a couple of kiddies. She'd recently had a pools win – not a great amount but more'n she'd had in her life before. An elderly woman from a nice house at Clanfield – her savings had been drawn from the bank. And two sisters in their fifties from Portsmouth.'

'These crimes, are they connected?'

'Yes, they're connected. All the victims were strangled, and all left with pieces of wood stuck inside their mouths, so they couldn't call out before they died. The speed with which this bloke insinuates himself into lonely women's lives is incredible. He must have the charm of the devil.' Daisy bristled and shook her head.

'Fingerprints? Don't you have fingerprints?'

'The clever bastard clears all traces. But stop worrying about other people, Daisy, these are my problems, not yours. Are you really all right for money?'

'At present, yes. The house is secure now so we're not about to be chucked out on the street. And all the debts are sorted...'

'I've got some put by.'

'I don't want your bleedin' charity, you can stick it up your bleedin' arse!' He laughed at her.

Daisy and Vera walked out into the car park at Portchester Crematorium.

'Not very nice to 'ave lived a life and leave it with bugger-all people to mourn you, is it, Dais?'

'A few of your girls, an me an' you, Vera.' Daisy pulled up the collar of her black wool belted coat.

'Did you ever in a million years think Alec would commit suicide, Dais?'

Daisy stopped walking and turned to her. The Crematorium gardens, alive with colour in the warm weather, were fading fast as autumn approached. In fact they looked as dejected as Daisy felt.

'If you want the honest bleedin' truth, no. I wish I could 'ave known sooner what he was goin' through. I never knew his depression was that severe.' She fumbled in her pocket for a piece of tissue, sniffing as she did so.

'Our flowers were nice, wasn't they?' Vera had changed the subject.

Daisy nodded. 'Chrysanths always makes a nice show.'

'Nice of you to foot the bill for everythin', Dais...'

Daisy couldn't hold on to her feelings any longer. All through the service she'd gritted her teeth and tried to be sensible; now she threw herself into Vera's arms. Her friend had no option but to hold her close and let her cry. After a while Daisy's tears abated and she said, 'I need to tell you somethin'. We'll go up on top of the hill an' I'll explain. It's my fault Alec's dead.'

Vera pushed her away. 'Don't be so fuckin' stupid.'

Daisy pulled Vera across the tarmac to her MG. After fumbling in her purse for the keys she got in and released the catch so Vera could climb in.

'Don't say nothin' 'til you've 'eard what I got to say,' Daisy said, starting up the small red sports car.

In silence Daisy drove up towards the top road that spanned the hill. The wind was noisy, rattling against the tiny car, and specks of rain hurled themselves at the windscreen. At the beauty spot's nearest car park, Daisy pulled in and killed the engine. The whole panorama that was Portsmouth was spread below them.

She turned to Vera who, for the occasion, was also dressed in black, her dark hair peeping from below her wide-brimmed hat. Vera's eyes held hers.

'You better tell me...'

'Remember the night of the fire? And Alec took me home?'

Vera nodded. And Daisy told her what had happened.

You could almost touch the silence in the car, thought Daisy, as she explained to Vera she'd made it plain after Alec had loved her that there was no future for them.

'It's my fault he hanged himself.'

'If you go on thinking that you'll send yourself round the bend, ducky. You ain't the first nor will you be the last to have an unwise quickie with a bloke you don't love but needs a bit of comfort from.'

Vera sighed deeply.

'But he'd have been alive now, if we hadn't ... hadn't...'

'Do you know that for sure? You can't look in a bloke's 'ead an' tell what goes on there. What if he was plannin' to kill 'imself all along?'

'But Alec's past was behind him and he'd got the drink under control, Vera.'

'You don't get better from bein' an alcoholic. It's always there, naggin' at a person to take just one sweet drink. *You* might have thought he had it under control, and his life an' all. Only, you can't know what was goin' on inside 'im.'

'But by sleepin' with 'im I messed his 'ead up even more...'

'Oh, don't be so fuckin' melodramatic! You could understudy Bette Davis you could!' Vera was now tapping her fingers on the car's windows and her heavy rings were clattering against the glass on the inside while the rain beat a steady tattoo on the outside.

'So what you tellin' me?' Daisy said.

'Look at me, and listen good. Alec made a deliberate decision to do away with 'imself. So don't that tell you he wasn't in 'is right mind? He ain't been in 'is right mind for years. It wasn't nothin' to do with you. You didn't do anything to hurt Alec. The person who meant him the most harm lived right inside his own bleedin' 'ead.'

Daisy listened to Vera. What she said made sense. For a few moments neither of them spoke. Daisy gave a huge sigh. Sometimes she felt like giving up. What was all the struggling in life for? Holding on, that was it, that's what life was all about.

Then Vera said, 'This bleedin' rain's getting on my tits. Let's get 'ome an' have a cup of tea.'

Daisy looked at Vera through damp lashes and smiled.

Gaetano Maxi, who now went by the name Bruno Pace, punched the pillow into a more comfortable shape and slipped it behind his back. The bed smelled faintly of her perfume and their lovemaking.

'That's better, Tammy. I can see you properly now.' He looked across the room to where his whore lay on the sofa. Her hair was long and blonde and she was sloppily dressed in a white and red filmy nightgown that had ridden up exposing her pale legs and bouncy breasts. 'You got nice tits. I like nice tits.'

He let his mind wander. Tammy was too beautiful to stand on the street with a red plastic skirt up to her arse and her tits hanging out of that – what was it called? – quarter bra. For one thing it was autumn and the nights were cold. Tonight had been drizzling with rain when he'd met her down by the gasworks.

Why have powdered cleavage? Why wear such garish eye-shadow and a ton of fuckin' lipstick? Most blokes prefer their sex with scrubbed-faced tarts, he'd thought.

Bruno looked into her eyes. They were blue and really quite small but the black mascara gave them depth. 'Pretty eyes,' he said, and a smile lifted the corners of his lips. He stared around the room. Wind chimes hung from drawing pins pressed into the ceiling. Ornamental china cats covered every surface wherever there was a shelf for them to stand. Tammy had stamped her personality on the room, and it showed. She loved cats because even the bloody curtains were printed with kittens playing with blue wool balls.

He yawned. He was tired but he wouldn't stay the night with her. It would be too risky. He glanced towards his jeans, folded neatly on the chair. He could almost see the roll of notes in their pocket. It hadn't been his money, but it was now.

He thought about the sex. They'd entered the room after climbing the tower of stairs to the top floor; he wrinkled his nose remembering the stairwell that stank of piss. Tammy had laughed and grabbed hold of him, rubbing his cock through his jeans as soon as they'd got inside her room.

Then her clothes were off and so were his but she'd slipped on that ridiculous froth of white. On the bed she'd put her hands to her cunt and spread her legs wide so he could look into her pussy. It reminded him of a flower, a red, juicy-looking bud that tasted of the sea.

And then she sat up, pulling away from him,

begging him not to make her come too soon.

'Let me suck you,' she'd said.

'Don't you like pricks inside you?' he'd asked.

'I can take anything you have to offer,' she laughed. She blew lightly on the throbbing head of his erection, then opened her mouth and her lips touched him, very, very lightly. She licked his hole and flicked her tongue around the rim. And then she took him deeper, deeper into her mouth.

'Get it down you, take me,' he'd pleaded, with her face pressed into his curly dark fuzz.

She sucked all of him into her damp warm mouth again. And then he was fucking that deep moistness and she was sucking it like it was the last thing she would ever do. Afterwards, he'd laid her gently, reverently on the sofa.

And now he got up from the bed and dressed in his underwear, shirt and jeans. From the street outside came the noise of traffic.

He combed his hair carefully, whistling 'Que Sera, Sera'. He shook his jacket before slipping it on and moved over to Tammy, kissing her lightly on her cool forehead.

'*Non ti scordar di me,*' he said. Then he opened the door and walked out without a backward glance at her, or the stick he'd jammed in her mouth, or the breadknife he'd screwed her with afterwards and which was still embedded in her lifeless body.

# CHAPTER 11

'I could give you a job.' Daisy glared at Vera. Eddie smothered a grin.

'That's defeatin' the object, ain't it? The object is to bring new money into the house not recycle the old!' His mum had on her old black jeans and a black polo-necked jumper. He thought she looked like a young girl with her blonde hair tied in a ponytail. Eddie thought he'd join in the banter.

'You wouldn't be a prossie, would you, Mum?'

'There ain't nothing wrong with the oldest profession in the world, son.' Daisy grinned at Eddie. 'But it's not for me.' She turned to Vera. 'Thank you for the kind offer.'

'You could start a bookstall,' said Susie. She was rolling out pastry for a jam tart. It was Saturday morning and they were all around the table for a conference except for Jamie and Joy. Joy was in the garden playing in her Wendy house and Jamie was around somewhere. The kitchen smelled of cake baking and vanilla polish.

'Sure I know the second-hand book business inside out but I'll leave that to your Uncle Bri. I don't want to be treadin' on his toes, do I?'

'Caff.'

'Come on, Suze, I can't afford to rent premises and fit 'em out, an' I reckon after all those years cookin' fryups in Bert's Caff I don't want to repeat the bleedin' experience.'

'I should be doing something,' began Lol, but she never got a chance to finish.

'Shut up,' said Vera

'Any more ideas?'

Silence reigned. Eddie smoothed Kibble's fur and the cat started purring. He moved the animal slightly to relieve the pressure of the flick knife in his pocket. It was his father's knife. His mother would go round the bend if she knew he kept it on him at all times when he went out. Normally when he was home it was in the top drawer of his bedside cabinet. He could hit anything with it. Even across a room his aim was spot on.

He tried to keep the knife hidden from Jamie though; no telling what would happen if he got hold of it, though he did sometimes wonder if his brother had been secretly playing with the knife. Once or twice he'd been sure it had been removed from the drawer and then returned.

Susie was spooning red jam in the tarts and the theme from *Rocky* was playing on the radio when Daisy finally spoke again.

'You know these car boot things what's been springin' up all over the place?'

'Where people clears out their rubbish and takes it to a field or barn and buys rubbish off another person what's taken their rubbish along?'

'Got it in one, Vera.'

'It's crap bein' moved about.'

'Sold, Vera.'

'We ain't got no crap,' said Susie. 'I keeps this place spotless!' She was all pink-faced from the heat of the oven where she'd put in the baking trays. Eddie licked his lips, he liked jam tarts.

'I know that, you silly cow!' said Daisy. 'I got to go an' buy some stuff.'

'Thought you was supposed to make a profit *selling?*'

'Got to 'ave somethin' for others to buy first.'

'Where you goin' to buy stuff?'

'Car boots and auctions.'

'Car boots an' auctions?'

'What are you, Susie, a fuckin' parrot?' Eddie laughed and Vera sat stone faced.

'I buy stuff cheap at car boots and sell it on, auction the choice bits. I can do this,' his mother said and Eddie believed her. His mum could do anything she put her mind to.

'You got enough money to start?'

'Don't really need all that much. If I start with a few quid and make a profit then I'm on to a winner. If I put in a lot of dosh and I lose it then I'm bleedin' stupid.'

'Don't they sell off paste tables?'

'I'll make do with putting me gear on an old blanket on the ground,' said Daisy. 'Buy tables later if it works out.'

Susie looked up. 'Actually there are two old tables in the shed. One's a small square plastic one with legs that unscrew and the other's a paste table but it needs nailing up a bit.'

Eddie said, 'I can soon fix that.'

Vera said, 'They won't go in Daisy's silly little MG, will they? In fact nothin' can get in that bloody machine except Daisy.'

Eddie thought for a bit then said, 'I know. Tyrone can use his mum's Mini.'

He saw his mother look at him as though he'd

gone mad.

'A Mini!'

'It's got four seats and a decent boot an' his mum won't mind if we put a roof rack on the top for the tables.'

'I ain't plannin' on buyin big stuff,' Daisy said.

'We bung Tyrone's mum a fiver 'ere an' there. Don't forget, Ty loves that car an' she knows he'll look after it.'

His mum was looking a bit down in the mouth.

'Now I got two people to pay an' I ain't earned any money yet!'

Just then Jamie came in and sat down at the kitchen table.

'Hello, love,' said his mother. Eddie smiled at him but Jamie scowled back.

Susie opened the oven door and took out the first tray of jam tarts she'd made earlier.

'Smell yummy they do,' Eddie said, licking his lips. 'Anyway Ty's mum's promised him the Mini if he passes his test which comes up next week. Her boyfriend 'as got a nearly new Cortina. Ty says her boyfriend reckons the Mini's no good to 'ave sex in, a Cortina would be easier on his back!'

Vera let out a laugh and then smothered it with a hand. 'Well, I never,' she said.

Susie looked up from the oven where a second tray of tarts were emerging. 'I bet you 'ave, our Vera!' And then Eddie laughed.

'I won't be needin' any of it yet, I'll just use me own car to buy a bit of stuff first.'

'That's a bloody stupid idea.'

His mother turned on Vera.

'Why?'

'If sellers sees you in that poncy little thing they'll think you got money. The same as when Gosport people knows you live in Western Way, they thinks you got money. It's a class thing. Folks don't realise you can live in a smart place an' 'ave a nice little car but be livin' by the skin of your teeth!'

'That makes sense,' Eddie said.

'Well, I'll 'ave to make sure I parks me *poncy* little car out of sight then, won't I?'

'Fair enough,' said Eddie. 'Can I come?'

'No, you bleedin' can't. You ought to be getting a trade – and not as an understudy to Roy Kemp.'

'A trade's not what I want.'

'He's right, Dais.' Eddie gave Vera a grateful look of thanks. She continued, 'Why don't you let 'im 'elp?' He could see his mother thinking quickly.

'If I say yes, will you promise me that if it all goes pear shaped you'll start learnin' a trade?'

'Yes!' He wasn't going to ask her what she considered a 'trade' or he might find himself promising to take on an apprenticeship to a tradesman. While that was good in theory and suited a lot of men, no way was he going to slog his guts out for a peanuts wage for years. Besides, he knew he was like his mother: she didn't like being told what to do by anyone else and neither did he. He wanted to be his own boss like she was and take whatever life threw at him. So far his mother didn't look bad on it. He grinned at her.

His mother got up and went to the sink to fill the kettle. While she was there she stole a jam tart off the wire tray where Susie had left them to cool.

Lol said, 'I can help.' But her plea was ignored.

'You'll need to get up early in the mornings,' his mother said through a mouthful of pastry.

'I can do that,' said Eddie.

'You'll also need to study these books I got from the library.' Daisy went over to the sideboard and took out three volumes of *Collecting Antiques* and laid them on the table.

Eddie was surprised; he never thought she'd consent. He picked her up, whirling her slight body around the kitchen.

'Put me down, you oaf,' she yelled, but he knew she didn't mean it.

'Anyone want a jam tart?' Susie asked.

'Yes,' chorused Vera and Lol. Eddie caught sight of Jamie's face. It was sour enough to turn milk bad.

## CHAPTER 12

Fuckin' hell, didn't the old bag ever stop opening her bloody mouth!

Her voice followed him as he carried the weighty glass-topped box into the garage, kicking open the door to the kitchen and thankfully sliding the box onto the table. And still the woman was yacking at him.

'Is heavy, this gold jewellery.' He cut her off in mid sentence. She'd followed him in and flopped her ample body on a kitchen chair. Her thighs draped themselves over the sides and he wanted to be sick. If he had to fuck her one more time he'd slit his own throat.

'There's a fair bit there, Bruno. We 'ad a good night at the auction, didn't we? Make us a cuppa, me little Italian love.'

He tuned out from the repeat of the boring conversation she'd had with a friend in the auction room to whom she'd explained her forthcoming holiday to Italy, and put the kettle to boil.

The kitchen smelled of her stale, sweaty flesh.

His eyes fell on the flight tickets on the draining board. He'd say she'd given him his in case they got separated on the way to the airport. If the police caught up with him when he came back from Italy he'd say he thought she'd decided not to come. Then another worrying thought struck him: when he returned he'd have to do something about that blonde bint of Roy Kemp's. He smiled to himself. Roy Kemp believed Gaetano Maxi was still in prison. However, under the assumed name of Bruno Pace he was out and he'd give that bastard Kemp plenty of grief; he'd see him banged up inside where *he* belonged.

Bruno thought about Roy Kemp's nefarious dealings with that fucking detective Vinnie Endersby. Together they'd foiled his nice little earner from the porno and snuff films he'd wanted to export abroad *and* got him a prison sentence. And that wasn't the only thing Roy Kemp had done. That fuckin' bastard had been the cause of his younger brothers' deaths too. Drugs for one and a bullet in the head for the other – but Italians were good at revenge and Roy Kemp had run his manor for too long. Bruno laughed softly to himself and tapped his fingers

111

on the table. Maurie Nelson was going to be the next king of the underworld and he, Bruno Pace, or Gaetano Maxi as he'd once been known, would reign with him.

But first he needed to raise some more cash. Money was what Maurie Nelson needed to finance the drugs takeover, and money was what Bruno would provide. Of course, Nelson wouldn't know how he came by the money. That Bruno killed women for cash didn't matter; what did matter was seeing Roy Kemp's empire topple.

Her voice intruded on his thoughts.

'So didn't I say to Marlene...?'

His head ached with the echo of her voice. It was only made bearable by the wallet full of money on the draining board in readiness to spend on holiday. Her savings, the silly cow. As if he'd ever settle for someone as ugly as her. A common market trader who sold gold secondhand jewellery bought at rock bottom prices at the auction houses. Still, that little lot in the box would bring him in a pretty penny when he took it round to a fence he knew.

He stirred the tea bag in the mug until the colour burst forth like brown blood. Two sugar lumps, just the way she liked it. He patted his inside pocket, smiled to himself and took the tea over to her, placing the mug on the table.

'You're a good boy,' she said. She'd taken off her plimsoles and the smell of her feet joined her body odour. He went behind her chair and started to knead her shoulder blades. Now she was talking about the auction again, but it wouldn't be long before she was silenced forever. 'That's it,' she said. 'Knead them knots from me muscles, darlin'.'

'*Non ti scordar di me,*' he said.

The blade was sharp so it slid easily through her meaty flesh. Not too deep, he didn't want to sever her head from her body, but he needed the cut to be just deep enough. She gave a choking sound, more of a gurgle really, before she slumped forward, blood pumping.

Bugger, he'd got some of the fat cow's blood on his shirt! He swore again, this time in Italian, thinking how oaths sounded so much more musical in his own language.

His hands were covered in bits of her gory skin. Nevertheless when he was finished, and stood back to survey his handiwork, he was pleased.

'That's shut up your fucking row,' he said.

Her tongue protruded through the slit in her neck.

'That's called a Brazilian Necktie,' he said. He wiped his bloody fingers on his shirt that he'd definitely have to dispose of now and began to laugh. 'An Italian Necktie would be a better name,' he said.

Eddie opened his eyes. Lol was shaking his naked shoulder. She caught his warm masculine smell that sleep had enhanced.

'Whadda ya want?' Kibbles, curled at the foot of the bed and disgusted at being disturbed, jumped down and slunk off into the darkness.

'I need to talk.'

'Oh, Lol, can't it wait?'

'No.' She meant business and she took a deep breath. 'I can get the money your mum needs for a bigger vehicle.'

Her hand dropped to the counterpane, her fingers twisting the material.

'Even if you could, you should know she wouldn't take money off you.' He wiped the sleep from his eyes.

'She's a good woman and I want to repay her for the kindness she's done me.'

'Don't worry about it,' he said. 'She wouldn't have done it if she didn't want to.'

'Too right I wouldn't.'

Lol turned her head towards Daisy's voice.

'I never heard you–'

'Don't you worry about me, I couldn't sleep so I was going downstairs to make a cuppa.'

'No, don't leave, Daisy. It's time you knew the truth an' all.'

Daisy sat down on an upright chair. Lol thought how tired she looked. The worry of keeping all her family together was beginning to tell on her.

'If you're sure I won't be in the way...' Daisy tightened the belt of her old off-white dressing gown.

'I was thinking I could go and work for Vera,' said Lol.

She saw the look of disgust on Eddie's face, closely followed by Daisy's anger that manifested itself by her tightening her lips into a thin line.

Daisy said, 'You got to be jokin'!'

Lol shook her head then tucked a strand of her long blonde hair behind an ear.

'It's what I was doin' in London.'

'I don't think I want to hear...' Eddie began.

'I want the two of you to listen. Why d'you

think that lot set on me down the ferry?' Eddie didn't answer. 'They sussed what I was on the boat coming to Gosport. I was hoping to get paid – the blond one was up for it – only he couldn't lose face in front of his mates so it turned into a free for all. All I needed was a few quid for a bed and breakfast.'

Daisy's tears weren't far away.

'I was hungry and I had no money.'

'You was running away from something or someone?' Daisy asked.

Lol nodded. She stared into Eddie's lovely green eyes, eyes he'd inherited from his mother. But they were cold and expressionless.

'The coppers raided The Crinoline Club in Soho. It wasn't the usual raid where we went upstairs with those that wanted it and Big Mick bunged the chief a wad to keep him sweet; this time it was for real. There's this snout shouting the odds about scams the coppers are in...'

'Wouldn't be Maurie Nelson?'

Daisy frowned. 'How d'you know that, Eddie?' she said.

'Roy's got problems with him, remember?'

Lol nodded. 'I squeezed out the lav window, thank God I'm skinny. I don't dare get my name on record because ... my father ... he's never accepted me...'

Eddie pulled the blanket free and wrapped it around her. She was as cold as ice and that's how her heart felt.

'I'll start with the good memories. When I was little I used to dress up in my mother's fringed shawls and dance in front of the mirror to

115

records. Jeanette MacDonald and Nelson Eddy; I'd swirl and tap my feet to the rhythm. I think I knew I was different even then. My mother's clothes smelled of the rose perfume she always wore. She loved to watch films so we'd sit in the dark of the auditorium together and I'd adore Joan Crawford's hats and Bette Davis's walk.'

'No wonder you gets on so well with our Vera,' said Daisy.

Lol treated her to a smile and nodded as Eddie chimed in, 'Bette'd stride in and take over the film like it belonged to her, which in a way it did.'

'My mother had some beautiful clothes. Long gowns and hats with plumes.'

'I bet you strutted around, loving it.' said Eddie. Lol knew he'd understand.

'Not really. Imagine being five years old and thinking that you're in the wrong body. My father called me a cissy.'

She shivered. 'It's all right,' said Eddie. He drew her close and she could feel the heat of his body. 'Go on.'

'I got sent away to boarding school. I remember Daddy being angry because I didn't like rugby, or running or even swimming. He was always asking me when I was going to stop looking in the mirror and toughen up. I never told him that I was raped at school. I was nine, the first time.'

'Oh, Lol,' Eddie said. She could hear the concern in his voice.

'Oh, sweetheart,' echoed Daisy.

'I remember living in constant terror of the beatings and sexual abuse. I pretended it wasn't my body they were putting their hands on,

116

pressing their pricks into. Squeezing my eyes tight shut in the darkness I pretended it wasn't really happening.'

'Don't say any more,' said Daisy. She'd risen from her seat and come over to cuddle Lol. The pressure of Daisy's hand on Lol's arm was warm and made her feel loved.

'I'd lie in bed after they'd finished with me and dream that one day I'd meet someone who'd love me for who I was. But that was a fairytale because I knew no one would love me as much as Mother did. She wanted me home with her but my father wouldn't allow it. He couldn't bear it that I was different.'

'How long was you at that school?'

'Forever it seemed, Daisy. Then I ran away. I was fourteen.'

'Some education,' Eddie said.

'I'd stolen money from a teacher's desk. I caught the train to London and I was sitting in this cafe wondering how I could eke out the cup of tea for a bit longer when this bloke came up and sat next to me. 'Hello girl,' he said. I didn't wear make-up in those days but you've no idea how wonderful it felt to be spoken to as if I wasn't an alien. 'Are you on the game?' he asked. I practised fluttering my eyelashes at him and then I answered, 'I could be.'

'You see, I figured if sex had been *taken* from me at school then surely I could sell it. At least that way I'd be able to rent a room for the night. It wasn't very comfortable in the back of his car but I liked the feel of the money in my pocket.

'He dropped me back at Waterloo and I walked

out of that station with a smile on my face. It was early evening, just getting dusk. At Piccadilly I met another girl. That was when I learned I was not the only one in the world like myself. Her name was Billie and she helped me put on make-up properly, not like when I'd daubed it all over myself in front of my mother's mirror.

'As time went on I found myself living at Billie's place. She was older than me and had this dear little flat in Westminster.

'We bought clothes, make-up, hair dye and Veet, and we used to drink in this cafe that had pictures of boxers on the walls. Inside there were other girls and I knew I had died and gone to heaven. We talked and talked and I saw inch-long fingernails and false eyelashes and sparkling clothes, and high, high heels. Flaunting myself to my best advantage became a drug and I soon got hooked. For a year I was truly happy.'

'Veet?'

'Darling Eddie,' she said. 'For hair removal. Even skinny girls can grow beards. I didn't want to be reminded I was in the wrong body, did I?'

'Didn't you get set on?' Daisy asked.

'Of course it wasn't always plain sailing, but there are things we make sure we do. Never look back when you think someone's following. Don't run. Walk faster, keep to where it's well lit and just hope.'

Eddie asked, 'So you were happy in London?'

'Yes, and free, until ... until Big Mick Ryan and some of the other tosspot club owners decided it'd be better to "manage" us girls whether we wanted to be managed or not. Apparently we were taking valuable trade that they decided they should profit from.'

'That means you had to work inside a club or get done over?'

'Done over is right, Eddie. Toni rebelled, she was a pretty little redhead. They found her pretty little head inside a suitcase in the Thames. The other bits of her started appearing all over London.'

'Ugh. Who did it?' Daisy was horrified.

'No one. What you got to remember is that even though Ken Drury, the head of the Flying Squad, was convicted for corruption charges, there's plenty of other coppers still taking backhanders.'

'I know about that copper,' Eddie said. 'You warm enough now?'

'How d'you know about Drury?' Daisy asked.

'Roy nearly went down when it all started coming out. Only the other week he was having a laugh about that quote of Commissioner Sir Robert Mark's that went, "A good police force is one that catches more criminals than it employs."'

'Some bloody hope that is,' Lol said.

Daisy asked, 'So you had no option but to work for this Big Mick Ryan?'

'Me and Billie started work in The Crinoline Club but we soon found it was like being kept prisoner. We had a room over the club where we serviced clients, but it was damp as well as dirty and pretty soon Billie got ill.

'She started picking up every ailment going, losing weight and seemed forever to have a cough. That bastard Mick Ryan didn't give a flying fuck, just told her to plaster on more make-up so the punters wouldn't see how sick she was.'

'Couldn't you just walk out? Get an ordinary job somewhere?'

'Not so easy, Eddie. Big Mick made sure we always owed him money.'

'How come?'

'Rent for the room, food, drinks. Everything we ate or drank was at bumped-up prices. We all knew we were trapped. I used to weep thinking of the times Billie and I had laughed over hairstyles in the cafe together and now she was sick and I could do nothing for her.' Lol's voice grew quiet. 'We used to pray one day we'd make enough money to go abroad and have an operation.'

'What happened to Billie?' Daisy could barely ask the question.

'Eventually she died. Her body was taken away, and I was left in the room alone – except for the johns.

'A week later the place was raided for real. We'd often had police searches. But we'd sleep with the coppers and Big Mick would bung them a hand-out and things went on as usual. This time it was different. I managed to climb out of the window and you know the rest. Oh, I also stole a wad of money out of Big Mick's desk while he was talking to the coppers.'

'But you said you didn't have any money when you got to Gosport?' Eddie was confused.

'I got smacked about on the train coming down to Portsmouth Harbour and it was taken off me.' She sighed and it seemed to shake her whole body. 'If ever Big Mick finds me, he'll kill me, I know he will. Still, the sailors left me with enough for a boat ticket,' she laughed. 'That's why I was hoping to make a bit from that blond. You saved me. I am so glad you took me in. I *can* help with this car boot thing, honest, Daisy.'

'The answer's still no, but I'm glad you've told me about yourself,' Daisy said.

Lol felt as though a huge weight had been lifted from her shoulders.

Daisy said, 'I'm goin' down to make a cup of tea. Anyone want one?' Lol shook her head. She felt herself getting angry with frustration. *Why* wouldn't Daisy let her help to earn money? And then she thought, bugger Daisy, she *would* find a way.

# CHAPTER 13

'I wish I was comin' with you, Dais.'

Vera spread Echo marge on the toast then pushed the plate towards Daisy.

'Well you can't. There ain't room in that poxy little car of Ty's for all of us.'

Eddie reached for a piece of toast and said through a mouthful of crumbs, 'He'll be here soon.'

'Don't speak with your mouth full,' said Vera.

'Anyway,' said Daisy, 'I thought you was interviewing a couple of girls today to take Samantha's place.'

'No one can take Samantha's place!'

Daisy realised she hadn't chosen her words well. The police had at last released Samantha's body and yesterday they'd gone to Portchester Crematorium to see her off.

'I'm sorry,' she said. 'I didn't mean to sound callous. Have a bit of toast. I'll put some marmalade on it for you.'

Vera smiled at her.

Susie was still in bed, so was Joy. In his own room Jamie slept like a log. The music stopped for the five a.m. news.

'When I went to identify Samantha's body,' Vera said, 'Vinnie drew the sheet back off her poor face an' she 'ad these nasty swellings on her mouth and her lips was cut at the sides.'

'You never told me that.'

'Well, I'm tellin' you now. You know what that bastard did? As well as takin' her hard earned money?'

Daisy shook her head. She certainly didn't fancy any more toast now.

'He'd put a stick in 'er mouth longways like to keep it propped open. That was 'ow she was found, 'angin' from a tree.'

'So the bastard strangled her with her own stocking then strung 'er up?'

Vera nodded.

'Why didn't you tell me this before?'

'No sense in both of us seeing it in our dreams, is it? Anyway, I really don't want to be on me own.'

'You ain't on your own, Susie's 'ere. And Jamie, and Joy and Lol. You gets on like an 'ouse on fire with Lol, you even let her fix your eyelashes. An' she loves you telling her about your exploits with the blokes. I should be back by dinnertime. I'll even bring you back a surprise.'

Vera's eyes were shining. 'What?'

'Wouldn't be a surprise then, would it, you daft tart.'

Daisy watched as Vera smoothed the fur of Kibbles who had jumped up on her lap.

'Just got up out of bed, have you, Kibbles?' Eddie reached over and plucked the cat from Vera. A hearty purring began.

'Just like a bloke,' said Vera. 'Always leaving me for someone else.'

'You got to face facts, Vera,' said Daisy. 'That cat's an old man now.'

'No you ain't, are you, Kibbles?' Eddie burrowed his face in the mackerel coloured fur.

Vera had opened the fridge and unwrapped fish. She paused with a piece of uncooked cod in one hand and a saucepan in the other. 'I 'ad 'im when I was first down Bert's Caff. He must be at least twenty years old. Came in the caff an' claimed me like a long lost lover and never left me. He wasn't a kitten then.'

'There's no doubt he's slowing up, Vera. We don't find him sleeping on the tops of doors or high up on wardrobes any more, do we?'

'If you ain't got anything cheerful to say, I'd really rather you went to Arundel, Daisy. You're suggestin' my boy's ready for the knacker's yard.' Vera covered the fish with water and set it to boil for Kibbles' breakfast.

A gentle knocking on the front door cut into Daisy's thoughts. 'That's Ty. C'mon, Eddie, you ready to go?'

She kissed Vera on the cheek and smelled her familiar Californian Poppy perfume.

'Don't forget me pressie,' Vera said, as Daisy ushered Eddie out, him twisting his arms into his leather jacket which he'd grabbed from the back of the door. 'And good luck.'

Daisy sat in the front of the car and flicked a tabby cat's hair from her black trouser leg.

'It's really good of you to lend a hand, Tyrone.'

'Think nothin' of it, Mrs L. It's good practice for me, bein' as I've passed me test now.'

Daisy had a few misgivings but she could see he was a careful driver.

'You been to this place before, Mrs L?'

'No, I heard about it from one of Vera's girls. Apparently there's a big sale every Saturday morning, starts around seven. It's at a place called Ford.'

'My brother's in Ford!'

'What, you mean he's going to be selling stuff today, Ty?' Daisy could hear Eddie laughing.

'No, Ma. His brother's doin' a stint in nearby Ford Open Prison.'

Daisy began to laugh as well. 'He definitely won't be selling stuff then, will he? I heard there's all sorts sold at the sale. Whole house clearances as well.'

Daisy didn't like admitting she was worried about paying bills and putting food on the table. It was one thing saying she didn't want help but another, being pushed back into the harsh reality of looking at every penny. She'd told Eddie she'd pay out for a few driving lessons so he could pass his test. Thank God she'd put that money by. He'd be seventeen soon and old enough for a provisional licence. It would be a nice birthday

124

present for him.

'There's the castle, Mrs L.'

Daisy looked to the left where Arundel Castle towered over the town. The road wound round to the right and soon they were going through the countryside again and over a level crossing where they had to wait while a train went by.

After a while she saw the airfield where the market was supposed to be.

'We're here,' she cried, looking at the overflowing parking area. 'Where's the stuff for sale, then?'

'I reckon it's up there in that enclosure,' said Tyrone.

'I'm goin' to stretch me legs for a bit,' said Eddie. 'I'm all cramped up in this car.' He got out and said, 'I'll wait up by the entrance.'

Daisy asked, 'I wonder how much the sellers pay for a pitch here?'

'Few pounds maybe,' said Tyrone. 'I expect it's like Gosport Market. The regulars pay less than the casuals.'

'Whatever you pay has to come out the profits,' said Daisy. 'Let's go and find Eddie, shall we?'

They walked down the concrete parking area together. It was going to be a lovely day. The sun was already shining and there was a bit of a wind, but nothing to worry about. Daisy felt for the money in the pocket of her fur jacket. She had no idea what she and Eddie would find but she'd brought only what she thought she could afford to lose if it didn't work. Actually it was the council rates money so she couldn't afford to lose it at all, but the rates weren't due for another couple of months so she'd make it up somehow if today wasn't a success. She'd already put some money by for petrol for Tyrone.

Ahead at the entrance she could see Eddie, talking to a girl. Daisy turned to Tyrone, who was blushing bright red and craning his neck so as not to miss anything. Suddenly the penny dropped. Tyrone fancied the girl Eddie was chatting to.

And the girl was Lol.

'What the bleedin' 'ell are you doin' 'ere? An' how the fuck did you get 'ere?' Lol tried to hide behind Eddie. Daisy could smell burgers and coffee. Eddie tried to shield Lol and Daisy saw the girl was frightened. Her heart went out to her. 'I thought you was asleep at home.'

'I want to pay you back for bein' so good to me. I *can* help. I got up early and managed to get a lift from a lorry driver. I knew if I asked you if I could come you'd probably say no, especially as there ain't much room in the Mini, and if you get some bargains that are a bit on the bulky side...'

'I ain't plannin' on buying a bleedin' three piece suite, girl...'

Lol said, 'I ... I know a bit about antiques. I want to help you all I can, Daisy.'

Daisy was secretly proud of Lol's ingenuity. She put her arms around the girl. 'Well, one thing's for certain, you ain't goin' 'ome with no lorry drivers!'

Just then the crowd began to surge forward, signalling that the punters could enter the compound. Daisy found herself being pushed along. She could feel her excitement rising. What would she find? Eddie had his hand clamped to her shoulder so she wouldn't get swept away in the crush of people.

The sellers had set out their wares opposite each other so that a wide path ran all round the enclosure, enabling buyers to come in one side and go out the other. Daisy pulled Eddie to a relatively quiet place at the side of a flower stall.

'Eddie, I'm givin' you some money.' She looked at Lol and Ty. 'Take them with you and see what you can find. Listen to Lol, she seems to have her 'ead screwed on right.' Lol grinned. 'But listen, son, I can't afford to lose this money, so whatever you get 'old of has to make a profit elsewhere, understand?' She handed over some notes. 'We'll meet in a couple of hours back at the car.'

She turned and walked away into the noisy crowd, knowing it would take time to examine all the sellers' wares. What she was interested in was the people who looked like they had genuinely cleared out their own attics and the blokes who had vans full of house clearance goods set out that she could rifle through.

Apprehensive but excited at the same time, she was ready for her new venture!

'Don't forget,' she called back. 'If you see any little trinkets for Vera, grab 'em while you can! And don't go buyin' any bleedin' Hepplethwaite chairs.'

'Hepplewhite!' chorused Eddie and Lol.

Daisy knew sod all about what she was doing. She was going to rely on her instincts. Roy was waiting for her to fail. She knew he wanted her dependent on him but that was one thing she'd never be. No man was ever going to give her hand-

127

outs or tell her what to do. And now she had to replace the rates money somehow, didn't she?

Her heart was light but, at the first pitch where she stopped to look, worn furniture was spread on the concrete and plastic containers filled with broken jewellery were sitting on paste tables. A pile of filthy curtains and bedding reposed on a blue plastic sheet on the ground. Daisy wrinkled her nose at the smell. Nothing she fancied here. She moved on.

People jostled her and trod on her toes, their body odours mingling with perfume and with the smell of burgers and chips and candyfloss.

She passed a clothes seller with a pile of shoes and handbags and a rail of clothes that looked fit for the dustbin, but Daisy couldn't resist picking over the shoes, wondering who'd worn them and thinking some of them looked too tatty to be sold. It was in the handbag pile – mostly plastic ones like she'd seen the old dears in Gosport tote about – that she saw it. A black, beaded bag with a deep fringe. She turned it in her hands, saw that the pearl clip was in perfect condition and opened it to find the inside clean. Daisy poked about again without seeming too interested, then casually asked the bloke who looked like he'd slept in his clothes, 'How much the 'andbags?'

'Fifty pence each.'

Daisy was quite unsure of herself but she had to become a businesswoman. Hadn't Vera told her she was too soft? Every penny of her money today *must* count.

'Take forty pence for one?'

He sighed and said, 'Go on then.'

128

She'd done it! Struck her first bargain. But she didn't pick up the bag until she'd paid him for it. Just in case he changed his mind and asked her for more money. She needn't have worried, for as soon as the coins were in his grubby hand he turned away from her to another customer. Daisy lifted up her treasure and popped it in her carrier bag.

The black beaded bag was almost exactly the same as one Vera had and which she claimed was a genuine 1920s handbag. Daisy's quick eyes had registered that the silk lining was perfect and every bead was in its place. If she couldn't get more than forty pence for it then she really was a fuckin' non-starter, she thought.

She'd allowed Eddie ten pounds and kept fifteen herself. She'd already decided that if either of them purchased something that wouldn't sell she wasn't going to moan about it.

The place was filling with people now. Some of the buyers seemed to know the dealers, and there was a great deal of handshaking and backslapping going on. Music was loud, with Abba singing 'Dancing Queen'. It made Daisy feel very lighthearted.

At a stall manned by a harassed young woman with a crying toddler Daisy pulled out a black velvet rose-flocked shawl. This, she decided, would make a lovely gift for Vera. She kept hold of it while she burrowed further into the rather musty-smelling pile of clothes. She uncovered an ornament. A greyhound with a rabbit at its feet on a green base, it was about ten inches tall. Daisy's heart flipped. The hound had a soulful expression. She turned it over in her hands. A Staffordshire greyhound, not chipped.

The woman was trying to stuff a dummy in the kiddy's mouth but the child was having none of it. Holding the piece of china in her hand Daisy asked, 'What you chargin' for this ornament, love?' Her heart was beating fast. It was plain this young woman had turned out her house or her mother's house and come along to sell the goods today.

'There's another one of those somewhere,' the woman said. 'I think it's in that box underneath.'

Daisy bent down and scrabbled through a cardboard box of used baby clothes. Her heart leapt as her hand closed over the twin ornament. And then plummeted as she saw the brown coating over the dog's ears. It looked like paint! No scratches or chips though.

'I got it,' said Daisy. She stood up straight and faced the woman. 'It's covered in paint.'

'You don't want to worry about that,' said the woman, smiling now the child had stopped wailing. 'My little 'un was playin' with it in the car. That's chocolate. I was goin' to ask for a pound for the two of them, but seein' as you got to wash that one I'll take seventy-five pence.'

'Well, if you're sure,' said Daisy. 'What about this shawl?'

'Twenty pence?' Daisy nodded and again she paid before the woman could change her mind. Her heart was beating even faster as she wrapped the china dogs in the shawl and put them in her bag.

'Me gran had those ugly dogs on 'er mantelpiece for years. Glad to be rid of 'em,' said the woman.

Daisy wondered if she ought to feel bad. The seller had got the price she'd asked for, but Daisy thought the dogs were probably worth quite a lot more. She'd seen a picture of dogs very similar to these in one of the antiques books and the suggested value was a hundred and fifty quid. But wasn't that what it was all about? Buying and selling? Daisy consoled herself with the thought that maybe she'd got carried away and the ornaments weren't worth any more than she'd paid for them. But then again, if she couldn't bump up the price she'd definitely chosen the wrong game to start up in.

A bit further along there was a table set out with jewellery. Some pieces had price tickets, some didn't. Daisy saw the man watching her as he leaned on the bonnet of his van drinking a mug of steaming tea.

'See anything you fancy, darlin', I could do a special price for you.'

I bet you could, thought Daisy, you bleedin' chauvinist pig.

'Just looking,' she replied, and smiled sweetly. Jesus Christ, but she so hated being asked before she'd had a chance to have a look at anything. If, as soon as she walked into a shop, some bit of a girl asked, 'Can I help you, modom?' Daisy didn't stay long enough to buy.

She moved along the glass-covered cases thinking there was nothing special until an orange necklace caught her eye.

The bloke set his tea down on the concrete and was over to her like a shot.

'I can see you like the coral,' he said, and before

she could say another word he had it out of the case and was pressing it into her hands. 'Belonged to my old mother that did, my dad bought it for her.'

Daisy didn't believe a word he was saying, but it was a pretty piece. Then she noticed the clasp was broken.

'How much?'

'To you, darlin', half as much as it's worth.'

'What's that?'

'Twenty pounds.'

Daisy couldn't help herself. 'Twenty fuckin' pounds? I didn't just come up the Solent in a bleedin' bucket, you know!' Talk about over-priced! She put the necklace down on the case.

'I'll take that as a no, then,' the man said. His face turned ugly. 'What about a tenner?'

Daisy shook her head and made to move off. It was a nice piece and, with a bit of luck, at a tenner she might even make a couple of quid on it, but then there was the broken clasp. He was looking at her dithering.

'If you ain't buyin' piss off, you bitch!' he said. 'And let some genuine customers 'ave a look.'

She could feel sweat running down the back of her neck, and she shivered. Take it on the chin, Daisy, she told herself. If you're going to make a success of this game you're going to meet all kinds of people and some of them are going to be right bastards. She knew then that she would always treat her customers fairly and with consideration. That's if she ever found enough stuff to sell on.

She stood for a moment in a shaft of warm sunlight. It was barely eight o'clock but the day was dry and warming up nicely. She watched the people like ants, scavenging around the piles of broken furniture, old beds, tables full of what seemed at first glance rubbish, and then she slid back into the crowd.

The brightly painted van stood out like a sore thumb and so did the young bloke in jeans and a tie-dyed shirt. He had a small table, some well polished fire irons displayed on it, an old metal fireplace propped at the side of his van, and two plastic tables dangerously overloaded with clutter. Beneath the tables were the usual boxes of books and smaller items.

He gave Daisy a lazy grin as she bent down and started rummaging. The smell of weed rose to meet her as she poked about. She came upon a black lacquered box with what she supposed was a Japanese design on it. Opening it she found it packed tight with jewellery. Old-fashioned brooches, a pearl necklace, some broken bits of what to Daisy looked like enamelled ear rings, and a couple of watches. Daisy shook the watches and they rattled. She laughed. She saw the brooch, a long bar with what seemed to be a piece of plastic stuck on it. It was filthy. Daisy knew the piece of plastic was ivory and the bar of the brooch gold.

'What do you want for this?' She held up the pretty box to him.

'It's goin' for a song, lady, a song,' he said.

Daisy laughed at him. 'I can't bleedin' sing. How much?'

'A quid? Just dump the rubbish inside back in the cardboard box, if you don't want it.'

Daisy thought quickly. A sort of lie was needed

here, but it had to be mostly the truth or she couldn't ask him. You can believe a thief but you can't believe a liar, her mother used to say. 'I got a little girl at home might find a use for the junk, making pretty things for her dollies,' Daisy said, handing over a pound coin. 'You want any more for what's inside?'

'No,' he said, pocketing the coin.

Daisy was happy, the seller was happy, and Joy would have great fun with the broken jewellery. If she wanted to make a success of this buying and selling she had to be ruthless. Didn't she have a family to support?

Still, you can't afford to be sentimental, she told herself as she walked away. Another thought struck her. So many people passed through car boots and salerooms she might even hear something to her advantage about poor Samantha.

An hour later she hadn't bought anything else.

It was as if the well had run dry, Daisy thought. She'd enjoyed looking at the stuff on display, the furniture especially. She'd seen some lovely pieces that she'd have liked to add to her own home, but she'd kept faith with herself. She had to be strong and not buy anything else she couldn't sell on, and – hopefully – at a profit.

The crowds had thinned to ordinary buyers. It looked as though the dealers had got their bargains and left. The smell of food was strong and she realised she'd give anything for a sit-down and a cup of tea. It was definitely time to make her way back to Tyrone's car.

She was peering into the car park's distance

when she felt a hand on her shoulder.

'Hello, Ma.'

She breathed a sigh of relief.

'I thought I'd never find you, Eddie,' she said. 'Where are the others?'

'Sitting in the car.'

'I've been up and down the aisles. Have you?'

'Not missed a trick unless you've been there first.'

She said, 'You ain't carrying nothin'.'

'It's in the boot.'

'Oh,' she said. 'What you got?'

'Not a lot,' he replied, but she could see his eyes were twinkling.

He took her bag off her.

'How much money you got left?' she asked.

'Nearly all of it. We only spent two quid.'

Daisy's heart fell.

'We won't 'ave enough to put on a paste table to sell then. Will we?'

'You told me to be careful, and Lol was a fount of bleedin' wisdom.'

'Really?'

'I don't know what the house was like that she grew up in but she knows her stuff.'

Daisy practically fell into the front seat of the Mini. Her feet were killing her. She'd soak them in a bowl of salt water when she got in.

'Well, at least there's plenty of room for you in the car, Lol.'

For a while no one spoke, then Ty said, 'Shall I go and get the stuff we bought out of the boot?'

Daisy felt the excitement well up again. Ty returned and set the bag on her lap.

Daisy said, 'Let me show you what I got first.'
She took out the items one by one.

'That bag's a right beauty,' said Lol. 'Wouldn't mind it meself.' Daisy laughed. Then she showed her the lacquered box and Lol, after opening it and poking around inside, gave a whistle. 'There's some nice bits in here,' she said.

'A quid,' said Daisy. 'That's what I paid for it.'

'The box is worth five times that,' said Lol.

'How come you reckon to know so much, missy?'

'We had some nice stuff in our house,' she answered. Daisy looked at her and waited. But all Lol volunteered was, 'You got a few bits of gold in here as well.'

Daisy almost purred. 'I know,' she said.

'These are bloody 'orrible ugly dogs,' said Tyrone, wrinkling his nose.

'This is a lovely thing.' Lol had picked up the shawl.

'Well, you can keep your hands off that, it's a pressie for Vera. I hope it don't fall to bits when she washes it.' Daisy carefully replaced the items and handed them to Eddie.

Then she opened the newspaper surrounding Eddie, Lol and Tyrone's offerings.

As she turned first the small pot, then the larger bowl in her hands, the brightly coloured designs seemed to come to life.

'Well I never...' She held the honey pot upside down and peered.

'Christchurch! Even I know this name. Clarice Cliff. Fancy this turning up in a place like this.'

'The pot'd been thrown in with a box of

gardening crap. Our Lol 'ere took both bits into the public lavatory and cleaned the dirt off.'

'Well I never,' said Daisy again.

'I reckon we should get at least a hundred and fifty pounds for them,' said Lol. 'I think I'm right in saying they're both from her Bizarre range.'

'Well, I nev–' Daisy clamped a hand over her mouth to stop repeating herself. There were tears in her eyes that started running down her cheeks.

Maybe, just maybe, she could get the finances of her family back on track, especially with the help of Lol. 'You done real good, Lol,' Daisy said.

'I also had this beautiful present bought for me.' Lol pulled from the inside of her shortie raincoat a black feather boa, glossy and plump. She held it to her cheek. 'You don't know what this means to me,' she said.

Tyrone was blushing as red as a post-box.

'We still ain't got enough to take to a car boot,' Daisy said. 'An' I can't see punters forkin' out big money for–'

'Auction,' Lol said. 'This stuff needs to be auctioned.'

'Brilliant,' said Daisy. Then she remembered the bloke who'd been rude to her. It was a sign she wouldn't find things easy. She had to accept that she'd meet people who'd try to do her down. But she'd have to take the good with the bad. Then another thought struck her,

'When you went in the lav to wash them things clean, which one did you go in, Lol?'

Lol opened wide her big blue eyes, 'Why, the ladies' of course!'

# CHAPTER 14

'Your lot ain't never goin' to put me away makin' fuckin' stupid mistakes like this, are you?' Roy could smell the sweat from the coppers' exertions as they puffed and panted while bringing in the gear from the van parked outside his pool hall, The Pocket. 'An' I see some of 'em need a spell in me gym next door, they look like pansies. But then I don't suppose you lot are as fit as my boys, we're used to luggin' pool tables an' other stuff about.' He glanced around the hall, a hive of activity.

DCI Vinnie Endersby turned his head away.

Roy continued, 'You cost me about two thousand pounds from this place alone while them fuckin' tables, money inside 'em an' all – an' *that* had better be all there, mate – while they been stored up at your fuckin' nick just because you thought I'd got 'em off the back of a lorry!'

'I've seen the receipts now,' said Vinnie, as though that explained everything. He sighed. Roy thought Vinnie looked smart today in a new suit and raincoat, but then Vinnie always was a clean-cut bloke. Didn't wear expensive clothes, not like his own Savile Row gear, nor was the copper's hair fashionably long and curling on his collar as his own was. But then they had rules in the force, a sort of dress code, didn't they...

Vinnie was talking again. 'And you got your wish,' he said. 'The same coppers who took 'em

138

out should bring 'em back.'

Roy winked at a stony-faced bluebottle who staggered past him with an armful of pool cues.

'A load of fuckin' wankers,' said Roy. He ran his fingers through his hair. 'Still, I ain't goin' on at you, you wasn't around when this fiasco started. Just your bad luck you was at the station when it was okayed to bring 'em back.' Roy could smell the freshness of Imperial Leather soap and reckoned Vinnie must have had a shower at the station. He put out his hand and extended it to him. 'Still a handsome bastard, I see. It's them eyes as gets the women, eh?'

Vinnie had different-coloured eyes, but far from messing up his dark good looks, they gave him a kind of mystique.

'Not women, just one woman. I'm still with Clare.' Vinnie accepted Roy's handshake.

Roy knew Clare was Vinnie's wife. While separated, Vinnie had fathered Daisy's youngest boy, Jamie. Even thinking about Jamie made Roy shake his head in exasperation. The boy was a little sod.

'Seen Jamie since you sent him 'ome?' He saw the red flush creep up Vinnie's neck. 'I'll take that as a no, then, copper,' he said. Secretly he was glad Vinnie had little contact with Daisy. He brought his thoughts back to the matter in hand. 'This ain't the way to clear up crime in London, or anywhere else come to that,' Roy said. 'Confiscating pool tables then returning 'em must be way down on your list. You should look after me a bit better, Vinnie boy.'

'You think I don't realise one word from you and my career is down the fuckin' Swanee?'

139

Vinnie gave him a long hard stare.

'Just because it's been necessary for us to bury a couple of bodies together it don't mean I'll shoot me mouth off. There are a few past crimes neither of us want bringing up,' admitted Roy. They moved aside to allow a fruit machine carried by four panting coppers to pass.

Vinnie looked about, making sure he wouldn't be overheard. 'We both know I wouldn't have risen to the dizzy heights of a DCI without you covering for me. And for some of the stunts *you* pulled, you'd be behind bars if it wasn't for me. It ain't me you got to worry about, Roy, it's Smalls and Nelson, supergrasses. Bobby Mark would love to have you behind bars and you know it. Jack Slipper got the Krays and he reckons that Smalls and Nelson are the greatest weapons the coppers have got today.'

Roy shifted from one foot to the other. 'I don't like the fat little bleeder and I'd hack him into a thousand pieces if I could, but you lot got 'im swaddled in cotton fuckin' wool, the cunt.' He walked over to the bar and selected a bottle of Glenmorangie from the back of the shelf and set it on the bar.

'Want a drink, Vin?'

'Only if it's some good stuff and not that watered down gut rot you sell the punters.'

'Single malt distilled in Ross-shire.' Roy poured two good measures. 'Anything in it?' The aroma of the whisky rose and he breathed it in. Its golden colour delighted him.

'Why spoil it?'

Roy laughed and pushed one of the tumblers

140

towards Vinnie. Then he said, 'Sorry you ain't drinking it out of cut glass but my usual customers wouldn't know cut glass unless it was stickin' in their bleedin' faces. Now I know you're not just 'ere to help set my pool tables back in their right places so what can I do for you?'

Roy watched Vinnie's body language. The man was ill at ease.

'Got a nutter parting women from their money...'

'Jesus fuckin' Christ, you askin' me about some poxy bloke–'

'Listen, Roy, it isn't as straightforward as it seems. This bloke takes their money and then strangles the poor bitches. He likes to leave their mouths prised open with a bit of stick... Or he gives them Brazilian Neckties, or worse.' Even to think about the breadknife made him feel sick.

'Fuckin' hell. I ain't heard of that stick business since the war. Used to 'appen in the concentration camps, so I 'eard. Men'd be strung up, hung like, but they wouldn't be able to close their mouths. The wood kept it propped open.'

Vinnie put his empty glass on the bar top. 'I don't need a bloody history lesson, Roy. Vera's girl Samantha was left like that.' Vinnie was savouring his whisky. 'We didn't publicise that,' he added.

Roy was taken aback. 'I knew Samantha,' he said quietly. 'She didn't strike me as a woman who'd flash her savings about. Working in the massage parlour meant that she was clued up on what information she gave out to the johns.'

'But suppose it wasn't a regular john?'

'C'mon, Vinnie, where's the girl going to meet

anyone regular when she's a bleedin' prossie?' He took Vinnie's empty glass back to the bottle on the bar and poured another generous measure. Then drank his own whisky straight back and refilled his glass.

'She was working behind the bar at Daisychains just before she was killed, Roy.'

Their conversation was halted as a constable came up to them, flushed, dusty and panting. He looked worn out, thought Roy. 'Sir, everything's back inside now.'

'Bloody good job an' all,' broke in Roy. 'I'll trust you've not left anything behind, I know what a thieving lot you coppers are.'

Vinnie said, 'Go back to the station, I'll be along later if anyone asks.' The man said, 'Yes, sir,' and left.

'Like being called sir, do you, Vinnie?' Roy saw Vinnie colour up. 'Let's get back to this girl. You say she was working behind the bar? She could have met anyone there, couldn't she? Obviously she kept it a secret.'

'But why? That's what I don't understand. Surely she'd have wanted to share it with the rest of her mates, especially Vera.'

'Vinnie, perhaps she didn't want him to know she'd made her money from lying on her back.' Vinnie went quiet and a frown crossed his forehead.

'Or just maybe it was him didn't want anyone knowing who he was,' he said thoughtfully.

'You think this has anything to do with the fire at Daisychains?'

Vinnie shrugged. 'You tell me. You're the bas-

142

tard with enemies, not Daisy Lane.'

'But I didn't own the fuckin' club!'

'Maybe the bastard didn't know that. You've had other clubs burned and damaged, haven't you?'

'Kids, that's all. I get damage done all the time. Rivals, fights, all in a day's work.' He tried to play it down.

'If that's what you'd prefer to believe.'

Roy looked at him. 'You thinking different?'

Vinnie shrugged. 'I don't know what I'm thinking, Roy.'

'What's in it for me if I come up with anything that'll help you? Though I must admit I've drawn a blank on all the enquiries I *have* been makin'.'

Vinnie said quickly, 'Fuckin' 'ell, don't you ever do anything for nothing?'

'Not where you're concerned, Vin.' Roy gave him a broad wink. The atmosphere was charged and it needed defusing.

'I'm only a small cog in a big wheel but look, Roy, what I can do is try and keep Bertie Smalls off your back as long as possible. But from what I hear you got Maurie Nelson hoping to take over your manor.'

Roy gave a big sigh. 'You lot don't give a bleedin' fuck about anything! I 'ad Keefie, my West Indian runner, knifed in a pub. The drugs 'ad gone, so 'ad the money, and no question Nelson was involved. Your lot got his fuckin' phone bugged so you even heard 'im tell his missus on the blower what to do with 'is bloodstained gear.'

'He was arrested—'

'Then let go for lack of evidence! Lack of fuckin' evidence! How much fuckin' evidence do

143

you need?'

'He's worth more on the streets, that's why.'

'An' what's the fucker doin' now? I'll tell you. He's movin' in on me an' it makes me want to spew up. He's small time. Ain't got the clout or the money but he'll work with anyone, an' your lot's protectin' 'im. Well, don't be surprised if he 'as a nasty accident.'

'You and me are tied tighter than a hangman's noose, Roy. If you bleed, I bleed. But I'd watch your back, if I was you, an' I wouldn't broadcast what you've just said to me. And look out for Daisy as well.'

Roy stared at Vinnie. He knew the copper's words made sense. Vinnie couldn't be account-able for what went on in the rest of the force.

But he made up his mind that if Vinnie couldn't help him then he'd just have to help himself. Wouldn't he...?

# CHAPTER 15

Eddie slipped his key in the door and went inside, following the aroma of a casserole in the kitchen. He smiled to himself. Susie had been cooking again and he wondered if it was his favourite beef in red wine, which his mother called by some other fancy name. Susie was getting quite adventurous with her cooking lately. Last night they'd had spaghetti bolognese. His mother had shown them the proper way to eat it, winding the spaghetti into the bowl of the spoon with the fork. She could do it real quick, so could Lol. Vera had got the hump about it because her spaghetti was falling about all over the place, and Jamie and Joy had had to have theirs cut up. After that Jamie had sat at the table giving everyone the evil eye and wouldn't finish his dinner.

There was a chocolate cake on the side. Eddie licked his lips.

He thought he was alone in the house until he heard the muted sounds of the radio upstairs playing 'Lonely Boy' by Andrew Gold. He looked at his watch. Both Joy and Jamie should be around; it was after school, so that meant someone, a grown-up, had to be in.

He went to the bottom of the stairs.

'Suze?'

'I'm ub 'ere. Don't feel well.' Her voice sounded thick.

He bounded up the wide staircase. He liked this house with its big rooms and the large garden that backed onto Stanley Park. At school the other kids thought he was posh because he lived in Western Way but they soon realised he was just a Gosport kid like the rest of them. The only reason they lived in one of the best roads in Alverstoke was because his dad had been a bleedin' gangster and made some good deals before he died. His dad, the first Eddie Lane, was a hard bastard by all accounts, but he'd given the house to his mum. It was well known he'd loved her to bits.

In Susie's room he found her cocooned in bed.

'You should see your nose,' he said. 'You'd give Rudolph the reindeer a run for his money.'

'I think I god a cold.'

'I think you god a cold an' all,' he said. 'I'm in now. You stay there an' I'll see to everything.' It was no skin off his nose to keep an eye on the kids.

She blinked at him damply. He eyed the sodden pieces of kitchen roll on the bedside table.

She asked, 'You sure?'

'Sure I'm sure.'

'I ain't done the veg for tea.' Her eyes filled with tears.

'Well, that's nothing to worry about. I can soon do 'em,' he said. He saw the kitchen roll had fallen to the carpet and he picked it up, tore off a couple of sheets and handed them to her then put the roll where she could reach it. 'You want anything? Water, cup of tea?' She shook her head.

'Sleep?'

She nodded and he backed out of the room.

In the kitchen he put the kettle on then ran some water in a bowl and found the potato peeler. By the time he'd started peeling the spuds he realised, apart from the soft music coming from Susie's room, how quiet it was.

So where were Jamie and Joy? He put down the peeler, wiped his hands, and went outside through the kitchen door. His mother had gone into town with Vera to see how business was going at Heavenly Bodies, and Lol and Tyrone had gone to the Forum for an afternoon showing of *Jaws*. He could see Kibbles curled into a tight ball, asleep in a patch of sunlight, on the edge of the fishpond.

Then he saw the brightly coloured Wendy house that had been a Christmas present for Joy, and a lad waiting outside. The kiddie was about eight years old. Three other small boys were kicking stones on the gravel drive near the side of the house and Jamie was waiting with them. He took what appeared to be money from one of the boys and slipped it in his pocket.

Eddie stepped back against the brick wall and watched, knowing he couldn't be seen, and was amazed to see a small boy duck down and come out of the Wendy house. The lad was giggling and gave a Pompey thumbs-up sign to Jamie, who nodded his head. The boy directly outside the Wendy house went inside. As soon as the first boy got back to his mates Jamie pushed one of the other lads towards the Wendy house.

Eddie had a feeling that something was very wrong. Where was Joy?

He walked over the grass to the toy house and peered inside. He straightened up and yelled at Jamie.

'Don't you bloody move!' Jamie's face went white. Eddie could see him weighing up his chances of escape or capture. The lads scarpered. The small boy, trapped by Eddie's bulk, looked as though he was about to burst into tears.

'I ain't done nuffink,' he said. 'I ain't done nuffink!'

'You'd better clear off home,' Eddie said icily. When he looked into the Wendy house again Joy was standing in just her vest. Her white knickers were on the small chair and her blue dress was slung over the back of it.

She grinned at him. 'Did you pay Jamie fifty whole new pence? You have to if you want to see

147

my minnie and my bum. Did you pay?'

'Someone's going to pay,' he said, the words catching in his throat. 'Get dressed, sweetheart, and come into the kitchen.'

He heard the kitchen door slam and guessed Jamie had made a run for indoors.

After a while the five-year-old emerged with her dress buttoned up wrong.

'Eddie, I don't think I've done it right.' Her curly red hair was tangled and her freckles had darkened with the sun.

'You're fine,' he said. He took her by the hand and led her to the wire-covered pond, where he sat her down on the broad stone surround. She peered into the murky depths.

'Look, a yellow fish,' she said, pointing to the lily-strewn surface.

'I need to ask you about the game you've been playing,' he said.

'It was ever so funny.' She wiggled her fingers into the holes of the mesh. 'Why is this all over the pond? Is it really like Auntie Vera says? The pond is dangerous?'

She stressed the word dangerous and he could imagine Vera saying it loudly just as she'd warned him when he was a kid.

Eddie took a deep breath. He didn't want to ask her but he had to know.

'Those little boys in the Wendy house, did they touch you?'

He waited, his heart sickened and beating so fast he thought she'd hear it. He stared at Joy, she was such a pretty little thing.

There were frown lines across her foreheard as

she turned her face towards him.

'Silly Eddie. It was fifty pence a look. Don't you know nothin'?'

'So, no touching?'

She was looking at him as though he was the child and she was the grown-up. 'Only Mum and Auntie Vera and Daisy touches me there, an' that's only for washing and drying.'

'Of course,' he said. 'I'm so silly.' Yet the relief he felt made him weak.

'That yellow fish is hiding,' she said.

No doubt Jamie would be hiding as well, he thought, as they went inside the house.

'Mummy's made a chocolate cake. Can I have some?'

He shook his head. Then he changed his mind. 'I don't see why not. As long as you promise to eat your tea,' he said.

'Okay.' She got the stool out and dragged it to the sink so she could wash her hands. He cut a small sliver of fragrant cake, oozing with chocolate cream, and put it on her special plate.

'Wash your hands properly,' he said. He knew she took ages.

He went upstairs and pushed open Jamie's door. The lock had long since been removed.

'Get downstairs,' he said quietly. 'If you wake Susie, I'll kill you.'

To his amazement, Jamie smirked at him, slid off the bed where he'd been pretending to read the *Beano* and went down the stairs. Eddie followed.

'Get out in the garden,' he said.

'Why?'

'Because I said so.'

Joy was standing by the table wiping her hands on a tea towel. 'Can I have my cake now?'

'Sure.' He put the plate by her seat.

Jamie was waiting outside the kitchen door. There was something about the swagger of the lad as Eddie pushed him towards the park end of the garden that annoyed Eddie intensely.

When Jamie reached the wooded end he lolled against the fence.

Eddie said, 'She's a little kid. What fuckin' game d'you think you're playing?'

Jamie brushed back the fall of blond hair from his forehead then put his hand in his jeans pocket and pulled out a handful of fifty pence pieces.

'What's the matter, Eddie, you frightened I won't give you a cut of the takings?'

Eddie hit him then. The force of the punch sent Jamie backwards and he lost his footing. He sank to the ground, and coins scattered, littering the garden like silver flowers.

Sudden guilt flowed through Eddie. *This was his brother he'd knocked down.*

He was just about to help him up when the lad rose nimbly to his feet. A red bloom on Jamie's chin was growing fast. He gave Eddie a smile that sent shivers down his spine.

'You'll pay for that, wanker,' he said, and walked away.

# CHAPTER 16

'You ain't changing your mind about me comin' with you, are you?'

'Vera, if I say a thing you know I bleedin' mean it.'

'Well, you didn't want me with you last time.' Vera's perfume filled the room along with her peevish voice.

Daisy got up from the kitchen chair and stomped over towards the sink. Wet footprints on the parquet flooring trailed behind her. She looked back at the bowl of warm salty water and grumbled.

'I can't even soak my feet in comfort without you going on and on and on. It took me ages to find a decent enough venue to try to auction off the stuff we bought from Ford on account of I know bugger all about auctions, and all I get for my trouble is you goin' on an' on at me. Lol's been more help than you; thank God she's got 'er head screwed on right.'

She turned to the kettle and plugged it in the electric wall socket. Vera was sitting on the bench with her feet in a blue plastic bowl and Kibbles draped over her lap. All four of his legs were hanging down. Vera looked Daisy in the eye, her head cocked to one side. Daisy narrowed her eyes too, ready to do battle, then decided against it. Vera had worries of her own.

'You want a biscuit with this bleedin' tea I'm makin' or not?' She stared down at her wet wrinkled feet which looked like prunes and said, 'All this is because I won't take any money from you.'

'Daisy, you can be very 'urtful sometimes.'

'I happen to know you're not doin' too well down at Heavenly Bodies.' Vera sighed, as Daisy added, 'I thought you'd taken on a couple of new girls?'

'One I got rid of the very next day. She'd been pinchin' money off the clients. I can't 'ave that. I runs a respectable knockin' shop!'

Daisy laughed. 'That's the first time I've ever 'eard you call Heavenly Bodies a knockin' shop!'

'Well, what else is a bleedin' massage parlour if it ain't that?'

Daisy went over to Vera and bent down and put her arms around her. 'I remember when you first opened that place how excited you were.'

'Dreams, Dais, just dreams. Now I feels like me dreams are fadin' and I'm just hangin' on. Me original staff is like me, getting a bit long in the tooth.' She waved Daisy away and continued, 'The regular girls has favourite clients who won't ask for anyone else to see to their needs. I don't just want bleedin' old codgers comin' in. There ain't no fun in takin' their pensions off 'em. I want new blood, and I thought these two girls would pull in the punters. An' now I only got one new girl.' She looked up at Daisy. 'I shouldn't be burdening you with my problems when you got no money comin' in at all.'

'It don't matter. We're mates, ain't we? We pull

152

together, Vera.'

The kettle started wailing and Daisy made the tea. She shook out a plateful of Bourbon biscuits, thinking she'd never seen her mate so low.

'I don't get the overflow of punters from Daisy-chains, now the club's gone,' Vera said. 'The blokes as couldn't afford the club's girls came round to me. No club, no blokes.' Vera was idly stroking Kibbles' fur then she looked up. 'Sorry, Dais,' she said. 'I won't moan no more.' She gave a half-hearted grin.

'Now you're really cheerin' me up, Vera!' A thought struck Daisy. 'This house is very quiet to-night, ain't it? Jamie's gone to 'is dad's, Joy's asleep, an' Eddie, Ty and Lol are gone to the pictures to see *Star Wars*, an' Suze – where did Suze say she was going?'

'She didn't. She's been actin' strange lately. Goin' out all tarted up and smelling to 'igh heaven of that bleedin' 4711 cologne she puts on by the bucketful.' Vera waved her hand in front of her nose. 'Perfume should be used sparingly.'

Daisy nearly choked on the biscuit she was eating.

'You reckon she's got a feller?'

'If she 'as, she ain't sayin'. But she has got a sparkle in 'er eye, an' as she went out she was singing 'Que Sera, Sera'. What d'you make of that?'

Daisy lay staring at the stars through the window. She felt cold, not just in her body but deep inside. Almost as if something bad was about to happen and she was going to be powerless to do anything except be swept along with the tide. It wasn't just the fire that had destroyed her livelihood, or the lack of money, or even her almost daily battles with Jamie. She was tired.

No matter what had happened the previous day, the next morning she used to wake up with a spark alight inside her. She'd be ready to take on all that life had to give her, bad things as well as good. Somehow that spark had now shrivelled and disappeared. When she'd had it, she'd taken it for granted. Now it was gone, she mourned its passing.

She got out of bed and opened the curtains wider, gazing at the stars as if they held the answers. What was the matter with her? She had a nice house, a good family and friends who rallied round in times of crisis.

She shivered. What the hell was this chilling numbness? And then a shooting star swam across the sky trailing a brilliant golden spray. It was an omen, she thought, but of what she wasn't sure.

At least she was feeling more settled than she had earlier today. This morning in the kitchen she'd come over quite peculiar, like she was going to faint.

A shower. She'd have a hot shower and see if that did the trick.

Leaning her head against the cold tiles with the water running over her body she willed her brain to slow, to stop, just for a few moments, so she could clear her head and start again. If she could do that all the negative thoughts would go down the drain with the shower water. Her eyes closed, her breathing slowed.

And then, in spite of the running water, she

heard soft knocking.

She knew every creaking board in the house. Every sound she could account for. Who would knock on her front door at this time of night?

She was out of the shower in a flash, grabbing her old off-white dressing gown and clutching it around her body as she peered through her bedroom window and down into the darkness then breathing a sigh of relief, then happiness, as she saw Roy's Rolls Royce. She flew downstairs and opened the door and fell into his arms.

He was holding her as though he didn't want to let her go, bending his head down so he could nuzzle into her neck. His familiar cologne and the recognisable strength of his arms was balm to her.

'You're all wet,' he said.

'I've just come from the shower.' She pulled him into the hallway and closed the door. He looked tired. 'What's the matter?'

He shrugged. 'I just wanted to see you, Dais.'

'You couldn't have chosen a better time, I was feeling sorry for meself.'

'You? I don't believe that. You're the happiest person I know.' He cocked his head on one side. 'Is that the water still running?'

She nodded then grinned at him. She wrestled his jacket off and dumped it on the bottom stair rail and took him by the hand. She turned and caught the familiar sweet smell of brandy on his breath. He went to speak but she touched his lips with her fingers.

'Shh! Everyone's asleep.'

In the bathroom she let her dressing gown fall and said, 'Well, what are you waiting for?'

155

He slipped out of his clothes, leaving them in a pile on the floor. His warm musky maleness filled her senses and her nipples grew hard. His cock stood out in front of him, swollen with desire. Daisy pulled him into the cubicle and closed the door.

Her arms went around him and, as he kissed the base of her neck, a piercing hot sensation ran through her. His lips trailed round to her face and lingered on her eyes, her nose, her mouth. She felt as if she had been kissing him for years and would never get enough of him.

Daisy looked down at his cock, at the milky fluid at its tip. He wrapped his arms tightly around her and hoisted her against the glass so he could enter her.

His movements began carefully.

She pressed herself against him, opening herself as wide as she could with the pleasure of having him inside her.

Stabs of satisfaction sent her into her world of total abandonment. And then it was as if he sensed her coming and she felt the swift shudder of his orgasm joining with her own. She clung to him as the shooting hot fluid filled her.

Slowly the convulsions lessened and he wetly kissed her face again and ran his hands over her body before he fell from her.

Later, in her bed, he clung to her. 'You know, I don't know what I'd do without you,' he said.

She sighed. 'And now I think you should tell me what's worrying you.' Daisy felt as though her strength had been renewed. She could cope with whatever life had to sling at her.

He suddenly smiled at her and it was like a rainbow had brightened the room. 'You and your bleedin' Karma,' he said.

Daisy didn't correct him. It had been her Eddie's father who'd said time and time again, what goes around, comes around.

She thought about Jamie. Even some kids who had stable homes started turning into little devils.

'Jamie gets me down at times,' she said.

'He's got a bad streak,' Roy said. 'Ain't nothin' to do with you, it's in him.'

'What can I do, Roy?'

'Love the little bastard,' he said. 'And I'll help you keep an eye on him.'

She'd once witnessed Jamie put a stone over an ants' nest so the poor little creatures couldn't find their way back into the hole. She'd kicked the stone away, but when she'd asked him why he'd done it he'd just grinned at her with that smile that made everyone's heart melt. Even now she'd think of his cruelty and that terrible smile and she'd shiver.

'Sorry,' she said. 'I shouldn't be lumbering you. Go on, I'm listening.'

'Maurie Nelson's watchin' every move I make,' he said. 'It's makin' me fuckin' paranoid.'

'I ain't never met 'im,' Daisy said.

'You don't want to know the wanker,' Roy said. She could feel the tension growing in him. 'By the time he was nineteen he'd escaped from a couple of remand homes and run out of Pentonville in bare feet.'

Daisy laughed.

'You might think it's funny but he was inside

then for armed robbery. In the sixties he got sent down again for robbery, and not long ago he got done for wounding. The trouble is, he's got a foot in both camps because he's provided the coppers with information about a Paddington bank job. Even the coppers don't like 'im. He's a burly dark skinned fucker that's a bleedin' menace. I wouldn't be a bit surprised if it hadn't been him that got the coppers to take my pool tables off me.'

Daisy had never seen him so distraught about a bloody nobody before.

'If that was all I 'ad to worry about I wouldn't care, but he's got heroin and cocaine on the go and he's dealing his shit on my manor. With the coppers on his side and the power that brings him I'm worried my time is running out. I've run my manor for so long that every so often I get a fresh young kid who thinks he can take me over, an' I deal with the silly bastard. But who knows? With police protection, Maurie Nelson could be the bloke with the control to step into my shoes. All he needs is the dosh for the drugs and then he'll flash it in suppliers' faces.' He sighed and Daisy could sense his tiredness.

'You got to see it through, Roy. Don't give up before the fight is done.'

'You always manage to make me feel better, don't you, Dais?'

Daisy wondered how that could be true when she couldn't make herself feel better.

'I've been hearing tales he's been doin' a bit of burnin',' Roy said. 'A Surrey country club went up in smoke–'

'That place didn't belong to you.'

'No, but I can't put the finger on who's setting fire to my properties. I wouldn't like to think Nelson would dare go that far. If I lose my patience...'

'Daisychains was arson. You reckon he did it?'

'If I thought ... well, it's only a matter of time before Nelson gets his comeuppance.' Roy's eyes were dark and thoughtful and his voice was low, and then he looked at her and smiled that smile she loved so much.

From the bed covers came the delicious male scent of him.

He yawned and his sweet breath was warm on her cheek.

He said, 'You should let me give you money instead of grubbing in the muck at car boots and–'

'Where there's muck there's brass,' she said. 'And I got to prove to myself I can pick myself up and start again. 'Specially at this auction tomorrow.'

'You want me to run you to this place?'

'Don't even think about it. Vera'll have me bleedin' guts for garters if it ain't just me an' her going off tomorrow.'

'Fair enough,' he said. 'Now about Eddie. I was thinking of making a big do of his seventeenth birthday.'

'Oh, was you? Nice of you to ask me!'

'Come on, Daisy, you know I love that kid like he was my own.'

'You'd never let him get into anything unsavoury?'

'Unsavoury? What the fuck's that? I'm a fuckin' gangster and you know it. But I can promise you the boy will be protected at all times.'

She felt the relief course through her.

Daisy pulled back the sheet and inspected his hard-on.

'I s'pose we better do somethin' about that,' she said.

# CHAPTER 17

'I never thought it was goin to be this fuckin' borin'.'

'You wanted to come to the auction, Vera. I never asked you. You moaned and bleated like a bleedin' sheep. Lol can come next time.' Daisy looked around the stuffy hall then back at Vera.

Her friend had pursed her mouth like a cat's arse and Daisy expected a torrent of abuse. Instead, as she smoothed down the red neck ruffles of her silk blouse, Vera said, 'Think I'll 'ave a wander about.'

'Good idea, Vera.'

Daisy stood up and slipped off her black suit jacket, leaving it on a chair. Just to make sure their seats wouldn't be taken she draped her scarf across both the chairs. She knew as soon as her back was turned Vera would be up and looking for some bloke to chat with. Daisy threaded her way past the seated people waiting for the auction to start.

No wonder Vera was tired. They'd driven to the auction site at the small village of Boarhunt, just outside Wickham, early in the morning to find the hall a hive of activity. Daisy was surprised to see all manner of items, machinery and furniture being presented for inspection.

'Our stuff's given a lot number so likely buyers can examine it before they bid,' Daisy told Vera.

'If this goes well and you really want to do it permanent, like, you'll 'ave to fork out for a van. Can't go on relyin' on Tyrone's Mini.'

Before Daisy had had a chance to reply, Vera was tapped on the shoulder. She'd looked round in surprise. ''Enery Sugden, fancy seein' you!' Daisy swore Vera was blushing beneath her pan-stick make-up.

The huge bear of a man with thinning hair whisked Vera off to a corner of the room where Daisy could see her giggling like a girl.

It had given Daisy a chance to walk around and examine some of the goods for sale. She'd stopped to look at some figurines. As her fingers touched the cold china a voice said, 'Those are not good. One has a chip and it devalues them.'

He really was a gorgeous looking man. Spanish? Greek perhaps? The dark suit he wore beneath the shortie raincoat was expensive. His aquiline nose was just the right balance for his tanned face. He brushed a hand through glossy hair that shone like a raven's wing.

'Kind of you to tell me.' She eyed his silk shirt and then his smile with very white teeth that made her heart beat just a little too fast.

He shrugged. 'I see you before at the place near Arundel and I guess you come here to sell the stuff you perhaps buy?'

'You're very astute,' she said.

161

'Now I see you with your mother and I want to talk to you but I am shy. Your mother, she looks very, very, how you say, *fierce?*'

Daisy laughed. If Vera knew he thought she was her mother she'd have forty bleedin' fits.

'You and I, we walk around the hall together?'

'Why not,' said Daisy. 'What's your name?'

'Is Bruno,' he said, 'and you are...'

'Daisy.' She knew Bruno was an Italian name.

He nodded. 'Sorry, my English sometimes is not so good.' He put his hand to her waist, guiding her to the next table where a jewelled bracelet took her eye.

'Nice piece,' he said. Daisy scribbled a possible price down in her catalogue. If she had good offers on her own items she might treat herself.

'I think so,' she said. 'Perhaps I'll be lucky and it won't go any higher than its gold weight value.'

He was wearing a tangy cologne Daisy recognised as expensive. She looked at him and smiled. A fluttering feeling began in the depths of her stomach but the feeling was interrupted by Vera returning to her side and giving her a very old-fashioned look. Daisy was about to introduce the Italian to Vera but he seemed to have melted into the crowd. Oh, well, thought Daisy, it saved her explaining things to her 'mother'.

'That 'Enery Sugden used to be a regular of mine way back when we lived down Bert's Caff,' Vera said. 'He was a live wire, he used to like–'

'I don't want to hear about your sex life,' Daisy had snapped.

'No, missy,' Vera said huffily, 'but you'll like it when I tell you I been makin' a few enquiries as

162

to the best auction houses and there's one in the New Forest that's well attended.'

Vera had handed her a paper on which she'd scribbled the location and dates. Daisy went to get them both some teas and Vera wandered back to their seats. Daisy thought Vera looked tired and fed up.

'Two strong teas and two bacon rolls with brown sauce, please.'

The blonde with an inch of black hair showing at her roots went off with her order and Daisy looked back at Vera sitting with the paddle on her lap.

'Just don't go waving it around for any old junk. I don't want to go home with a set of bleedin' golf clubs or a piano,' Daisy had warned Vera.

After only slopping the teas a little bit Daisy reached her seat again. The sale was due to start any minute. Vera took the rolls off her and Daisy stashed the teas under her chair.

'Ain't this exciting, Dais?' said Vera through a mouthful of bacon roll.

Daisy grinned at her. 'I thought you was bored,' she teased, and glanced through the catalogue.

''Enery Sugden told me there's a lot of stuff in 'ere that'll be sold off cheap, boxes of bits. They'll go for a quid or so. Car booters and secondhand shops'll buy them and sell the good pieces individually to make a decent profit.'

'I saw loads of boxes of books.'

'Buyers got to be careful there. Got to examine 'em. Couple of good sellers on top makes the naive buyer think the whole boxful is a bargain.'

'Mr Sugden's been teachin' you well, 'asn't he, Vera?'

163

'Yeah, an' I showed him a few things when he was a customer of mine...'

Daisy glanced at Vera who had a bit of brown sauce clinging to her chin. But for once her eyelashes were on straight. Daisy smiled and put out her finger and wiped off the sauce. Then she squinted at the catalogue sheet again.

'One hundred and ninety-eight lots. We got the bag at number eight. The dogs is forty-six and the china's one hundred and seven. The jewellery ain't until last. They don't pay out until the very last lot's gone.'

'We'll be needin' another cuppa before the end, won't we?'

A whistle sounded and the sale commenced.

It seemed that in next to no time it was the moment for Daisy's beaded bag to be auctioned...

'Did it go as well as you hoped?' Lol asked. She was sitting on the sofa in a floaty green dress that made her look more fragile than ever.

'It was fuckin' nervewrackin', I can tell you,' Daisy replied. She threw the bundle of notes on the coffee table. 'I'd put a reserve on the Clarice Cliff, just like you told me, and the bids didn't get anywhere near. So I brought the stuff home again. I want you to come with me next time, both for the buyin' and the bleedin' sellin'. I got fed up with Vera givin' me earache.' A grin split Lol's face from ear to ear.

'You might need to go further afield to sell the china,' Eddie chimed in. He'd been sprawled over an armchair when Daisy first pushed open the sitting room door, but had now risen to go into the kitchen to make her and Vera a cup of tea.

'Trouble is,' said Daisy, 'I made enough money today to settle up bills that's escalated but I'll need to put some real hard graft in to make this lark work. I was thinkin' I would sell jewellery at car boot sales an' markets.'

'You'll 'ave to get up bleedin' early for that,' said Vera, coming in. Daisy saw that she'd already changed into her fluffy mules and black silk dressing gown.

'I think me days of lyin' in bed are well an' truly over,' Daisy admitted. 'But I won't need a whole market pitch, not for a card table an' a case of pretty things, will I?'

'You can't always rely on finding little treasures to sell at auctions,' said Lol. 'What 'appened at Ford was a fluke, a piece of luck, but it ain't always goin' to be that way.'

'I'll cut down on expenses by using me own car...'

'You ain't 'alf goin' to get tired, Mum.' Eddie looked worried sick.

'Hard work never 'urt no bugger,' said Daisy. She stared round the room. It was her room, in her own house, and she'd work her fingers to the bone to keep her family and this house together.

'I been thinkin' while you been out,' said Eddie. The kettle was whistling and Daisy was gasping for a cuppa.

'Me an' Tyrone is goin' into the house clearance business—'

'What! Usin' a bleedin' Mini?'

'Nah, we'll get hold of a van. That way *you* can have your pick of the smaller items. Some people die an' don't 'ave relatives and 'ave been keeping little knick-knacks for years. There's money in this, Mum. You said I could help you an' I think this is the way to go.'

'Will you take up a *proper* apprenticeship like I asked if this don't work out?'

'Okay.' A shadow crossed Eddie's face then just as quickly was gone. 'I promised you, didn't I?'

Daisy shook her head. He was like her, this big lad who could pass for a man. He'd work all right, and bloody hard, but he'd only work at what he wanted to.

'Where you going to get rid of the stuff I don't want? The bigger stuff like wardrobes and that?'

'Southampton Market, Ford – there's plenty of places. The rubbish can go to the local tip.'

'It's not a bad idea, son,' said Vera 'The pair of you are strong, 'ealthy blokes.'

'Tyrone's mother's boyfriend says he knows where he can pick up a big van cheap.'

Daisy was mulling all this over in her mind.

'It could work,' she said. There were tears threatening to rise. 'You're doin' this to help me, ain't you?'

Eddie shrugged. 'I want to make a bit of dosh an' all. An' I'll need somewhere to store stuff.'

'The garage?'

'Fine!'

Eddie went into the kitchen to finish making the tea just as a key clicked in the front door and Susie came in, bringing cold air with her.

'Where you been, all dolled up like that?'

Susie blushed which made her pink cheeks pinker than ever. She ignored Vera's question.

166

'Is Joy asleep?'

'Like an angel,' said Lol.

Suddenly Vera asked, 'Are you seeing some-one?'

'No!' Susie cried a little too fiercely.

'You're telling fibs. I can always tell,' said Vera. 'We'll find out eventually, you mark my words. If you wanted to meet a bloke, an auction is the place. Teeming with 'em. There was this really 'andsome Italian eyeing up Daisy.'

'Stop it,' said Daisy. She knew she was blushing. 'Don't start on me or I'll tell 'em about that bleedin' ol' birdcage you bought at the auction for a quid.'

'I bought it to paint up an' then I'll put a plant in it and hang it up. It's very decorative, Daisy.'

'It's a fuckin' broken birdcage, Vera.'

And the room was filled with laughter.


## CHAPTER 18

The noise from the fruit machines was doing his head in. Three days now he'd been playing this fuckin' game of giving her the eye. He already decided if the stupid bint wasn't about to take the bait tonight he was moving on.

The blonde smiled at him as he asked for change for what seemed the fiftieth time that night. He tried to touch her fingers but the glass separating the customers from the assistant in the change kiosk didn't allow it. The bottom slit was only big enough for money to pass through.

'You want I wait for you when you finish tonight?'

What would the cunt say? Yes or no?

'I don't usually walk home with anyone,' she said. No, he thought, I bet you don't, you ugly bitch.

'I watch you for days now. You and I we should be friends, good friends.' The music was loud. David Soul was giving it his all with 'Don't Give Up On Us Baby'. The song was telling him what to do and he liked that.

She was weakening; he gave her a smile. Come on, you dozy bitch, I bet you don't get many offers. Who else is likely to fancy a fat cow like you in this Godforsaken place? Hayling Island, full of old dears with zimmer frames. He'd only ended up here because things had got a little too hot for him in Portsmouth. But he'd go back, maybe not to Pompey, but he had some unfinished business with that little blonde in Gosport, didn't he?

He stood aside while a couple of teenage boys changed some money then he grinned at her again. She bit her nails. Down to the quicks. It made him cringe. He wouldn't think about that while he was giving her one. Lull the bitch into a false sense of security, then he could take the money and run.

There was a rattle of coins somewhere behind him. Someone had hit the jackpot. The machines were a mug's game, he thought, no one ever really won much on them. They were fixed to pay out coins few and far between. Only the owners of the slot machine arcades won and they were

168

quids in all the time.

'I here tonight just to see you.'

She nodded.

'You notice me?'

Fuckin' cunt couldn't help but notice him; he'd made a big enough show of wandering around and giving her the eye.

'I've noticed you,' she said. Her eyes were blue, watery blue. Outside it was dark and he knew the arcade closed at midnight. It was cold for autumn and soon the whole of the beachfront would close down for the winter. Already the funfair was being repainted. Her skin was pale like it had never seen the sun. She'd probably been in here every night of the summer amongst the fag smoke.

'That's good.' He opened his eyes wide. He knew the women loved his dark brown eyes with their long lashes. 'You must like me a little bit to notice me? Yes?'

She smiled at him then.

Jesus Christ, this was hard work, he thought. 'I wait.' He looked at his watch; it said eleven forty-five. 'I walk you home, please? Or my heart will break.'

'All right,' she said. 'But you mustn't stay in the arcade. The manager comes to make sure I've got everyone out.'

'Why?'

'We can't have people left inside with the money in the machines. And I have to cash up the takings.'

'You do this?'

'Yes, then he trusts me to put the takings in the night safe.'

169

'Why *he* not do this?' He knew full well why the spotty-faced youth didn't do it. This girl lived in one of the static caravans and the bank was just up the road from the site. The manager lived in the opposite direction and was too lazy to do his job properly and go to the night safe.

'It's my job,' she said. 'If you wait along the road near the bus shelter I'll be as quick as I can.'

He grinned at her. He'd never doubted he'd win the bitch over. He looked around the now deserted arcade and pulled his mackintosh around him, then he left.

There were stars in the sky and he could hear the rush of the waves on the shingle beach.

He knew Hayling Island was a resort but it was a bugger to get in and out of in the holiday season. Sometimes the traffic was nose to tail. Apart from pubs and the funfair and the car boot on a Wednesday morning nothing much went on to entice the youngsters to come and stay.

He walked along the deserted road. The street lights were few and there was no pavement along this road which led to the small community of caravans.

He knew she lived alone. Knew the caravans either side of her were empty.

All he had to do now was wait.

In the height of the short summer season Hayling Island could be a little goldmine with its fish and chip shops, bars, pubs and holiday camps, but in the winter it was like Siberia. Another few weeks and the first of the winter winds would make sure the beach was left to the gulls once more.

Looking back to the arcade he saw the lights darken, heard the music fade and muted voices that he guessed was the manager and herself, bidding each other goodnight. Marie ... that was her name, wasn't it? Then there was silence until he heard the clop-clop sound of her scuffed white high heels on the tarmac.

He looked expectantly for the heavy bank bag. Yes, she had it with her, he could see the top of it peeking from the plastic holdall.

As she neared he stepped from the shadows.

'Hello, Marie.'

'Hello.' She stopped walking and waited expectantly. 'I ... I don't know your name,' she whispered.

'Bruno,' he said. 'I have something for you.' He took from his mac pocket a flower, a rose. Probably the last rose still flowering before winter came. He'd stolen it from a nearby garden. He presented it to her. He could see she was impressed.

'Thank you.' She took the flower.

The girl was simpering. Oh, for fuck's sake let me get this over and done with, he thought, the stupid, stupid cow.

'Where you live?'

She pointed further along the lane. She didn't know that he already knew.

'I would like very much to kiss you,' he said. He put an arm around her shoulder and inclined his head towards her. Oh, God, she stank of sweat and stale cheap perfume.

His lips met hers and he had to steel himself not to throw up. He could feel her heart was beating fast beneath the flimsy dress she wore under her white cardigan. Thank God her mouth was dry. He hated wet and slobbery kisses.

She tried to cling to him but he pulled away. He knew the cow wanted more, they always did. The old women were the easiest to fool, they were so fuckin' grateful for any small favour. One woman had told him when she'd turned fifty it was as if she'd become invisible to men. That made it all the easier for him, didn't it?

'We walk?' he said. He wanted to get his hands on the money. But he was forced to go through this rigmarole to get it.

It wasn't as if he really liked killing them. He didn't. It was simply that it was necessary, otherwise they'd be able to give his description to the police and he didn't want that, did he?

So far luck had been with him. By leaving the women with pieces of wood in their mouths they'd think they had a psycho mass murderer on their hands. The police wouldn't be looking for *him*. He left no indication at all of being near the dead women.

The money was growing. And Maurie Nelson could do nothing without money. But when he had enough he'd be able to move in on that bastard Kemp's manor and Bruno would be there as Nelson's right-hand man. Money would buy cocaine from a source Nelson knew in Colombia. Money would make more money.

Bruno knew things about Kemp he wouldn't like dragged out in the open. It wouldn't be long before a jury would send Kemp to prison and throw away the key. There were murders instigated

172

by Kemp that'd been hushed up – including the boxer Valentine Waite who'd mysteriously disappeared some years ago. It'd come through the prison grapevine that Waite had abducted Daisy Lane, Kemp's lady. Kemp and that bastard of a detective Vinnie Endersby had offed the boxer. Because Waite was such a national treasure the truth had been hushed up. Not for much longer, though.

Maurie Nelson was a supergrass, hated by criminals because he was hand in glove with the coppers. But a few bribes here and there ensured the criminal fraternity still worked with him.

Wonderful what good fortune a jail sentence could bring. Bruno and Nelson had roomed together at Winchester nick. Nelson was inside for a robbery he said he didn't commit, and when it came to trial the evidence was lacking so he'd been freed. Nelson and him had been together long enough to plan to take over Roy Kemp's patch.

What Roy Kemp didn't know was that one of his blokes was getting paid by Maurie Nelson to spill the beans about pending drug consignments. Poor Roy Kemp had a cuckoo in his nest and he didn't know it. Bruno laughed. Kemp was going to get a big shock when he found police waiting at Langstone Harbour when his consignment of drugs came in from Africa.

Bruno wanted revenge on Kemp so badly.

It all started with Roy Kemp's fruit machines. His two younger brothers had stolen from the machines. Roy Kemp went to the flat and nailed the sixteen-year-old's hand to the table with a serving fork. He'd left drugs on the table to ease the boy's pain, telling him anyone stupid enough to steal from him deserved all he got. That was the start of his brother's drug habit. The boy had later gone on the streets, selling his arse for drugs. He was dead now. The other brother had got shot in crossfire when a rival gang had decided to take on Roy's men.

And then there was Bruno's prison sentence. The coppers had never been able to prove Bruno'd had a hand in the murders of the girls used in the snuff movies he'd made, so he'd gone down for collusion. He'd provided those snuff movies for Kemp to sell abroad. But when Kemp had sussed he was killing the girls and filming their deaths, Kemp and Vinnie Endersby had turned Bruno in to the rozzers, leaving him banged up in jail.

Yes, he had a lot of scores to settle with Roy Kemp.

And what did a few arson attacks on Kemp's clubs matter? It helped to slow the bastard down and make a dent in his takings. That club by Gosport's ferry had seemed a nice little earner. He smiled to himself. Well, it wasn't an earner at all now, was it?

It was there he'd met that dozy Samantha, serving behind the bar and trying to make customers think she'd come up in the world to a barmaid instead of the slag she really was.

And now he was about to get his hands on the arcade's takings. He looked at the girl. 'You all right?' he asked.

She nodded her head.

He could tell by the way her arm was straining

that the bag was heavy. One thing for sure, he wasn't going to offer to carry it for her.

He admired Nelson. The bloke even had legitimate businesses to back up his earnings: scrap yards, car lots and a thriving van hire business. He had the know-how all right, but what Bruno admired most was that Nelson was doing all this on Kemp's patch, right under the bastard's nose, and Kemp couldn't do a thing. Not about the protection rackets Nelson had set up, nor about the lorry hijackings of Kemp's vehicles. Nelson was a busy boy, a busy police-protected boy.

And now Nelson had an ally in Bruno. Revenge would be sweet. Wasn't that what Italians were good at?

'It's not far now, that's where I live.' Marie pointed out a dark hulk of a static van and then said, 'Come with me along the road a bit. I have to deliver something.'

'We no go into your home?' He bent to nuzzle into her hair that smelled of chip fat.

'I have to do something first.' She made to pull away but he could tell she liked him kissing her hair, her neck.

'Afterwards,' he said. 'Plenty of time.' He twisted her around so she could look into his eyes and he said soulfully, 'I wait very long for you. *Non ti scordar di me.* I think you no like me. Perhaps I better go, leave you?'

'Oh, no!' she cried. 'Don't do that. What's that foreign language mean?'

He pulled her to him and held her close. 'My little forget-me-not.'

He knew he'd got her hot for him now.

They walked through the open wooden gate and within moments she was unlocking the van's door.

She switched on the light and inside was exactly as he'd thought it would be. A tip. A million rancid smells came at him.

'Would you like tea? Or a drink? I have whisky.'

His stomach hurled itself about looking at the small sink stacked with chipped unwashed mugs and plates. No, he definitely didn't want to put his mouth against one of those filthy cups.

'I want you.' He shrugged himself from his mac so she could see his neat dark suit and his crisp white shirt. He bet she didn't get many blokes as fastidious as him in this dump.

He put his mac on a cushioned bench and led her towards the unmade bed. She put the heavy bag down on the floor with a comforting thud.

He pulled her clothes from her body one by one until she was naked in all her fat glory. She went to undress him but he couldn't bear to think of her hands on his clean clothes.

'I do it. You sit so I can look at you,' he said. He folded his clothes and set them on top of his mac. Then he turned and held out his arms to her.

She eased into them.

She put her hand down and touched his cock. He didn't want her feeling him, dirty bitch. He moved out of her reach.

'I need you,' he said pushing her onto the bed. The sheets stank. Stupid cow looked as though she believed him. What he really meant was I need that money to help ease my way into Nelson's confidence and I want this over as soon as possible.

'I think I love you,' he murmured. Closing his eyes so he wouldn't see her, he pushed his swollen cock into her moist opening.

It slipped easily into her and she cried out. He was proud of the size of his penis. Not quite the twelve inches of Teddy Baird but a good size for a man who wasn't as tall as he'd like to have been.

Surprisingly she had a tight cunt. He began a leisurely movement but she wanted a more furious pace. Thank God, he thought. He could have this over and done with in no time.

He thrust his hips, entering deep. She pushed forward and began with short frantic motions but each time sliding from a different angle, opening up whole new sensations for him

'I love you,' he whispered because he knew she'd expect it. And then he took over, jabbing at her until that furious flame shot from him.

After the final shudder, he lay still until the nausea of her got to him, then he moved and said, 'You like?'

He ignored the undisguised disappointment on her face. He hadn't given her a chance to come, but then why should he? The cow should be grateful that he'd fucked her.

His soft voice melted her anguish. 'We try again in a moment. It has been so long for me and I think of you so much I can't help myself.'

She smiled at him. He'd got her now, the silly cow.

'I'll make a cup of tea,' she said.

He watched her fat arse and floppy tits swing about as she got up from the bed.

He too slipped from the bed and fumbled

inside his clothes. While she had her back to him, busying herself at the sink, it was simplicity itself to slip the wire over her head to her neck and pull until she stopped quivering and was quite still.

After he'd jammed the stick into her mouth and laid her on the bed he felt content.

It gave him great satisfaction to leave her with a gaping mouth.

His father had told him that sticks were often inserted into prisoners' mouths to stop them screaming when they were hung in prison camps during the war. He rather liked the idea.

The sticks? He thought it was a neat signature. He bent his head and smelled his armpit. Jesus Christ, but he was rank, and all because of the fat cow. He couldn't wait to get back to the pub he was staying at in Gosport and have a bath.

After dressing, he carefully wiped down the caravan. It wouldn't do to leave any fingerprints. He picked up the bag containing the money and turned off the light.

He was whistling an old Doris Day song from the fifties, 'Que Sera Sera', as he walked back along the road, thinking of the blonde in Gosport.


## CHAPTER 19

'Before I take you shopping I've got a bit of business to attend to. Don't mind, do you?'

He looked into her long-lashed green eyes and inhaled her Chanel Number 5 perfume. Daisy squeezed his hand. 'Why should I mind?'

Roy Kemp shrugged. He didn't like combining business with pleasure but this lunchtime he had no option. The Star Tavern, with its bright show of autumn hanging baskets and lanterns, was a stone's throw from Teddy Baird's mews house home and if Baird was willing to take him up on his offer of ten thousand pounds for five minutes' work he'd be a happy man.

'Do you want another drink?'

She nodded, pushing strands of her blonde hair out of her eyes and crossing her knees. He looked at her slim legs and smiled. Dressed in black, with a single gold bracelet on her wrist and the diamond brooch his mother had given her pinned to her shoulder, Daisy looked fantastic. She loved that brooch. She might be selling jewellery now but she seldom wore more than those two choice pieces. The gold bangle had been given to her by her first love, Eddie's father, and Roy had never seen her without it. The brooch was worth a small fortune and was reserved for special occasions. A warm feeling ran through him.

He'd seen the punters in the drinking place swivel their eyes towards her, then, when they'd spotted him, fear had made them turn their eyes elsewhere.

Roy got up and took off his overcoat with the velvet collar. He put it over the back of his chair, then made his way to the bar. He knew he was gathering looks from the customers. And why shouldn't he? He was a face.

The blonde barmaid refused his money but gave him generous measures. The easy way she moved reminded him of Eve, the girl he'd been shagging in London. He felt no guilt over that; perhaps he should, but Eve meant no more to him than a woman to fuck when he needed it.

As he turned, with the drinks in his hands, he heard the familiar laugh of his mate Biffo Baird.

He called across the smoke-filled room. 'I suppose you want a drink, mate?'

The barmaid touched his arm. 'Leave the drinks, I'll bring them over. I know what Teddy likes.' Roy treated her to a smile. Everyone, he thought, knew what Teddy liked, from his drink to his drugs to his women. And everyone liked Teddy Baird. He was a big man with a ready laugh and a twelve-inch prick, and as long as you didn't cross him he would be your mate.

Teddy Baird was also skint.

Back at the table, Roy slapped an arm across Baird's broad shoulders. Ever the casual dresser, he was in his usual jeans and a sweatshirt and looked settled in for the day, making Daisy laugh.

'That good-looking model still putting up with your wild ways?' teased Roy.

Baird grinned at Roy.

'Of course,' he said, the corners of his eyes creased with lines. 'Daisy won't 'ave me. Why she prefers you I ain't got no fuckin' idea.'

Daisy starting laughing again, her mouth wide open, showing her small white teeth. Roy liked to see Daisy happy. Lately, though, she was beginning to look tired and she'd lost weight. No wonder, given how early she had to get up to drive off to auctions and car boots all over the place, either to buy or to sell stuff. It was hard on

180

her feet and she was out in all weathers, but he'd given up trying to get her to take money off him. The feisty little bitch had told him where to stick his hand-outs. Still, he admired her for her earning power and her determination to look after her family in her own way. And he felt honoured she'd agreed to go shopping with him today.

'Sorry to break the party up,' Roy said, sitting down on a velvet-topped bar stool and stretching his long legs out in front of him. At that moment the barmaid chose to set the tray of drinks down. She gazed at Baird as though she could eat him. But then, he had that effect on women.

'I'm financially embarrassed, so if you're expecting me to buy a round in return...' said Baird. His hair tumbled across his forehead and he wiped it away lazily. 'Thanks, Cath,' he purred and ran his hand over her generous backside.

Roy sighed. 'You got debts way beyond your assets which amount to a couple of hundred quid, right?'

Baird eyed him suspiciously. 'How the fuck do you know that?'

'If I want to do business with you I make it *my business.*'

'So, what do you want with me?'

'How about you take ten grand off me?'

Baird spluttered into his beer. 'You must want me to off someone.'

'Am I saying that?'

'You want me to off someone because you don't want to be seen to have any part of it. You or your henchmen.'

'Not just a pretty face, are you, Biff?'

He saw Daisy was watching as the pair of them bandied words back and forth. Her face was expressionless. He knew she'd say nothing until the deal was finalised, and then she'd forget she ever heard them talking. He liked her for that. She hated being lied to but there was never any need for him to tell her an untruth.

'I don't think I need to tell you who is getting on my bleedin' wick just lately, do I?'

Baird gave him a steady eye-to-eye gaze. That was another thing Roy liked about Biffo. He'd grown up a strong-willed bloke having come from a working class background. The streets of Fulham had taught him a lot. He was hopeless with money, even as a lad when the one-armed bandits and fruit machines captivated him. He'd been a born fighter and leader, and if he wasn't leading his mates into trouble he was taking it on himself. Roy smiled to himself, remembering that Teddy Baird had started his criminal record when he was aged eleven for breaking windows in a derelict building. He was pulled in for malicious damage. Since then the cop shops had had their fill of him. Growing up in Fulham, Baird, like most of the other inhabitants, had an eye to getting a foothold with the big guys, the gangsters. Biffo continued to eyeball Roy and then suddenly grinned at him.

'Probably the same fuckin' tosser who gives me the shits. Where and when?'

Roy knew Teddy Baird was no friend of Nelson's. Baird was a hard man and had spent more than a few terms locked up as a guest of Her Majesty. Roy also knew Teddy's money troubles had taken on a life of their own when he'd earned good money as an actor but never bothered to give the tax man any. But that was Teddy all over. If he had money he spent it. Living for the day was his mantra.

Roy said, 'I'll leave that in your capable hands.' Baird touched Roy's glass with his own.

'Cheers,' he said. Roy drank back his brandy and saw Daisy's glass was empty.

Baird reached down and exposed a shining Bowie knife he kept inside his boot. 'I could give him this little gift.'

Roy nodded then turned to Daisy. 'Are you ready, Daisy?' He helped her on with her black, belted coat and slipped his own coat over his shoulders. He twisted back again to Baird. 'She's a bugger to buy anything *for.*' He wanted to lighten the atmosphere. 'But when I say we're going shopping, we're goin' shopping.' Then he pulled out his wallet and peeled off a few bills. 'Have a drink on me,' he said.

Teddy Baird half rose to shake his hand. 'It'll be an expensive afternoon, Roy. You just spent ten thousand before you even hit the bleedin' shops.'

'So you're paying out to get Nelson off your back?'

'Did I say that?'

Daisy shook her head. They were in an exclusive shop, where she was trying on a black suede coat that looked as if it had been made for her. She twisted this way and that in front of the mirror.

'If you insist on forkin' out money left right and centre then I'd like this coat—'

And then, suddenly, with her hand covering her mouth, she thrust the coat towards him, and ran for the ladies' as though a bat out of hell was chasing her.

With the coat over his arm Roy walked to the lavatory and banged on the door. 'Daisy,' he called. 'Are you all right?' The assistant was hovering.

After a while Daisy emerged, looking none the worse.

'That was a funny thing,' she said, dabbing at her mouth with a piece of tissue. 'I threw up. But I'm fine now.'

'Eaten anything to make you feel sick?' He was worried about her. He knew she didn't eat properly nowadays. Too many burgers and chips from the vans at car boots. Still, he'd make sure he got a nice fat juicy steak inside her on the opening night of his new club. He was planning on inviting her whole family and making a party of it.

Daisy shook her head, then suddenly grinned.

'Probably that extra large brandy and lime on an empty stomach.' Then she poked him in the arm. 'Thought you was paying for that coat for me? You still got it over your bleedin' arm. They'll be thinkin' we're goin' to pinch it.'

She took it from him and passed it to the assistant, nodding her head to show she wanted it. The assistant walked with it towards the till, and Daisy slipped her arm through Roy's. He liked her doing spontaneous things like that, but then she whispered, 'You really gonna get Baird to kill Maurie Nelson?'

Roy knew Daisy hated any kind of violence. 'I didn't tell 'im to kill him, but it's either Nelson or me. Last night I had a big fight in my Kingston

184

club. A lot of stuff got broken, an' some of my blokes got hurt so much they won't be workin' for a while. The fuckin' coppers couldn't give a shit.'

Daisy looked up at him as she slipped her own coat on, then she asked him the same question she'd asked many times before.

'Do you think it was Nelson who fired Daisy-chains?'

'Probably – possibly. He might have reckoned I was still the owner.'

'Do you think he had anything to do with Samantha's death?'

'Again, it's possible. I just need to shut the bleeder up before I end up sitting down with the Kray twins for lunch, permanently. The fuckin' filth would love to put me back inside.'

The worry in Daisy's head deepened.

'I see,' was all she said.


## CHAPTER 20

'You got a fella, I know you 'ave.'

Daisy saw Susie colour up beneath Vera's probing gaze.

'Leave 'er alone, will you. You're like a bleedin' dripping tap trying to wear 'er down.'

Susie gave Daisy a grateful smile, which she returned, and went on peeling the potatoes. The meaty smell of a steak and kidney pie escaped from the oven.

'These spuds can see better'n me with all the

bleedin' eyes they got,' Daisy said. She looked into the saucepan and asked, 'Ain't this enough, Suze?'

Susie peered over Daisy's shoulder. 'Not if you wants to feed the kids as well, it ain't.'

Daisy gave a huge sigh. She hated cooking and anything to do with it. She looked back at Vera and said, 'We always 'ave spuds with everything an' I'm sick of peeling them. An' why are you sitting on your arse?'

Vera looked up from the *Evening News* she was reading. 'Dais, did you read about that girl being strangled over in Hayling Island?'

Daisy shook her head. 'How could I when *you* got the paper an' *I* been out all afternoon?' Her feet were killing her and it'd taken her ages to get warm after queueing with the crowd of people ready to pounce on bargains at St Mary's Hall. The tabletop sale produced no bargains, nothing more exciting than a couple of secondhand books – Nell Dunn's *Poor Cow*, and *Rosie Darling*, Rosie Swale's book about sailing across the Pacific in a thirty-foot catamaran. Daisy looked forward to sitting on the sofa with her feet up and starting to read... Vera coughed for attention.

'What's it say then?' Daisy dug out another eye then moaned at Susie who was pricking sausages, 'Where did you get these bleedin' spuds?'

'It says the money she was supposed to bank for the arcade where she worked was taken an' she 'ad a piece of stick propped inside her mouth.'

Daisy heard the crack in Vera's voice. She threw the potato peeler in the sink and within seconds was at Vera's side, putting her arms around her. It seemed to her that Vera would never get over Samantha's death, and she could do nothing except witness Vera's pain. Daisy noticed how Vera's bones seemed nearer the surface than usual and there was a line of grey roots showing in her dark hair.

'Suze,' Daisy ordered, 'put the kettle on.'

'That's what they did to my poor Samantha.' Vera was sobbing. 'They took *her* money as well...'

Daisy put her fingers beneath Vera's chin and tipped her face towards her. One of her eyelashes was off centre. A great wave of emotion washed over Daisy.

'You got to stop thinkin' about Samantha,' she said.

'But if I 'adn't given 'er 'er savings she might still be alive.'

'The whole fucking world is full of ifs and buts, Vera. You ain't responsible for Samantha's murder.'

Daisy dabbed at Vera's mascara'd eyes with the end of the tea towel but only succeeded in making the black smudges worse. Tenderly, she pressed the left eyelash back in position.

'He's in this area, Dais. Who's goin' to be next?'

'Well, it won't be none of us, 'cos we ain't got no money,' said Daisy.

'You sure? I wouldn't be too certain of that, Dais.' Vera motioned towards Susie clattering with the cups and saucers. 'Madame over there got a bit put by. Insurance money from buryin' Si a few years back. You wouldn't accept any of it, remember?'

'I offered it,' protested Susie, scattering sugar from the teaspoon all over the formica top. 'Shit,' she said. 'Now look what you made me do!' She slid the spoon back in the bowl.

Daisy shook her head. 'An' I still don't want it. You got a little girl who might need that money, and we'll manage. I just wish that first bit of good luck I 'ad at Ford had continued.'

Vera chimed in. 'Ain't been so lucky for a while, 'ave you, love?' She reached across the table and took the teas from Susie.

Daisy shrugged. 'Win some, lose some,' she said, picking up her cup.

'Yeah, que sera, sera,' said Susie, 'What will be, will be...' Just then a loud pop made Daisy drench herself with hot tea. 'Fuck!'

Vera didn't bat an eyelid but passed the tea towel to Daisy. 'Wipe yerself down with that. I told you you shouldn't give Jamie an air rifle, but you wouldn't bleedin' listen...' Another crack rent the air.

Daisy sighed again. She put the half empty mug down and picked up the cloth, dabbing at her black jeans.

'When Eddie was Jamie's age I let 'im play in the garden with an air rifle so I can't not let Jamie 'ave the same privileges, can I?'

'You can when the bleeder might kill someone with it. Or 'ave their eyes out!'

'Don't be silly, Vera. He's got a round target pinned against one of the oak trees at the bottom of the garden. There's nothin' he can hurt there.'

Daisy looked at Susie who was shaking like a leaf. She was peering out the kitchen window. 'I can't see 'im.'

Daisy said, 'He's been really good lately.' Vera

188

raised her eyes heavenwards.

Eddie came into the kitchen rubbing his eyes with one hand and carrying Kibbles in his other arm. He passed the purring feline to Vera who promptly kissed her cat on the nose then settled him on her lap.

'What's that little shit up to now? You know I was tryin' to get a bit of shut eye.'

'Shouldn't stay out so late, then.' Daisy couldn't resist a dig at him. 'Just teasing,' she said.

Susie clutched at her heart as another shot rang out.

Eddie said, 'I'm gonna...'

'Leave 'im,' said Daisy. 'He's not 'urting anyone.'

She ignored Eddie's look that could kill and went over to the draining board to refill her mug from the teapot. She wasn't surprised to see Eddie leave the kitchen and stomp into the garden.

Then came the shouting that was loud enough for them all to hear.

Daisy was first out the door, her mug of tea overturned.

She rounded the corner of the house just in time to see Eddie strike Jamie so hard he fell to the grass. Her heart was in her mouth as she looked for the air rifle. It was lying on the concrete. 'Leave him!'

Eddie looked at her. She'd never seen him so angry. Ignoring her, he reached down and pulled Jamie to his feet as though he was a rag doll. Jamie tried to squirm away. Eddie pulled his arm back and slapped Jamie's face with such force that the younger boy flew backwards and lay in a crumpled heap on the lawn again.

'Didn't you hear me, I said fuckin' leave 'im!'

Daisy launched herself at Eddie but he was too quick for her; he gripped her by both shoulders and kept her at arm's length. She heard screaming and crying and realised it was herself making all the noise. She was aware then for the first time that Eddie was trying to look into her eyes. In his she saw anguish and pain and something more, something incomprehensible. She stopped struggling to listen to him.

'It's over now, Mum. It's over.'

A sort of calm descended on her, and she allowed him to draw her towards him. And then she was aware she was breathing heavily and sobbing at the same time.

'Give her to me.' Daisy felt herself being transferred to Vera's arms and enveloped in her comforting smell.

'Get hold of Jamie,' Susie said. 'The little bastard.'

'Don't let Mum see 'ow many he's killed or she'll 'ave fuckin' nightmares,' Eddie said.

Daisy's head was spinning. All she kept reliving in her mind's eye was the sight of her two sons fighting. How had it come to this?

Vera said, 'Let's get back into the 'ouse.' Then Daisy heard her say, 'I just hope the 'orror of what you've accomplished stays with you, young Jamie.'

Daisy tried to twist away.

'Oh no you don't, my girl. A cup of tea's what you fuckin' need.'

'If you won't let me see, for fuck's sake tell me!'

'All right, all right.' Daisy could feel the anger

in Vera's voice. 'Your son 'as been feedin' the birds an' squirrels on the table out back 'ere and then he's been shootin' them. There's fuckin' feathers and guts all over the place. Now you 'appy you trusted 'im with a fuckin' rifle?'

Daisy gasped, 'I never...'

Eddie said, 'Suze, you start digging a hole and I'll bury them poor creatures.'

In a blur of rose-print dress and white cardigan, Susie walked across the grass towards the shed to find a fork and shovel.

'Thank Christ it rained last night,' she grumbled. 'At least the ground will be soft.' She shivered. 'Cold though. I expect I'll soon warm up with a bit of digging.'

Vera, having got Daisy inside, said, 'If you'd seen what he'd done, you, with your love of animals, would be sick for a fuckin' month.' She pushed Daisy onto the bench at the table and then plugged in the electric kettle. Daisy put her arms on the table, her head on her arms, and sat quite still. The events went round and round in her head like a never-ending whirlpool. She heard Vera open the kitchen window and shout:

'Dig the 'ole deep enough or else we'll get the badgers and foxes dragging the poor little bleeders up again.'

Vera shut the window. Daisy lifted her head and looked across the table at her.

'I went for Eddie,' she said. Her voice sounded as though it didn't belong to her. 'I went for Eddie. I ain't never laid a finger on 'im in all 'is life an' I went for 'im.'

'Don't you worry about that, now. He's not

likely to 'old it against you. He could see how upset you was.'

'I wasn't thinkin' straight. All I could see was my two boys fightin'. I love 'em more than life itself, an' Eddie was beltin' ten bales of shit out of 'is little brother. I only wanted it to stop, Vera.'

'Well, it 'as. And if you ask me you should 'ave been the one to knock ten bales out of that boy years ago. We wouldn't be 'avin' all this trouble if–'

'You saying I'm a bad mother?'

'No, I'm sayin' you loves 'em both too much. You can't see Jamie's faults.'

Just then the door opened and Eddie came into the kitchen from upstairs. His face was like granite. Daisy was shocked at how like his father he was and even more so when he spoke in a quiet, serious voice.

'Jamie's sitting in bed reading a Dan Dare comic. Don't jump down my throat for letting 'im do that,' he said. 'I've been talking to 'im...'

'Talking?'

He sighed. 'Yes, talking. A bit later he's coming down to apologise to you for causing so much trouble.'

Vera sniggered. 'Does he mean it though? An' he can't apologise to all them mutilated creatures, can he?' She got up from Daisy's side to go and yell through the kitchen window once more. 'How's that bleedin' 'ole comin' on, Suze?'

'We shouldn't be leaving Susie out there with all them dead pigeons.' Daisy got up and went to Eddie. 'I'm sorry I went for you, Eddie, love.'

He looked down at her and kissed her on the forehead.

'Forget it.' It was his natural instinct to forgive easily. Vera caught hold of his sleeve.

'What did Jamie say?'

Eddie spoke quietly to Vera but Daisy had sharp ears.

'He said at first, "So what, they're only pests."' Daisy saw Vera raise her eyes heavenwards once more.

Daisy said, 'He'll grow out of this, you'll see...'

And then a scream punctuated the air.

'Fuckin' hell, that's our Suze!'

Daisy was out the door like a shot. Susie was staring into the hole as though she was mesmerised. Eddie and Vera pushed Daisy to one side.

'It's a bomb! It's a fuckin' bomb!' Susie was pointing down into the freshly dug dark earth that smelled like ferry silt.

'Let me look! Daisy, get back!' commanded Vera. 'We'd better phone the police! Eddie, phone the police!'

Daisy stood back and let the three of them peer into the abyss. She took a glance at the bird table where blood and feathers and shattered bodies were proof of her son's handiwork, and the tears rose in her eyes. She could see the fresh bread he'd put out to lure the hungry creatures to their doom, and she knew then Eddie was right to have had a go at Jamie. She should have tightenened the leash on him a long time ago, Vera was right. She'd spared the rod and spoiled the child long enough.

She turned away from the carnage.

Eddie said, 'Is it ticking?'

'No,' yelled Susie, 'but it might go off any minute. We got to phone for the experts. Vera, whatever are you doing?'

'Vera, get back!' Eddie tried to pull Vera from the edge of the hole but before he had a chance to grab her she'd slithered down into its depths.

'Vera! Vera!' Daisy shouted.

'Get back, everyone! Mum, take cover!' Eddie took charge and thrust Susie away from the hole, then he dropped to the ground, pulling Daisy with him and covering her head with his hands.

From inside the hole Vera could be heard scraping away at the earth. Daisy could see the dirt flying out. It was like a dog digging frantically for a bone.

'Vera, you'll kill us all,' shouted Susie.

'It's a bleedin' bath!'

There was silence for a while until Eddie said, 'Vera, what d'you mean, it's a bath?'

'It ain't a bomb. Come an' look.'

Eddie and Daisy crawled over and peered down into the depths and saw an iron clawed foot sticking out of the dirt. The foot was connected to curved metal and Vera was uncovering a second foot.

'Well I never,' said Susie. 'It's an old cast-iron bath someone's buried.'

'Of course it is,' said Vera. 'Didn't you see the bleedin' plug-hole, our Suze?' Eddie began to laugh and so did Vera. 'You ain't 'alf a silly bitch, Suze, mistaking an upside down bath for a bleedin' bomb an' frightenin' us all nearly to death.'

Daisy started to laugh as well.

Until she looked up and saw Jamie's pale face staring coldly down at them from his bedroom window.

# CHAPTER 21

'For fuck's sake, Tyrone, I can't believe it. We can't drive the van like that... You know I promised that woman we'd be there first thing in the morning... Well, if you reckon, take it, pay for it, an' I'll sort you out in the mornin'.'

Eddie put down the receiver and went into the kitchen. There were two freshly cooked apple pies on top of the oven and the fruity smell tickled his senses.

'First house clearance job we gets an' Tyrone tells me the van's got a puncture.' He looked at his mother, who was dusting Vera's cat ornaments that she'd taken from the top of the dresser.

'Put the bleedin' spare on then, dimwit! Don't forget I'm supposed to be coming with you to see what little treasures I can pick up.'

'The spare's got a puncture as well, Tyrone never got it fixed.' Eddie was well and truly pissed off.

'Eddie, there's some big places with cars in and men in overalls with tools, an' what they do is fix cars. Garages, they're called. Heard of 'em?'

'Yeah, that's what I told Tyrone, but this late in the day no one wants to know. It's nearly knockin' off time, ain't it?'

She looked at her watch. 'What you gonna do, then?'

'Ty's pumped up the tyre an' he reckons he can

195

make it to this place round the back of Moreland Road...'

His mother looked at him and narrowed her eyes. 'Desmond's?'

He nodded. 'Is it okay?'

'They're doing a roarin' business. They're taking a lot of trade away from the other small garages round there on that site. You must 'ave heard what they're up to?'

Eddie shook his head then sat down on a bench by the scrubbed table. Kibbles promptly crawled about a foot along the seat and collapsed on his lap. He began stroking the cat.

'You gonna tell me?' It was obvious his mother knew something he didn't.

'Right, son. There's three blokes, two youngsters and an older man. He's a grey-haired, scruffy git. They know a bit about cars, not that brilliant, but they can do the basics while you wait. But the reason they're makin' money hand over fist is because they got a couple of girls there.'

'Girls can work in garages, Mum. It ain't the bleedin' dark ages.'

'That's the point, it is the dark ages for these two. While you're waiting for the repairs to be carried out you can fuck these girls for extra on your bill.'

At first he thought he hadn't heard her right.

'You mean it's a knockin' shop garage?'

His mother nodded.

'What a fuckin' good idea!'

'Thought you'd say that, you bein' a bloke. But apparently the two girls is drugged up to the eyeballs, so you can imagine they ain't got no say

196

in what 'appens to 'em. An' they're only bits of kids. Jail bait.'

'If they don't like it, why don't they up an' leave?'

'That's the problem, they can't. Desmond keeps 'em drugged up an' locked up.'

'How long's this been going on? Surely the coppers...'

'Not long, but long enough to make Vera's takings go even further down the pan. She was moaning before about lack of trade, now she's moaning even more. Casual trade won't pay Vera's prices when the blokes can get it for next to nothin' from Desmond's. What's more, when a customer pays by credit card, he gets a bill for repairs that ain't been carried out, side by side with the proper repair amount, and the total for fuckin' the girls goes through on his card with no one bein' any the wiser.'

'So the johns claim on their tax or whatever?'

'An' the wives only see car repair bills.'

'How d'you know all this?'

'Vera. She's upset about the girls, an' her own trade.'

'Coppers?'

'Desmond gives someone in South Street nick a kickback.'

He sighed. 'I can't let Ty go there by himself. I'll take a walk down and see what's going on,' he said.

'Not without me, you ain't. Besides, I got a message to pass on to Tyrone from Lol.' His mother took off her frilly apron, slung it over the bench and had slipped her feet into her flat shoes before he'd taken his jacket from the back of a chair. Eddie knew better than to argue with her so he said:

'Them two seems to be getting on okay, don't they?'

His mother smiled at him as an answer.

Minutes later they were out the door, planning on walking down Vectis Road, then past the hospital and along Whitworth Road, where they could cut through the alley and into Moreland Road.

Eddie thought about the brothels in Gosport that Roy Kemp owned. Not as posh as Vera's salon; Roy's places catered to the lower end of the market.

Moreland Road had a number of lock-up car lots and repair shops. The pavements were oil-stained and the buildings shabby. Piles of old tyres and rusting car components spilled out of yards. At one end was a huge breaker's yard, and the smashed-up vehicles were hoisted on top of each other in precarious piles. The whole area stank of rubber and oil.

He spotted the van jacked up and a young bloke screwing on the wheel nuts. Tyrone was sitting on a filthy kitchen chair in the waiting room, which was a wooden shed tacked on to the front of the lock-up. He was chatting to an old bloke and when he saw Eddie his face split into a huge grin.

'Wotcha, mate ... Missus.' He nodded and smiled towards Daisy.

Eddie nodded at him and his eyes met the older bloke's stare. 'You ain't getting him to have any-thin' else done along with the tyres, are you?'

The bloke laughed, showing yellowed stumps of teeth.

'You don't need to tell me who you are, you're

the fuckin' spit of your ol' man. I knew the 'ard bastard well.' He looked at Daisy and said, before spitting a large gob of yellow phlegm at her feet, 'Well, Daisy Lane. You sure I can't introduce your son to our little extras?'

'The other extra we wanted was the spare wheel fixed. You done it?' Daisy replied.

'They 'ave,' said Tyrone. Eddie thought he looked uncomfortable. Then he noticed the pile of mucky girly mags at his feet that Tyrone had probably just been sifting through.

'We got a couple of real nice fringe benefits you can 'ave for a little extra cost,' said the bloke. He came out from behind the table that served as a makeshift desk. The bloke hadn't seen a razor for about a week and his stubble was grey.

Eddie saw the disgust on his mother's face. He willed her not to speak as he answered:

'I 'eard about the attention to detail you give. I reckon I could do with a service.'

He winked at his mother and realised, as she smiled back at him, that she understood perfectly and wouldn't interfere. Tyrone stared at him.

'But we can go. The van's almost fixed, Eddie.'

'You can please yourself, mate, but I like to know I'm getting me money's worth.' He saw the look of revulsion on Tyrone's face.

The bloke laughed. 'Cash or card?'

Just then in came the young bloke who'd been sorting the car and said, 'She's all done. Spare's in the back. I put two new tyres on the front, the back ones are fine.' He handed the keys to Tyrone, who got up from the chair then put his hand in his breast pocket to take out his wallet.

'Not yet, mate, we ain't finished,' said Eddie. 'C'mon, Desmond, where do we go? Only the two of you 'ere?'

Desmond grunted. 'Me other mechanic left at lunchtime.'

'I think I'll take a walk. Don't forget to ask the relevant bleedin' questions,' said Daisy. 'Oh, that reminds me. Lol said to tell you she'll be ready about seven tonight, Tyrone. Will you be long, Eddie?'

'Only as long as it takes, Ma,' said Eddie with a grin.

Eddie followed Desmond through a door that he unlocked and into a room where Eddie had to wait until his eyes adjusted to the gloom.

Desmond waved his hand.

'Take your pick, 'ave 'em both if you like. I'll put it on your bill.'

Eddie saw the girl, who looked as though she was asleep, lying on a stained mattress on the iron bedstead. She was naked. There was a heavy stench of shit and piss in the clammy room.

He went over to her and turned her to face towards him. Her dirty blonde hair was matted, there were bruises on her upper arms and between her thighs. Her pubic hair was non-existent and her breasts small.

'That one ain't exactly a virgin but you can do what you wants.'

'She's a kid,' said Eddie.

'Adele is fourteen, an' when she comes to, you'll find she's a regular little tiger. Tammy, she's different. She'll take it any way you wants.'

Eddie heard a sniffling sound and looked

towards a corner where a young girl crouched. Her body was shaking and her eyes were wild. Her nose was running. Eddie felt sick. How could anyone treat kids like this?

He turned to face Desmond then he said, 'I'll 'ave the both of them, but first I'll 'ave you, you fucker,' and his fist landed fair and square on the older bloke's nose. Eddie heard the bones crack.

'Get the young bastard before he runs,' Eddie shouted. He needn't have asked – Tyrone already had the mechanic with his arm pinned behind his back.

'What the fuck!' The old bloke, recovered, was slinging punches wildly as Eddie ducked. 'Them girls belong to me, I can do what I likes with 'em.' Eddie shook his head at him.

'You're too old, you bastard, to fight me.' He stepped back, avoiding another wide punch from Desmond, and put his hand in his pocket and brought out his knife, flicking it open. As soon as the man saw it he fell to his knees on the wooden floor.

'Don't cut me,' he begged. 'I got money in a tin in the desk, take it. Don't cut me.'

Eddie bent down and gripped Desmond's grubby clothes at his neck, pulling him towards him.

'Listen, you cunt. I'm takin' these girls an' you ain't stoppin' me. The only reason I ain't slashin' you to buggery is because I want you to tell me all you knows about that prostitute's murder.'

The bloke, tears in his red-veined eyes, looked confused.

'I didn't 'ave nothin' to do with that!'

'What about the firing of the club down by the ferry?'

Eddie thought the bloke would shake his head off. Waves of rank sweat floated up from his frantic movements. Those were the questions his mother had wanted asking and he'd drawn a blank. She'd left him and Tyrone, knowing the old man and the boy were no match for the pair of them. He knew where she was now, just as he knew the next steps he would take.

'You fuckin' piece of shit. Tell your mates Eddie Lane took away your little extra earners an' Eddie Lane held a knife to your throat. His father's knife. Anyone else fancies startin' up a little game like this again, you tell 'em not to bother because I'll 'ave the fuckers. Got it?'

The man was shaking with fear. Eddie threw him to the floor. Then he peered intently at him.

'Jesus Christ, I never told you to piss yourself, did I? Now you just crawl out of 'ere an' get off 'ome like a nice man.' He turned towards Tyrone, who had a smile on his face as he watched the old bloke shuffle off on his hands and knees.

'What you want me to do with this one?' He still had hold of the young mechanic.

'Let him go, Ty. Go home, kid. Don't work for scum like that,' Eddie said, and saw the grateful look in his eyes as he slid out the room.

'Go an' turn the place over, Ty. Find the money.'

Tyrone stared at him 'That was real clever, makin' sure the vehicle was fixed first.' Eddie clicked the knife back and slipped it in his pocket. He didn't want Tyrone to see he was shaking.

'You found that money yet?' Tyrone left him to

go into the office. Eddie heard him shout, 'You're goin' to get a reputation like your dad's. What d'you think of that?'

'I don't think fuck all,' Eddie said. 'When you're finished searchin', we'll get these two up to Chestnut House along Forton Road.'

Tyrone came back holding a tin. 'This is it, fair whack in 'ere. Isn't Chestnut House a knockin' shop?'

'Yeah, but it's one of Roy's places. Rosa, the woman who looks after the girls, is a mate of our Vera's so she'll look after these two.'

Tyrone said, 'They're well out of it, drugged to the fuckin' eyeballs, ain't they?'

Eddie bent down to the girl in the corner and put out a hand. She shrank back in fear. Eddie's foot crunched on a needle and he looked down to see foil and vomit everywhere. 'Get one of those blankets.' He managed to pull the girl from the corner and swathe her struggling bony body in the thin cover. He carried her to the cab of the van.

Tyrone said, 'I'll stay with her, you get the other one.'

The second girl was making moaning noises and blinking wildly at the light.

Eddie looked at the girls and his heart was crying.

Roy Kemp owned many brothels and the girls came and went. But they were looked after. Vera's girls were like her second family. Pricey girls, yes, but Vera had trained them well and they were worth every penny.

Eddie drove the van and parked it outside the gate that led up the path of the Georgian property called Chestnut House in Forton Road. So named for the huge chestnut tree that dominated the garden.

'You take one, I'll take the other.'

Eddie managed to open the gate and they carried the girls up the steps of the old house.

Rosa stuck her head out the upstairs front window.

''Bout bloody time,' she called down. Her head was full of curlers. Behind her he could see his mother and she was smiling.

'Bring 'em in,' his mother called. 'I've already given Roy a bell.'

Rosa and his mother were already in the living room when he carried his girl inside. The room was comfortably furnished with chiffon scarves draped over table lamps and there was the smell of incense in the air. He saw Rosa's eyebrows rise as she got a closer look.

'They're very sick,' she said. Red-haired Rosa had been working for Roy a long time and she was proud to be in charge of the girls at Chestnut House. Now he saw she had tears in her eyes.

'They're kids,' she said.

'Will they be all right?' Daisy looked worried.

'I'll do me best,' said Rosa. 'It's what Roy'd want.'

'Do you know anything about 'em?' Daisy asked.

'That old bugger's second wife ran off last Christmas because he knocked her about. This one,' she pointed to the blonde, 'is his step-daughter.' She pointed to the other girl, 'This one is his own fuckin' girl!'

Eddie thought he was going to spew up.

'You mean he's been lettin'... But why?'

'Who knows what goes on in men's 'eads.'

'Why ain't no one, like friends or coppers, done nothin' about this?' Tyrone asked. Eddie looked at him; his mate's face was like stone. Eddie shrugged.

'Who's gonna talk if they're on to a good thing?'

'Word had it in Gosport that his wife had taken the girls away with her,' said Rosa.

Eddie couldn't listen to any more and neither could he look at the wrecks lying on the sofas. He turned to his mother.

'How come you knew I'd bring 'em here?'

Daisy said, 'You're too much like your father to have done anything else, an' I knew those two dimwits wouldn't get the better of you. I don't like you carryin' your dad's knife but I guess this time it served its purpose.'

Eddie left the room before his mother could say any more. He was back shortly with the tin of money in his hand.

'Take this,' he said to Rosa. 'It's their money, they earned it, poor bitches.' It flashed across his mind that perhaps now Vera might find she was taking more money down at Heavenly Bodies. He bloody hoped so.

'I've already phoned for Doctor Dillinger,' said Daisy. 'He'll dose 'em up, sort 'em out, and pull a few strings to get the poor bitches over to St James' on a drug rehabilitation programme.'

When the three of them got back to the van, Tyrone said, 'I didn't think you was goin' to give all that dosh away. We're practically skint...'

'Well, I'm proud of the pair of you,' Daisy said. 'And you, son,' she ruffled Eddie's hair, 'if your dad was 'ere he'd 'ave been proud too.'

Tyrone looked pained. 'We should 'ave kept some of the money.'

'Shut up,' said Eddie. 'We got our van repairs done for free, didn't we?'

# CHAPTER 22

'You got to tell 'er, mate,' said Eddie.

'Timin' ain't right.'

Eddie turned the wheel of the van, passing a police car in Willis Road. He didn't have to worry about getting picked up, not now he'd passed his driving test. He liked it that the sun shone and it was very cold and clear. There was a sharp white frost on the grass in St George's Field.

'Looks like a Christmas card, don't it, Ty?' Eddie felt at peace with the world.

'Ain't you listening to me? There ain't never goin' to be anything really serious between me and Lol.'

Eddie said, 'Tell 'er. Tell 'er it ain't workin' out the way you thought it would. We all goes into relationships with high 'opes an' most relationships don't last. It's her you should be telling this to, not me.'

He could feel Tyrone staring at him. He knew Lol would be gutted when Ty told her how he felt.

He'd be there to pick up the pieces but he could do no more than that. He remembered when Lol first came to live at the house and Ty had felt drawn to her. A bit like the lure of the unknown.

Well, his cousin, Summer, had captivated him when he was a little boy, with her long red hair and the freckles on her upturned nose. He smiled thinking about her. Summer still didn't even know he existed.

His thoughts drew back to the job in hand.

'We've had a fair few house clearances in a short time, ain't we, mate?'

'That advert we put in the *Evening News* certainly did the trick.' Ty bent forward and took an orange Spangle from the packet on the dashboard, then said, 'Yeah, but to get a letter from Wales with the key an' all to clear a place in Mayfield Road...'

'The daughter has a subscription for the paper; she likes to know what's goin' on in her home town. Anyway it's work for us.'

'I can't imagine that the daughter don't want to come an' look over the place before we shifts the stuff...' Ty's voice was muffled as he sucked and crunched.

'Not much point, mate. She said her mum has nothin' she wanted.'

'You got the letter with you?'

'Sure. You think we want to enter a house in Mayfield Road without some kind of say-so? Mayfield Road residents look after their own; we mightn't come out alive!' Eddie laughed. 'Even the coppers walk around in twos down there.'

Tyrone joined in the laughter then asked, 'Ain't the mother gone off to Italy to get married?'

'Daughter ain't best pleased about that, neither, bein' as her mum's a bit long in the tooth.'

'Live an' let live, I say.'

From Dock Road Eddie crossed into Mayfield. He looked at the terrace of houses, searching for the right number. A black cat sat sunning itself on a tumbledown wall.

'Other side, I reckon. Could even be that end one,' said Tyrone, peering out of the van's window.

'Ain't often you're wrong but you're right there,' said Eddie, drawing up outside the small house. He noted that it was freshly painted and the net curtains crisp and white. 'No neighbours, I see.' He pointed at the To Let notice next door. Then he killed the engine and slipped out of the van.

Some kids were playing football and the ball rolled Eddie's way. He gave it a good kick, sending it back to them, and the boys cheered. Tyrone was soon at his side.

'S'funny, ain't it, how every time we step into a strange house it's a bit like goin' into the un-known.'

'For Christ's sake, Tyrone, what's the matter with you today?'

Eddie slipped the key in the lock and turned it, then pushed open the front door. He kicked away the pile of mail and newspapers then looked back at Tyrone who immediately put his hand to his nose.

'Fuckin' hell, don't it stink in 'ere!'

Eddie said, 'Been shut up, ain't it? What d'you expect?' He looked at the pictures hung on the walls and the coat rack with coats standing al-most to attention. On the hall floor sat three pairs of shoes in a neat line. They were sturdy and well polished. He wondered if the old dear had decided to buy all new stuff to go away with.

Eddie opened the kitchen door. Flies buzzed over a sink filled with dirty dishes – two plates, two cups and saucers, several saucepans – and the rancid remains of what he supposed was food was in the pans, covered with mould.

'She was a dirty bitch to walk out and leave the place in this state,' said Tyrone. He scratched his head then put his hand over his nose again. 'Jesus, 'ow can people live like this?'

'We should be thankful we got the bleedin' job.' Eddie had quoted a good price for the clearance. He went over to the window above the sink and opened it, letting some of the flies out.

Tyrone said, 'What I like about this job is it's like bein' paid twice. We charges 'em to 'ave us clear out the stuff, then we sell it.'

'True, but it's a bleedin' shame to have no one care about the stuff you've surrounded yourself with for years. Every object in this house must have had some meaning for the old girl, yet the daughter couldn't give a flying fuck.'

'Let's get out of this stinkin' kitchen and 'ave a look round,' said Tyrone.

In the neat living room with its chintz-covered furniture and well polished wooden sideboard, Eddie opened a cupboard door and peered inside. He found a battered shoebox and took off the lid. Inside were photographs: a little girl in a ballet dress, holiday photos taken at a beach, snapshots of a baby, and a brown envelope containing a will and the woman's birth certificate and passport.

'She probably didn't want them,' said Tyrone, looking over Eddie's shoulder.

'Imagine the old girl looking fondly at them and reliving her memories, then leaving them behind. I can't understand some people,' Eddie said.

'That fuckin' stink seems stronger. You'd think the neighbours would 'ave complained,' moaned Tyrone.

'What neighbours? This is an end house with an empty place next door.'

Eddie wandered back into the kitchen which seemed as though it was in a fifties time warp. There was an old mangle, the kind which screws to the sink, standing in the corner and next to it a washboard.

'Something's worrying me,' he shouted back to Tyrone. 'Her passport. She'd need her passport to go to Italy, wouldn't she...' No comment from Ty, and Eddie opened a kitchen cupboard that revealed pots and pans blackened by years of cooking. Another cupboard exposed rotting food – potatoes, onions, carrots and cabbage in a string bag. Milk, cheese, and a jug of what once might have been cream sat on the top shelf. They smelled revolting.

'Found the stink, Ty,' he called out. 'Want a bit of cheese with a fur coat on?'

But Ty had wandered off, so Eddie continued his search. There was a nice toolbox beneath the sink with some fine old tools in it. They'd fetch a good price at auction, he thought.

He shrugged and tried to turn his mind away from the woman who'd lived here and whose daughter didn't want to know her. This could be a killer of a job if you let it be, he thought.

'Ty!' he shouted, at the top of his voice. 'You want to start loading the furniture?'

Tyrone grunted a reply from out in the garden.

'I'm gettin' a breath of fresh air. Don't know 'ow you can stick that disgustin' smell.'

Eddie climbed the stairs to see what was in the bedrooms. From the layout of the house he knew there would be two of them. In the back bedroom, he examined a carved wooden box lying on a single unmade bed. The box was empty. Likely the woman had emptied it of her jewellery before she left. Also on the bed was a Post Office Savings book. There'd been over a thousand pounds in it but it had been withdrawn in three payments. He put the book back on the bed and opened the wardrobe. It was full of everyday outfits, and lovely twenties and thirties dresses and capes of velvet and satin. His mum might like those to sell on.

The smell was stronger now.

He wandered back to the hallway at the top of the stairs and paused outside the second bedroom door. A curious humming sound was coming from inside. He pushed open the door and a cloud of flies flew angrily past him.

'Jesus,' he cried, batting them away then putting his hand over his nose and mouth. A stench like he'd never smelled before had hit him.

Sitting on a chair was a woman, or the remains of a woman, in a nightdress. Blood had been splashed on to the wall and on to a bedside lamp. The woman's eyes were expressionless. Dried blood like spilled paint covered the carpet, the chair and the front of her. It looked like it had pooled in her lap. She was wearing slippers with bobbles on and her legs were thin. Eddie realised how defenceless the poor woman had been. Her neck had been cleanly slit and a stick propped open her mouth. Her face and body rippled with maggots and insects.

Eddie backed out of the room, fighting a wave of nausea, and closed the door behind him. He practically fell down the stairs.

'I feel better now,' Tyrone said walking aimlessly towards him. He'd left the front door open. 'Hey! Mind out, mate, you'll 'ave me over,' he shouted as Eddie cannoned into him then turned his face away, bent over, and vomited on the hall floor.

'What's up, mate?' Tyrone's voice was full of concern.

Eddie wiped his mouth with the back of his hand and drew himself up straight. Using his friend as a support, he fumbled inside his wallet. 'Go and phone this number.' He passed Tyrone a slip of paper. 'Say you're with me. Tell him he must come.'

Tyone stared at him then at the scrap of paper. 'What d'you want Vinnie Endersby for?'

'There's a dead woman upstairs.'

Tyrone stared at him, his mouth open. After a few moments Eddie could see his words had sunk in.

'That's where the stink's coming from, ain't it?'

Eddie nodded.

'Where will you be?'

'Sitting on the front step with the door closed,' replied Eddie. 'Ty,' he said quietly. 'Fuckin' 'urry

212

up, mate.'

Eddie went out into the street, pulling the front door shut behind him. He watched the van roar into life after a couple of false starts as Tyrone went in search of a phonebox. The exhaust fumes enveloped him as he sat down on the cold step. Then he turned his head to one side and spewed again.

'You stumbled on a pretty scene here,' said Vinnie Endersby. The van's door was open and he'd a hand on Eddie's shoulder and one black shoe on the rubber mat in the front. He was leaning into the vehicle. Eddie caught the smell of his cologne and breathed it in. It was a hell of a lot better than the stench of rotting flesh.

'I hope I don't need to go back in there,' Eddie said, nodding towards the house. Tyrone was by his side and he'd hardly uttered a word since Vinnie had got there.

A crowd of onlookers had already gathered and were chattering and asking questions. A copper was putting up tape to keep them away from the crime scene.

'I need to ask you some questions.'

Eddie fumbled in his pocket and drew out the front door key of the house and the letter he'd received from the daughter of the dead woman.

'You might need these to show I was 'ere legally,' he said, and watched as Vinnie scanned them.

'Fine,' Vinnie said. Eddie thought how clean-cut the detective looked. This was the man who was his brother Jamie's father, the man who'd been in his life for as long as he could remember.

213

This man had taught him all he knew about MGs. He might be a copper but he was a kind man, a just man.

The local coppers, once they realised he was Eddie Lane's son, would definitely give him and Tyrone a rough ride. They'd probably try and tie him to the woman's death. He needed to have someone on his side and who better than the DCI?

'I'll 'ave me bleedin' fingerprints all over the place,' grumbled Eddie.

'So? You had a right to be there, this letter proves that.' He got another pat on the shoulder from Vinnie.

Eddie stared at Tyrone who looked pissed off. 'You all right?'

Tyrone looked up and shrugged. 'My prints'll be in there as well.'

'Stop worrying,' said Vinnie. He took off his hat and laid it on the seat beside Eddie then ran his fingers through his curly dark hair. 'You two are in the clear. You might have to go down Gosport nick to answer a few more questions ... maybe make a statement...'

'Not more bleedin' questions...' wailed Tyrone.

'It's just a formality,' explained Vinnie. 'As will be the fingerprinting.'

'This is the same bloke as killed Samantha, ain't it?' Eddie's voice shook.

'I can't say for sure,' Vinnie said.

'If he cut her throat why did he prop open her mouth?'

'If it is the same bloke he's telling us he did it,' explained Vinnie.

214

'That poor woman was planning on a new life and he snuffs her out of this one. I bet she gave him her jewellery and savings,' Eddie said.

Vinnie shrugged. 'Be careful how you tell this to Vera, you know how sensitive she is about Samantha's death.'

'Does that mean we can go?'

Vinnie nodded and stepped away from the van. Then he asked, 'You had any comeback from that Desmond bloke for takin' away his girls?'

'How d'you know about that?' Eddie grinned at him. 'Can't keep no bleedin' secrets in Gosport. No, an' I don't expect to.'

'That was a brave thing you did, rescuing them. I hear they're doin' fine over at St James' in that rehabilitation programme.' Vinnie put his trilby back on.

Eddie looked at Tyrone who suddenly grinned at him. Then he asked Vinnie, 'You coming up to London for the opening of Roy's new club?'

A shadow passed over Vinnie's face.

'Not this time, I'm having Jamie that weekend.' Eddie's heart lightened. No bleedin' Jamie!

'What's Roy having built on the part of the land near the ferry where the club was?' asked Vinnie.

'Ain't got the foggiest,' said Eddie. Vinnie shut the van door and slapped it, signalling them to leave. Eddie turned the ignition key. He grinned at Vinnie. 'Maybe he'll tell us at the opening of his London place.'

'I'm goin' up to London,' said Tyrone. Eddie thought he looked pleased with himself.

'Better get yourself a suit then,' shouted Vinnie with a wave. 'Suited and booted that lot'll be.'

215

# CHAPTER 23

'I mean, I don't even know where I'm gonna bleedin' sleep, do I?'

'If you didn't come to London you'd be moanin' about being left out, and now you're moanin' about where you're goin' to sleep! When you was on the game I don't suppose you gave a flying fuck where or whose bed you was goin' to end up in. I just think you likes moanin'!' Daisy went on looking out of the window at the sprawl of used-car yards and greasy-spoon caffs. The inside of the Mercedes car was filled with the scent of Vera's Californian Poppy.

Vera looked at her and went, 'Hrmmph!'

'I think you're as flattered as buggery to 'ave been invited to the opening of Roy's new club.' Daisy stared at Vera's eyelashes just in case one needed to be restuck, and breathed a sigh of relief that both were properly in place.

'I am. I just 'ope Suze is feedin' my boy properly, an' that she cleans up any little mistakes he makes. My Kibbles ain't been well lately.'

No, he ain't, thought Daisy, but that's because the poor ol' bugger is coming to the end of his run. But no way was she going to say that to Vera and start her off moaning again.

As the car that had been sent to collect them from Gosport drew up to the small terraced house, Daisy smiled inwardly.

Freshly washed white nets, a gleaming brass knocker, and a shiny green-painted front door showed Violet's fastidiousness. Before the driver had lifted the overnight bags from the boot and put them on the pavement, the door opened and Violet flung herself into Daisy's arms.

'It's so lovely to see you again,' she crowed, pulling them inside the terraced house.

It must have been about eighteen years ago when I first came to this house, thought Daisy. Roy's wife Moira lived here then.

Daisy and Moira had been firm friends but now Moira was living in a nursing home in Spain. About six months ago, when Daisy had flown out to see her, it had broken her heart to find Moira no longer knew who she was.

'Come into the kitchen,' said Violet. Daisy could smell the violet perfume she always wore following her as she walked ahead of them.

The house had changed little, thought Daisy. Gaily coloured cotton curtains up at the spotless windows and the same photograph of Ronnie and Reggie Kray, the two Violets and Roy on the window ledge above the sink. As always, the room smelled of fresh baking.

'I'll put the kettle on,' said Violet. She hardly seemed to have aged at all, perhaps a little slower in her movements. 'Pity young Susie's little one's got measles, though,' she said. 'Anyway, you can tell me later on all about your Eddie finding that body. I'm sure it gave him quite a shock.'

'Put the fear of God in 'im more likely,' said Vera. 'As to Suze, I reckon she got a feller. D'you mind if I takes me shoes off, Violet?'

Violet shook her head. 'Treat the place like it's your own,' she said, rattling cups and saucers.

Vera began rubbing her nyloned feet. Daisy glared at her.

'You two can go upstairs and settle in if you want. I'll call when the tea's ready.' On impulse Daisy put her arms around the small woman with the bubble cut of blue-rinsed hair and wearing a wraparound pinny.

'It really is lovely to see you, Violet,' she said. Violet's smile was as wide as her face.

'You know what time the others are getting 'ere?' Vera asked.

'They wanted to travel by train,' said Violet, 'so I told 'em to please themselves. As your Jamie's spending a few days with his father I don't have to worry about him.' Was it, Daisy wondered, her imagination, or did a wave of relief cross Violet's face?

'You sure you got enough room 'ere, Vi?'

'Course, Vera. I figured Daisy can either sleep with you or Roy. I've put you in what I always think of as Daisy's room. The boys can have sleeping bags down here. Lol I've made as comfortable as I can in the meeting room. I got one of them chairs that turns into a bed. I got some of those foam rubber mattresses so everyone should be quite comfortable. That leaves me and Charles in our own room at the front.'

Daisy knew that long ago Violet had given up sleeping upstairs due to the arthritis in her knees. Violet had been a widow for many years until she'd married Charles, who'd been Roy's father's friend. He'd loved her for years. Daisy could see being married had put an extra twinkle in Violet's eyes. Her blue-rinsed curls bobbed as she started preparing food. Daisy knew they certainly wouldn't starve while they were with Roy's mum.

Daisy said, 'C'mon, Vera, let's go an wash our 'ands.'

They picked up their cases and went upstairs.

'I might 'ave a shower before I get ready,' Daisy said. She recalled that it was in this very house she'd luxuriated in the first shower she'd ever had in her life.

'Where did you say 'is new club is?'

'Soho. It's called Les Girls.'

'So it's another brothel then?'

'Vera!'

'Well, a brothel where you can do a bit of dancin' and play cards.'

'Probably,' said Daisy. 'You're in there.' She pointed towards the room she used to sleep in. Vera disappeared inside and Daisy pushed open the door to Roy's room. It smelled of Roy's citrus cologne. There was a James Bond paperback on his bedside table.

Across the hall was the meeting room where once upon a time Roy's mum and she had carried up trays of tea and food to the Kray twins, the Richardsons, and even Teddy Baird. Such a lot of water under the bridge now, she thought.

Daisy put her hand to her mouth and only just made it to the bathroom before she was sick. When she'd finished and was wiping her mouth and pressing down the lever to flush the toilet she felt Vera's presence behind her.

She smiled at Vera. 'I think it was the travelling. Bit of car sickness.'

Vera gave a long drawn out sigh, came into the bathroom, turned and shut the door, put the lid of the toilet down and sat on it.

'How much longer are you goin' to deny to yourself that you're 'avin' a bleedin' baby?'

Daisy heard her words but couldn't for a while comprehend their meaning. Then her forehead creased and she allowed her mouth to set itself in a thin line before she said, 'Don't be so fuckin' daft!'

'Daisy, I can see it in your eyes.'

'Don't be so stupid!'

Vera shook her head. 'There's only you an' me in this bathroom an' no one else will know if you don't want to tell 'em yet. You been throwin' up, faintin' and feelin' like somethin' my Kibbles 'as brought in, right?'

Daisy still couldn't get her head around Vera's words but she said, 'Yes.'

'Well then?'

Realisation hit her. Then a huge wave of happiness swamped her and she threw her arms around Vera.

'Roy'll be over the moon,' she gabbled. 'I thought me periods 'ad stopped because I ain't been eating properly an' I've been rushing around like a bleedin' blue-arsed fly. Vera, I never realised...' Daisy touched her breasts. 'Yes, they're tender. Oh, Vera, how wonderful, I thought I might be goin' through an early change as well...'

'Slow down, girly.' Vera got up, grabbed hold of her and forced Daisy to look into her eyes. 'It ain't only Roy you slept with, remember?'

Daisy felt all the air leave her body. She gripped

hold of the side of the bath to stop herself falling and said, 'Roy so wants a child of his own.'

'Tell 'im he's gonna be a dad then. You wouldn't be the first woman to be unsure of her baby's father. It might be Roy's, Daisy. But you got to face facts. If it's born with a paintbrush in its 'and then it's Alec's.'

'You girls ready for a cuppa?'

The disembodied voice came up the stairs.

'Don't say anything,' begged Daisy. 'Give me a chance to get used to the idea.'

'Silly bitch! As if I'd give away your secrets.'

Daisy squeezed Vera's hand, then she looked at her reflection in the bathroom cabinet. She looked just the same. Could there really be a tiny baby growing inside her? A son? Or a daughter … she'd like a little girl.

'You got to pretend everything is normal. You got to witter on like you usually do. Come on, let's go downstairs before Violet comes up to find us.'

'I'll try,' said Daisy. 'Oh, Vera, I'm so happy.'

Vera frowned at her. 'I'm glad, now shut up,' she said. 'Remember, witter!'

'I bet she's made scones,' said Daisy.

'I bloody 'ope so. I'm starvin',' said Vera. Then, 'Who's goin' to be there tonight?'

'Dunno,' said Daisy. 'We'll see when we get there.'

Downstairs Violet was putting dollops of cream on top of home-made jam in the scones. The teas were already poured out in her best cups and saucers, laid out on the scrubbed wooden table. Daisy went up and gave the small round woman another big squeeze. She'll make a lovely granny, she thought.

Daisy wondered whether Violet's wraparound pinny was the same one she'd first seen her in all those years ago. Either that, or she had a drawer full of the aprons.

'Roy won't be long, he's with my Charles,' Violet said, disentangling herself and giving Daisy a beaming smile. 'Your Bri and his wife Jackie an' their young Summer is coming, but they didn't want to stay the night. Roy's arranged for a car to take them home.' Daisy nodded, her mouth full of crumbly fragrant scone.

Bri was Eddie Lane's brother and young Eddie's uncle.

Violet said, 'That Summer's grown into a pretty little thing, hasn't she?'

'Yes,' Vera said, 'but she knows what she wants out of life.'

A key turned in the front door and Roy swept in like a raging forest fire, leaving Charles to follow and close the door. He kissed Daisy, kissed his mum, grabbed a scone.

'Don't I get a kiss?' said Vera.

'Bugger off,' he said, with his mouth full.

# CHAPTER 24

'What d'you reckon, Dais?'

'Roy's new club's everything I thought it would be, Vera.' She squeezed Vera's hand lying on the starched white tablecloth. 'It reminds me of

Daisychains, all red and gold, and the piped music playing.' She looked about her and took in the chandeliers, the polished dark wood and the bar with blokes lined up like skittles, ready to buy drinks. Long-legged, pretty girls dressed in figure-hugging clothes were everywhere. Eddie, Lol and Tyrone were dancing and most of her family members were in a clique chatting to Violet Kray.

'I recognise plenty of high-profile coppers,' Daisy said, catching a whiff of Vera's comforting perfume. She smoothed the skirt of her black wool dress and flicked off an imaginary piece of fluff. Beside the competition she felt under-dressed. Not Vera, though; for once her friend was dressed in black as well, with a tight skirt with a slit at the side and a frilly blouse that had the top button undone showing the swell of her breasts.

'You don't need lots of jewellery,' said Vera. 'Your gold bangle and that fuckin' great diamond brooch sets you well apart from the bleedin' scrubbers 'ere.'

'I'll take that as a soddin' compliment, shall I?'

'And who is giving out compliments?'

'Never 'eard *you* creep up.' Vera grinned at Roy, who bent and nuzzled into Daisy's ear. 'Did you find the meal to your liking, ladies?'

Daisy put her hand over her stomach remembering the huge succulent steak she'd eaten. 'Delicious,' she said. Roy was facing her now, squatting on one knee and looking into her eyes. She could smell the freshness of the shower he'd taken before leaving the house.

She thought then that he'd make a lovely father for her child. But could she tell him it was his baby when she wasn't sure? When it might be Alec's? Trouble was, she couldn't lie. She couldn't tell Roy she was having *his* child because her conscience wouldn't let her. But she'd make an appointment at the hospital and get a due date. Her mind wandered, thinking about the child and how pleased she was.

'I wish you'd move in with me,' Roy was saying. Daisy put her hands on his shoulders, feeling their strength beneath his jacket. He pushed back his hair and once again she was reminded of his dark, gypsy looks, his likeness to David Essex the singer.

'We've been over this so many times, Roy. I don't want to leave Gosport and you need to live up 'ere in The Smoke...'

And as she listened to her own words, she realised what she was saying. Did it really matter *who* the baby's father was? She wasn't going to leave her home. The child was *her* child. Daisy suddenly leaned forward, cupped Roy's face in her hands and kissed him for a long, long time.

She broke away when Teddy Baird's loud laugh interrupted the kiss. He was holding court at the bar, and there seemed to be more noise coming from his party than from the rest of the people in the club. A man sitting in the corner was watching Teddy Baird from beneath dark brows.

'Who's that man?' Vera asked.

'Maurie Nelson,' said Roy, straightening up.

Daisy frowned and said, 'I thought you couldn't stand the bloke.'

'I can't, but I'm tryin' to keep on the right side of the fucker. Being a villain *and* an informant to the Flying Squad makes him a nasty bloke to cross. You know what they say, keep your friends close and your enemies closer.'

'I see,' said Daisy.

'Eddie told me about the woman he'd found–'

'Shook him up,' interjected Vera. 'Shook poor Tyrone up more.' Vera took a sip of her gin and tonic and pulled a face. 'Don't know why I drinks gin, it's got such an 'orrible taste.'

Baird, oblivious to Daisy and Roy watching him, bent down and took out the huge blade from one of his cowboy boots. It was obviously one of his party tricks to show people the knife.

'Is there goin' to be trouble, Roy?'

Daisy was surprised to hear fear in Vera's voice.

'No, I don't think so. Nelson's happy, he's got another scam going. He receives lorry loads of stolen goods, keeps 'em hidden, then the owners claim the insurance. The goods must be missing for more than twenty-four hours.'

'How come Nelson is happy about that?'

'Because, Vera my sweet, he sells the goods and shares the claim with the lorry drivers.'

Daisy gave a huge sigh. The more she heard about Maurie Nelson the more she decided she didn't like him. Whether he had anything to do with Samantha's death she had no way of know-ing, nor, it seemed, did Roy. She shivered, think-ing someone in this very room might have killed the generous, soft-hearted girl. Her thoughts slid to Daisychains and the fire. Don't get maudlin, she told herself.

As though Roy had read her mind he said, 'Nelson loves setting fires. The burning of my places, yes, he's got a hand in that, I'm sure of it.

225

He wants my territory and all that goes with it. But wanting,' he smiled, 'is one thing. Getting what he wants is another.' Then he passed Daisy her brandy and lime.

'This is a great party,' slurred Tyrone.

'For fuck's sake don't drink any more,' said Eddie. 'I thought you were gonna talk to Lol?'

It didn't seem right for Tyrone to be treating Lol as though she had the fuckin' plague or something, he thought. Ty hadn't danced with her, had hardly spoken to her all evening, and the pain on her face was there for everyone to see. And what was Ty doing? Getting falling down drunk to cop the easy way out.

'Look, it ain't really any of my business, but you'd feel better if you got it off your chest and told her it's all over between you two. She doesn't deserve to be hurt any more than necessary.'

'Couldn't you tell 'er? You bein' my mate, like?'

'For fuck's sake,' said Eddie.

'I s'pose that's a no?' Tyrone seemed to pull himself up. He put his glass down on the bar and took a deep breath.

'As long as we're telling truths then I got somethin' to say to you. I don't want to do the 'ouse clearances no more.'

Eddie stared at him. For a moment he was lost for words, then he realised it wasn't such a shock. Since they'd found the body, Tyrone had been apprehensive about entering premises, even houses where the owners or relatives had been there to greet them.

'Don't look at me like that!' Tyrone picked up

226

his glass and knocked back the alcohol. 'Fuck, I needed that,' he said, then, 'I'm sorry, man.'

'We won't be finding bodies in all the houses,' Eddie said. He knew as soon as the words left his mouth he wouldn't be able to change Tyrone's mind. And it took a lot of guts for Ty to tell him because Ty was leaving him in the shit. Eddie couldn't move furniture on his own and he wasn't sure he wanted the bother of looking for another partner. Him and Ty were good together, but he understood how his friend felt.

'Fair enough, mate,' he said quietly. 'No hard feelings. Only now you got that off your chest, go over and talk to Lol.'

Eddie stood at the bar, feeling empty inside.

He saw Tyrone push through the dancers, touch Lol on the arm and take her to a deserted table and sit down. Eddie turned away.

He was near enough to his family to hear Violet Kray saying how much she liked watching *Softly, Softly* on the television. Another roar of laughter from Baird at the end of the bar and Eddie saw he'd got his cock out for everyone to admire. Eddie's eyes searched the dancers on the crowded floor until they settled on Summer.

He didn't have the guts to go up to her because there was every chance she'd tell him to piss off. She was like that. As fiery as her hair. And yet he wanted her with every fibre of his being. She was wearing a long green dress, gypsy sandals, and a green scarf that floated from her hair and danced along with her own sinuous movements. She must have guessed he was staring at her for she suddenly turned and looked at him; their eyes locked until she gave a half smile and turned away again.

'Little cow,' he mumbled to himself. He knew from the stares he was getting from women in the club that he could have them if he wanted. The heavy furniture he'd lifted had given him muscle, had thickened his body where it needed it. He was athletically fit. Vera kept on saying how much he looked like his father and from the few photographs he'd seen of him, Eddie didn't mind a bit.

Maurie Nelson over in the corner was attempting to get out of his seat but when he stood, he stumbled and fell. Eddie was there like a shot.

'Whoops, up you get, mate.' But he needn't have bothered, for several of Nelson's minders quickly surrounded him, then about a dozen of Roy's men turned up. Eddie decided it was best he ignored Nelson's foul-mouthed references to Teddy Baird. He realised there were just as many gangsters' henchmen in the club as there were punters.

Eddie helped pick up the broken glass then went to the bar and got another large whisky for Nelson. He took it over to the table and said, 'Here you are, mate, compliments of the house.'

Nelson looked at him strangely then squeezed out the word 'Thanks.'

Eddie glanced towards Roy and the big man nodded as though to tell him he was doing the right thing.

'Want to dance, Daisy?' asked Roy.

'Yeah,' she said. 'At last some nice slow music.' The group had been playing popular music and rock. 'Where did the lovely piped music go?' she wondered, and got to her feet. She slipped into Roy's arms, but suddenly she felt faint, light-headed; her mind went blank and her legs turned to water.

'Whoops! I think you got up a little too quickly. Want to sit down again?' Roy's arms held her protectively.

Daisy shook her head. After a second or two her mind and body were beginning to feel they belonged to her again. She was fighting to control her emotions and was embarrassed at the way her body was betraying her.

Her nipples had hardened immediately Roy's hand had touched the small of her back and drawn her closer to him.

Over his shoulder she could see women eyeing him, brazenly wishing they were in her place. She wondered how many women he'd slept with when he wasn't with her. Once upon a time that would have made her feel threatened but now, strangely, it didn't. She was the one who held his heart in the palm of her hand.

Daisy kissed his cheek then buried her face in the warmth between his wide jaw and broad shoulder. She loved the shape of his face and the way his mouth slipped into a ready smile. She loved his slate-grey eyes that could be so warm, and the next moment like steel if he grew angry.

She clasped him tightly to her as their bodies danced in tune with each other and the music.

'I love you,' he whispered into her hair.

Hardly had the words left his mouth when she heard a scream. Lol!

Roy bounded away from her and Daisy's eyes

followed him. On the far side of the room she saw Eddie taking a swing at a large bald-headed man with a paunch. Through a sea of legs she could see Lol on the floor. She pushed through the crush of bodies to get to her, but she wasn't quick enough to stop the violent kick Lol received from the bloke before Eddie hit him.

Roy separated Eddie from the man, and Daisy saw Lol was curled like a foetus on the wooden floor.

Daisy yelled, 'Jesus Christ, look at the fuckin' blood!' The man's nose was streaming. Tyrone was holding back a well-built tattooed bloke who was trying to get at Eddie.

'What the fuck's going on 'ere?'

Already half a dozen huge men were at Roy's side. Teddy Baird was there ready to do battle.

Daisy fell to the floor and cradled Lol in her arms. There was already a bruise appearing on the side of her face and the top of her wispy dress was torn.

'Never thought that fuckin' tart would 'ave the nerve to show 'er face back in London,' said the bloke, trying to straighten his tie and stem the flow of blood at the same time.

Eddie edged away from the man and bent down to Lol, helping her to her feet.

She was shaking and very scared. 'Do you know who he is?' Eddie asked gently.

'He's that bloke... That bloke...'

'Who kept you a prisoner?'

Lol nodded. She began to cry and Daisy enfolded her in her arms.

The man started to justify his actions. 'She was

one of mine 'til she fucked off durin' a raid...'

'Don't mean you can spoil my party,' said Roy. His face was inches from the man's. Daisy's heart was beating fast.

'She owes me money...'

'She owes you fuck all,' said Roy quietly. 'Now do you want another drink? There's gear out the back if you fancy it. You don't ever want to become an enemy of mine, do you, mate?'

'You don't have to be scared any longer.' Daisy was trying to reassure Lol.

Tyrone had the beginnings of a black eye.

'Go and sort yourselves out,' said Roy, then he turned to the bloke. 'Let's say you and me go into the office and have a little chat.'

'I don't think I should stay here any longer,' Lol said. 'I'm getting to be more of a liability than an asset.'

'You're going nowhere unless it's home with me,' Daisy declared.

Vera had joined them and she said, 'Let's get back to Violet's, I've 'ad enough excitement for one day and, besides, Lol's got bruises that need looking at.'

Later there was complete silence in the car until Lol said, 'I want to work in Heavenly Bodies, Vera. How about it?'

'Ain't you overreactin'?' Vera said.

'No. I'd have volunteered before but I thought that Big Mick would find me. But now that he has and he can't touch me again, I can be my own person. Besides, me an' Tyrone ain't going anywhere. I can see that now.'

'But you don't want to go back to bein' made

231

to fuck, surely?' Daisy couldn't understand why Lol was asking Vera for a job.

'But that's just it,' said Lol. 'I won't be being made to do anything I don't want to. I'll be doing it because I choose to.'

'I'll think about it,' said Vera. 'It's possible you might just put my place back on the map.'

Daisy was in bed when Roy opened the door. 'Are you asleep?' he whispered.

'Yes,' she said.

'That's a shame, because I want to fuck you,' he said.

Daisy was filled with desire and anticipation. She'd been waiting for him.

He bent over her and kissed her. 'Don't move,' he said. 'You're beautiful, do you know that?' His voice was tender yet strong. Daisy's body wanted the warmth of his. He wrapped his arms around her and kissed her face, her mouth, her nose.

And suddenly she was crying. Suddenly, she had to tell him.

'I'm pregnant,' she said.

He pulled back and sat looking at her; it seemed as though he stared into her eyes forever.

Then he kissed her shoulders, her throat and her breasts.

'My darling girl,' he said. 'Is there anything you want?'

'Yes. To find out who killed Samantha.'

# CHAPTER 25

Fuck me – I feel just like Scarlett O'Hara did when she woke up after Rhett Butler carried her upstairs and had his wicked way with her, thought Daisy. She stretched luxuriously, then leaned on one elbow and traced a finger down Roy's nose to his lips. He stopped gently snoring, opened his eyes and took a playful bite at her finger, but missed.

'Morning,' he said. 'Any regrets about last night?'

'What d'you think?' Daisy grinned. 'Anyway, what 'appened?'

'That memorable, eh?' He laughed and pulled her down to him. He smelled of warm sexy man. 'It'll never be over for us, Daisy, never. And you don't know how happy I am.'

He pushed her away and studied her for a long time, until she grew uncomfortable beneath his gaze.

'You've lost weight, and you look tired, girl.'

'I can't expect much else, can I? It's bleedin' 'ard work getting up early and attending sales all over the place, looking for bargains *and* arranging to sell what I've managed to find – *if* I've managed to find anything.' She sighed. 'Some blokes have been doing this lark for years an' I'm only a beginner, so I got to put in the extra bleedin' effort...'

He stopped her flow of words with a kiss then,

as they pulled apart, he said, his breath warm on her cheek, 'Well, now you don't have to work. I can give you more money than you'll ever make grubbing in the dirt... Think of the baby, Dais...'

'But I don't want that, Roy.' She untangled herself from his arms and got out of bed.

'I love you, Daisy Lane,' he said. 'I want the two of us to be together—'

She turned from the window where the curtains had been left undrawn and cut him off. 'Stop it! I can't get on that ol' merry-go-round again. It messes my bleedin' 'ead up too much. Anyway, we're all right as we are, aren't we?'

'Are we, Dais?' She saw he was watching her carefully.

'Sure.' Daisy pulled his silk robe from the back of the door and slipped it around her. She made her way to the bathroom, thinking about his words. No, she didn't want to live with him. She didn't want to live with any man. The only man she'd ever really wanted to be with had been Eddie's father and he was dead and gone. Force of habit made her glance at the gold bangle he'd given her. In her mind's eye she could see the handsome bastard grinning at her on that Southampton street, holding the box containing the present of the bangle. Jesus, but she'd loved Eddie Lane. Always would, she guessed.

But now she was her own person, earning her own living, even though her fortunes fluctuated. Though she loved Roy Kemp, it was a different kind of love. She'd grown up, she guessed. And Roy? So what if when she wasn't around he dallied with some little slapper? What did it really matter

234

to her, or to the past they shared between them?

On the way back from the bathroom she pondered whether to go downstairs to make tea but decided against it. The whole household was still asleep. Why should she disturb them? No, she was better off in bed with her lovely man, wasn't she?

Daisy could see Roy watching her as she let his dressing gown slip to the floor.

'Move over,' she said. 'I'm cold.'

'So you are.' He pulled her into him. She could hear the beating of his heart.

'I been thinking, Dais,' he said.

'Could do you an injury that,' she said.

He ignored her. 'About Eddie.'

'And?'

'I want to give him a proper birthday present. I want to do something for him, make him independent.'

'You don't reckon he's doing all right on 'is own?'

'Sure he is, but I want to give him something permanent.'

'Like what? I don't want him gettin' into bad habits!'

'Not everything I own revolves around drugs.'

She sniffed. 'Well, it does seem to.' She knew he had negotiated for a large shipment of cocaine to come into Langstone Harbour. She also knew he was worried sick because if Nelson got to hear of it, Roy could lose the consignment. Lose his freedom too. Nelson could end up with the drugs – *and* a pat on the head for helping them nail Roy Kemp.

'I want to give him a business.'

'He's got a business.'

Roy shook his head. 'Tyrone don't want to help him no more. Finding that body has left him in a bit of a state.'

Daisy shook her head. This was the first she'd heard of it.

'A pool hall.'

'A pool hall?' Daisy's brain clicked into gear once again.

'Yes, by the ferry at Gosport. I'm in the process of rebuilding two businesses on the site of Daisychains, and I'm opening another club.' He stared hard at her. 'One that'll be run my way, so it'll make money.' Daisy knew it would be a place where punters would be able to get anything they wanted. 'And though it won't be so big or stylish as Daisychains it'll draw the punters,' he said. 'The pool hall will be a separate enterprise; what do you think?'

'I don't want him dealing in drugs.'

'Why should he when punters can get anything they want next door?'

'Are you asking me if Eddie'll accept?'

Roy frowned.

Daisy said, 'He'd be a fool not to take you up on your offer. Why're you doin' it though?'

'I think his father, if he was still alive, might be pleased I was looking after his son, don't you?'

'If he's looking down on us, he might be thinking it's only right, bein' as how you offed him!'

Roy sighed. 'I care about the boy as if he was my own.'

Daisy leaned into him. 'I know you do. And what about Jamie? You care about 'im?'

236

'Your youngest is a law unto 'imself. He's got his own father, Dais.'

'Jamie don't really want 'im though. An' he's jealous of Jack, Vinnie's older boy, who's the apple of his eye.'

'Shhh! Daisy.' He put his fingers across her mouth. 'What I'm tryin' to say is I'll look after both your boys, keep 'em safe. I can't say fairer than that, can I? Eddie though, he's proved he can run a business. Even though he ain't got the years on 'im, he's already gaining the experience.'

Daisy looked into his slate-grey eyes. She was melting inside. 'It goes without saying this new baby,' he ran his hand over her stomach, 'will want for nothin' either.'

'Thanks,' she said. 'Underneath that bloody gangster tag, you really are a very sweet and fair bloke. But I want you to know this baby is *mine*.'

'I always wanted a child with you, Daisy.' It was as though he hadn't listened to a word she'd said. 'You don't know how proud I am...'

Would it really be so bad if she let him believe he'd fathered her baby? After all, he might very well be the father, and what was the alternative? A child whose probable daddy had committed suicide? Imagine the stigma the poor little mite would have to live down. But wasn't she worrying about something that only *might* be? Why shouldn't she give Roy the happiness he so deserved? Hadn't he already proved he was a good father figure to Eddie?

'You'll be a father who doesn't live with us. Can you get your head around that? I will always need to be my own person without the interference of

237

a man.'

'Daisy, you don't have to tell me anything I wasn't already fully conscious of. It won't stop me loving you.'

'I'm fed up with this conversation now,' she said.

Roy laughed, that deep throaty chuckle that she so loved. A thought crossed her mind. 'What you calling these two new places?'

'Eddie's,' he said. 'And perhaps Daisy's for the club?'

'You're bloody daft, you are,' she said. 'Come 'ere, I got a present for you.'

'What's that?'

'Me,' Daisy said.

## CHAPTER 26

'Tyrone doesn't want me any more.'

Eddie didn't answer Lol.

She shrugged. 'It had to come sooner or later. I knew Ty didn't like us being stared at when we were out together.'

Eddie saw the glitter of tears in her violet eyes.

'It's him you should be talking to, not me.'

'That's just it, I couldn't talk to him. Nor him to me, not at the end. Apart from last night when he came over to the table to say...' Her face crumpled in on itself. She ran her fingers through her long hair and then wiped her eyes with the back of her hand. 'Men think they can handle the pressure of being with me but they can't. I thought Ty might be different... I think you could be different. Have you ever thought me an' you might have got it together?'

He took a while to answer then said, 'Not really. I've only got one girl in my life...'

'She doesn't want you. At least, not until you have enough money to keep her in frills and furs.'

Eddie could see Lol in his bedroom mirror. She was standing in the doorway watching him comb his hair. He put his comb back in his top pocket.

'I suppose you mean Summer?' The bruises on Lol's face had changed from mauve to green and the swelling had gone down.

'Who else?'

He turned towards her. 'You don't know what you're talking about.'

'I'm right and you know it. All those fine suits you've taken to wearing and all that smelly stuff you stick on ain't going to cut any ice with that bitch.'

He sighed. He didn't want to argue with her. He wished she'd walk away, go downstairs, leave him alone. She was feeling mixed up about Tyrone and wanted to take her temper out on someone.

'I'm not stupid. You wanted me even when I was out there on the Ferry Garden, even after I'd been fucked. I saw it in your eyes.'

He couldn't deny it. But that had been then, this was *now*. And though he wasn't going to be a monk because Summer was too young, he didn't want Lol. For a few fleeting moments he *had* fancied her, but that was before he'd known she'd started life as a male. All he could say was, 'I'm sorry.'

'Trouble is, if I was a proper girl we'd 'ave got it on just like that.' Lol's eyes filled with tears. 'I am a proper girl. I AM!'

Eddie went and put his arms around her. Her bones were fragile as a bird's. 'You're angry because of Tyrone. And it didn't help when Big Mick hit you last night.'

Lol put her fingers over his mouth.

'Don't say any more,' she said. 'I'll say it for you. I'm a transvestite, without the proper gear to give either of you what you want, but working for Vera will give *me* what I want.' She laughed. 'And one day I'll meet my big tall man to love me.'

He held her close again. He could feel her body heave with the tears she was trying not to shed.

'It's a fuckin' shitty world, ain't it?' Lol said. 'You think I don't know men? They all want to try me but they don't want to buy and keep me. Roy Kemp did me a big favour getting Big Mick to leave me alone because I'm going to work for Vera and get some money together, then I'll have the operation that'll make my world a better one. Thailand's the place for that!'

Lol swept away out of his bedroom and Eddie heard the click of her door lock.

'I can't falsify figures for you, Vera. I would if I could, but the facts are there in black and white.' Gloria, Vera's manageress at Heavenly Bodies, shook her head and her dark hair tumbled around her face. 'We're just not making the money we used to.' Glo slapped the red accounts book down on the glass-topped counter.

Daisy looked around the waiting room. Two

luxurious blue leather sofas, shelves filled with boxes containing wind chimes and crystals. A bunch of Michaelmas daisies displayed to their best advantage on a coffee table. The place smelled of perfume and it looked inviting. But there wasn't a man in sight.

Daisy knew the cubicles down the short passage were just as comfortable, but four girls were chatting in the kitchen area so her and Vera didn't need Gloria to tell them the place wasn't doing well.

Daisy could see with her own eyes that Heavenly Bodies was no longer the little gold-mine it used to be. She said, 'I just don't see how you can turn her down.'

She squeezed Lol's hand. She looked like a schoolgirl with her fair hair in plaits and a white blouse and short black skirt.

Vera said, 'I did think it would be a good idea, but now I don't know...'

'What's not to know? It's not as if I ain't done this kind of work before.'

'But you was bleedin' glad to get away from that seedy joint in London, wasn't you, Lol?'

'Look, I know how to make blokes happy...'

Daisy said, 'See, Vera, you could be back on your feet in next to no time.'

'But you've been like a daughter to me.' Vera stroked Lol's cheek.

Daisy said, 'Well, she ain't bleedin' running off, is she, you silly cow? She's wanting to follow in your footsteps.'

'Sounds good to me,' said Gloria. 'She can live 'ere with me. There's the other bedroom in your flat doin' nothing.'

'I ain't never allowed no blokes in me flat except my little man, my Kibbles...'

'But this ain't a bloke, this is Lol.'

'Please say yes, Vera? I don't know of any other way to make the money I need for the surgery. I trust you. You look after your girls, and you'll look after me. I want you to mind my money for me until I've earned enough to go to Thailand.'

Daisy punched Vera's arm good-naturedly. 'Think of the money you'll make, Vera. Just the lift this place needs,' she said.

'But I still don't understand why you was trying to get out of 'aving sex with blokes in London and now you want to go back to 'aving sex with blokes in Gosport?'

'Here it'll be my career.' Lol gave a pirouette and slung her feather boa dramatically round her shoulders.

Vera asked, 'Daisy, what do you think?'

'I think Lol should be allowed to do what she bleedin' well wants.'

'Jesus Christ, can't I even 'ave a fucking drink in peace?'

Roy removed his coat from the grubby velvet seat in the corner of the Thames Club to make room for his mate Biffo to sit down. He motioned to the woman behind the bar for more drinks. He didn't need to tell her what Baird was drinking; she knew. Anna knew the tipples of all her regulars. What he liked about this place was it served drinks after normal pub hours and his kind of people could always be found in here. It was also a hole of a place. Not far from the river Thames but you had to get to it along a rubbish-strewn arch beneath the District line near Putney Bridge. Bushes and weeds in the alley practically disguised the depressing entrance doorway.

'What's the matter with you?'

Baird sat down and stretched his legs out. 'Ain't me. It's you should be worried,' he said.

Roy looked at the big bloke sitting opposite him. Handsome feller in a rough cut way. He didn't think he'd ever seen him in a suit. Always dressed in casual gear and those bloody cowboy boots of his.

'Why should I be worried, mate?'

'Word's out that you got a big consignment of stuff comin' in?'

'Have I now? Who the fuck told you that?'

'I don't grass no fucker up, you know that, but Nelson knows all about it.'

Just then a couple of very large drinks were set down in front of them. Roy took out his wallet and put a note on the table, trying hard not to let it fall in the wet.

'Keep the rest, love,' he said. Roy grinned as he saw Teddy watching the arse on it as it swung back to the bar. 'Don't you ever stop thinkin' about fanny?'

Teddy threw back his head and laughed, showing his white teeth. Roy could see why the women liked him; and they liked him even more when they saw the size of his prick. And Teddy was proud of it, he'd show anyone who asked him.

A thought flitted through Roy's brain. 'Princess Margaret's gettin' a divorce from Snowdon at last. You ain't gonna be the next on her list, are you?'

'I get on better with 'er than I do with Maurie Nelson.'

'He doesn't like you, does he?'

'So the bastard don't like me,' admitted Baird. 'I heard tell it was because I had parts on telly an' got a few films under my belt. He certainly don't like it that I get the pick of the girlies.' He took a swig of his drink then wiped his mouth with the back of his hand. 'I reckon he's jealous of me, an' he's jealous of you because you got your manor sewn up.'

'An' I'm goin' to keep it,' said Roy. 'Where's he livin' now?'

'Might be up Elmer's End but I did 'ear he got another gaff in Tulse Hill. Your mate Vinnie Endersby an' his mate Terry Babbidge would like to see the back of him.'

'The scumbag's under the coppers' wing though. He's got a mouth on him an' they bang up whoever Maurie Nelson puts the whisper on,' Roy said.

'The coppers don't trust him. I don't 'ave to tell you this, but he's after your drugs.'

Roy pondered his words. It was a bugger of an inconvenience, but he'd have to change the port of entry and the delivery date. That fucker Nelson wasn't homing in on his territory.

'He still got that scrap yard?' Roy asked. He drummed his fingers on the sticky table.

'An' a van hire business. I'm just warning you 'cos you're my mate an' I reckon I could do with that ten thou you promised me.' Baird laughed.

244

'You got to admit, everyone wants a piece of the action.'

'Drugs makes the world go round until they make the world stop. Look at Elvis, who'd 'ave thought it?' Roy had only mentioned it because Elvis was singing 'Heartbreak Hotel' on the radio. 'You're a good 'un, Teddy. What you workin' on at present?'

'You know Elvis never came to England to see his fans?' Baird's voice was like scraped gravel and he didn't wait for Roy's answer. '*Trial by Combat's* out on the rounds and so's *A Choice of Arms*. They ain't gonna set the film world on fire but I got a spot coming up in that TV series *Hazell,* an' there's talk of me playing a drug dealer in *Quadrophenia*. But nothing's settled yet.'

'That should be right up your street, but I'm bettin' the way you can't keep money in your fuckin' pocket that you're skint, and that's why you think it's time to off Nelson. I was leavin' it up to you, timewise, Biffo but it can't be too soon for me. Did you find out any more about Samantha's murder? I got a lady who's breaking her heart about that girl.'

Baird swigged back the rest of his drink and treated the barmaid to a grin that meant fill up the glasses again. He waited until he saw her at the optics before he carried on. 'I don't know whether this means anything, but one of the dead women, the one young Eddie discovered, was bragging about going to Italy.'

'You reckon Nelson instigated these crimes?'

'Can't see 'im doing the actual killin'. It's not his style. I reckon this bloke, whoever he is, is trying to amass a decent wodge of the readies... Unless Nelson can get his hands on your shipment – an' I think you'll be too clever to let 'im do that – he'll need money, a lot of money, to finance himself if he wants to play with the big boys.'

The barmaid was setting down the drinks on the wet table. Roy pulled over a stained beer mat and lifted his brandy on to it. He watched as Baird slugged at his drink, all the while eyeing the barmaid. Roy drank back half the alcohol and waited until his mate had finished flirting.

When the girl had left, Roy took out his bulging wallet. Under cover of the table, he went on peeling off large notes, then shoved the pile towards Baird.

'What's this for?'

'Let's just say, you do things for me an' I do things for you. Ain't that the way mates behave? Now, let's finish this drink.'

'Cheerio, Suze, 'ave a nice time.'

Daisy heard the front door click shut. She had no idea why she'd called that to Susie, but seeing her in her best rose-printed dress and white high heels and smelling of 4711 perfume as she'd passed Daisy's bedroom, it just seemed the right thing to say. Especially as some kind of magic seemed to have settled over her friend just lately. She was always laughing, but then she might suddenly gaze out of a window with a dreamy look on her face. Vera reckoned she was either having a few wins at Bingo or she had a secret feller.

Daisy sent the hairbrush in long strokes over her hair. When she was satisfied she'd brushed for long enough she studied her face in the dressing table mirror. A few lines, a few wrinkles, and a bit of sagging here and there. Her life showed in her face; didn't everyone's? She'd always thought her eyes were her best feature, that shade of green that men seemed to like. Joan Collins eyes, someone had once said. Being pregnant suited her, gave her skin a special softness.

She sat back on the green velvet padded stool, rubbing her hand across the back of her neck to relieve the tension. The house was quiet.

Vera had gone to see Lol, who was loving living in the flat above Heavenly Bodies. Eddie was out. Joy was at a friend's birthday party and Daisy had to collect her at five o'clock, and Jamie was downstairs.

He was very quiet.

Daisy went down the carpeted steps and into the kitchen that smelled of the vanilla cake cooling on the top of the kitchen cabinet.

Her youngest son was bent over the table busily sawing at something just out of her eyeline. Standing behind him she said, 'What are you doing, Jamie?'

As the words left her mouth she could see what he was doing. She put her hand to her mouth to stop herself gagging. He looked up at her, his big blue eyes filled with innocence.

'Dad told me when they get dead people in, the police have special men who cut them up to see what's inside them. That way they can tell how the dead people died.'

The white wood scrubbed table was stained and bloodied. Four small legs were placed side

247

by side on a saucer. With Eddie's knife Jamie was in the process of cutting a lizard down its belly. The sight made Daisy want to retch.

She walked to the sink and, gripping the edge, stared out into the garden. And all the while she was swallowing down tears as well as her nausea. Her immediate reaction was to grab the boy and smack him – hit him and knock ten bales of shit out of him. Instead, she gripped the sink so tightly it took her a while to realise she was inflicting pain on her hands.

Daisy turned to him. 'Put the knife down, Jamie,' she said, more calmly than she felt. 'And come out into the garden.' She steeled herself not to look at the carnage on the table.

'All right,' he said, leaving the knife amidst the entrails and getting up. His face broke into a smile as he looked at her.

'Wash your hands,' she said. She waited until he'd finished then led him out into the garden towards the fishpond where she sat down on the edge of the raised crazy paving. Below the wire netting yellow and orange shapes darted amongst the shiny lily leaves.

He sat down beside her. 'It's cold out here, Mum.'

'I suppose it is, but it's a nice place to sit for a while out in the fresh air, isn't it?' He shrugged and snuggled in closer to her. Daisy took a deep breath. 'You shouldn't be touching Eddie's flick knife. I don't even like him having it, do I?' He shook his head. 'Where did you get it?'

'He left it in the bottom of his drawer.'

'And you took it? Why?'

248

'It's very sharp.' Daisy could understand the logic in that.

'But it's not yours, so by taking it, that's stealing, isn't it?'

'I guess. But I was going to put it back so he wouldn't have known.'

'But don't you see that's still being dishonest?'

'I guess so.'

'Right, sweetheart, I want you to tell me if you're happy at school?'

Was there something going on she knew nothing about? His teachers reckoned he was above average intelligence so she knew he wasn't finding the work difficult.

'It's okay,' he said. Typical answer, she thought.

'How about here at home? Are you worried about anything?'

He shrugged, then shook his head. 'No, Mum.'

Daisy felt as though she was banging her head against a brick wall with this boy of hers who she loved dearly but didn't understand one little bit.

'You do know it's cruel to hurt creatures?'

Daisy couldn't hurt anything. Even a spider was captured and set free. She knew it was silly but she imagined them going home to their families.

Jamie twisted round to look up at her. 'I wanted to find out what was inside the lizard. Did you know, Mum, even when I'd cut its legs off it was still moving?' And the smile he was giving her put the fear of God in her heart.

# CHAPTER 27

As the shadow fell across her, Daisy woke up. Sitting on the wooden bench provided by Pagham Sailing Club and facing the sea had seemed a luxurious way to catch the last of the sun's warmth before winter came. Lulled by the waves splashing across the shingle she'd dozed off.

'Oy, do you mind,' she said to the figure. 'You're standing in my sun!'

Daisy squinted as the man moved and sat down beside her.

Momentarily she was annoyed. She'd had the bench to herself during the past hour or so but it was, after all, a club bench and she wasn't a member.

She'd stood in Chichester market this morning since eight o'clock selling jewellery and was glad of a cup of tea, a tasty ham roll and a bit of warmth in Pagham's caff near the amusement arcade. She was passing time until the car boot started. It usually attracted a fair few people and, hopefully, she could sell more items there.

She loved Pagham with its pretty beachfront houses. The road journey through the farmland and fields to this funny little spot that smelled of burgers and candyfloss and was just like a miniature seaside resort made her feel happy.

'Are you buying or selling? I know good money can be made at this site from the holidaymakers who are staying at the caravan park along the coast.'

She recognised the voice immediately. Even without the fawn shortie raincoat over a dark suit she'd have known him and that attractive accent. She turned on the seat to face him.

'Selling,' she said to the Italian. 'And you?'

He laughed.

One of the best things about attending the Pagham boot was that the public weren't allowed in until the designated time. Then, when the sellers had set up their stalls and tables, the owner of the site encouraged the sellers to mingle so they could buy from each other. The queue of people waiting to get into the boot's compound was always long, tailing sometimes right around the back of the caff. She stared at Bruno.

He smiled at her. 'At this moment I am looking at you, Daisy.' His dark brown eyes seemed to bore inside her. But Jesus Christ, what a corny chat-up line, she thought. He was certainly a good-looking bastard. And he'd remembered her name, just fancy that! 'You looked very beautiful asleep.'

How did she reply to that? Part of her knew he was spinning her a line but another part quite liked it! She decided on a safe reply.

'Thank you,' she said. He took a packet of cigarettes from his pocket and offered her one. She looked at his hands, square with their long fingers. Her heart dropped like a stone.

'No, er, no,' she stuttered. 'I don't smoke.'

She forced herself to tear her eyes away from his hands. Her heart was beating furiously as she looked around her. Apart from him and her there were very few people on the beach. A hundred yards away a young mother sat on the pebbles reading; her child was presumably asleep in the wind-protected pushchair.

'You come with me for a cup of coffee?'

That was the last thing she wanted. Or was it? She thought of the small caff that would be over-flowing with buyers and sellers. She'd be safer there.

Some sixth sense made her look at her watch.

'Jesus,' she cried, rising from the seat. 'I forgot about the time. I have to collect my car from the car park and get in line for when they open the gates. The first car in gets the best site! I'm sorry,' she said. 'I really have to go. Another time per-haps...' She didn't wait for a reply but left him, running for the car park, searching inside her handbag for her keys at the same time.

She started the MG and drove onto the field, where she was waved into the first line. She breathed a sigh of relief.

Daisy looked about her for the Italian. Perhaps he'd gone to the caff anyway. Perhaps he'd walk around the sale area. Perhaps she wouldn't see him again.

In her heart of hearts she knew he'd find her though.

Lying in bed that night Daisy tossed and turned. She'd tried going downstairs and making tea, she'd tried reading, but it was no use. Her brain was in overdrive. The whole house was sleeping and in darkness; the only light was that from her bedside lamp.

She was afraid of the shadows, and had been ever since that maniac boxer Valentine Waite had abducted her and kept her prisoner in a dark room. It had taken years for her to come to terms with her rapes and beatings. The meeting this afternoon with that fucking Italian had brought all those fears back. And why?

Because he was wearing Samantha's ring!

How she'd got through the sale without her mind fully on her work, she had no idea. How she'd arrived home safely with her brain constantly thinking of him and the ring and Samantha was an even bigger miracle.

Daisy had even tried to persuade herself that it wasn't the same ring, but she knew it was. Samantha wouldn't take it from her finger. Nor would she allow anyone else to try it on.

So what did this mean? How had Bruno come by Samantha's ring?

Was he Samantha's killer?

Just because the Italian had the ring didn't mean he *was* the killer, did it? He could simply have come by the ring *via* the killer.

Daisy sighed. Her instinct told her the Italian creep was in this up to his neck. She needed to confide in someone. But who?

Not Roy, not yet at any rate. He had enough on his plate with his own problems.

Vinnie? She'd had little contact lately with Vinnie. It was funny, she thought, that for a woman and a man who had loved each other enough to have a child, they now needed distance from each other.

Eddie? Definitely not! There was no telling

253

which way his anger would turn, and Daisy wanted to keep Eddie out of trouble, not land him in it.

To confide in Susie was out of the question. She didn't need problems thrust upon her. The death of her husband had nearly tipped her over the edge and if she hadn't had the baby to keep her sane... No, definitely not Susie, not when she was now happier than she'd been for ages. But if she didn't stop singing that stupid 'Que Sera, Sera' in her off-key voice maybe Daisy would *kill* her.

So, what was she going to do?

She needed more proof.

Only then could she hand Bruno to Roy and Vinnie.

She was in no doubt that the Italian wanted something from her, that these meetings weren't simply chance.

She'd never seen him buy a thing at any of the auctions. Why go to auctions if he wasn't buying or selling? Nor did he have a pitch at salegrounds. Even today, he'd merely disappeared into the ether after meeting her.

A shiver went through her as a horrifying thought struck her.

*She* was next on his list.

Eddie parked the van on the driveway. He climbed out and stretched. Today was his last day of work with Tyrone who on Monday was starting at an MG garage in Stubbington. Christchurch, but he ached all over. Him and Tyrone had been up at Southampton all day after leaving at five this morning, and even Ty had said, when he dropped him off, that all he wanted was a bath and bed. Eddie looked at the van; it was about a quarter full of rubbish that needed to be taken to the tip. Already it was dusk, so tomorrow would do fine for that.

In the kitchen he made himself tea and sat down on the bench at the table and closed his eyes. A scrabbling sound outside the kitchen window made him start. He went to the window, opened it wide and called Kibbles, surprised that the cat didn't appear. Then he poured himself another cup of tea. Eddie had the house to himself and relished the peace. He could smell something good and meaty, and a covered plate set over a saucepan of water on the top of the stove had a note with it: 'Left you some dinner, Suze x.' He smiled to himself. It was a good feeling to be cared about.

No doubt Susie and her daughter had gone on one of their mysterious jaunts. He looked at his watch. Jamie had been muttering something about going to the pictures to see *Superman*.

He slugged back the last of his tea, remembering he'd left the key in the van. He swore, tempted to leave it, but he knew he'd never forgive himself if the bloody van got nicked. Just because it was in the driveway didn't mean it was safe. This was Gosport, after all.

He opened the front door and walked over to the vehicle, pausing to look along Western Way, where he spotted the outline of someone in the distance.

The man was running. Eddie saw him pass beneath the light from the lamp post and then darkness claimed him. Unease formed in Eddie's mind. Where had he seen that figure before...

He shrugged off the feeling. He needed a bath and then he'd heat up that meal Susie had left for him. He hadn't even lifted the top plate to see what it was. Didn't matter, he thought, whatever it was, it would be bloody good.

He sang as he scrubbed. Since there was no one indoors to tell him to shut up he sang out 'Tonight's The Night' at the top of his voice. Vera said he had a voice like a saw going through rock! He thought he sounded a little like Rod Stewart.

Back in his bedroom he buried his face in the cat's warm fur. Kibbles was curled up on the bottom of his bed but moved to butt his head against Eddie. That's when Eddie noticed the damp spot.

'You've done a wee on my counterpane in your sleep, boy. Didn't you know?' Not expecting the cat to answer him but nevertheless used to chatting away to the animal, he carefully moved him along on the bed. 'You been eating your fish properly, boy? You're a bit bony.'

It seemed to him that Kibbles had lost his bulk. He hadn't lost his purr though. The noise was loud, and in the quiet of Eddie's room, comforting.

Eddie went along to the bathroom and came back armed with Vosene shampoo and a toilet roll and proceeded to clean the bedding. Luckily, the thick counterpane had soaked up most of the urine so it hadn't gone through onto the blankets and sheets. When he thought it was clean enough, Eddie made a sort of tent using a paperback book to let the air get to it and dry it.

'Tell you what, Kibbles,' he said after getting rid of the evidence. 'I won't tell if you don't.'

Downstairs he heated up the meat stew and dumplings, and thought about Lol.

She hadn't exactly taken Samantha's place in Heavenly Bodies, no one could do that, but by all accounts she was drawing in the punters and making money for herself and Vera. It seemed as if Samantha's murder had been put on a back burner by the cops. Vinnie hadn't a clue and Roy was up to his eyeballs in his own business, but Vera talked about Samantha constantly.

Eddie had a lot to thank Samantha for himself.

He'd been fourteen and waiting for his mother and Vera to return to the massage parlour in the High Street. They'd been delayed and it was a quiet day at Heavenly Bodies.

Samantha had been sitting on the blue leather sofa watching him when she'd suddenly said, 'C'mon, boy, let's see what you're made of.'

She'd led him down to her cubicle and stripped herself and him. Even now he could see those luscious breasts jiggling beneath her white coat of a uniform, and when they'd been released it was like they'd become alive in his hands. He'd been terrified. Terrified and excited, both at the same time.

Beneath the white coat she'd worn black fishnet stockings and suspenders.

He'd come almost straight away.

But she'd held him and whispered that it didn't matter.

'You'll be fine,' she said. 'It's my job to make you fine.'

And she did.

She took her time with him.

'This is what a woman likes, Eddie. This, and

257

this, and this.'

When he crept out of the cubicle to resume his wait for Vera and his mother, he felt ten foot tall.

'Our secret,' she said. And it always had been their special secret. Of course he knew the value of her teachings. Samantha had taught him how to make a woman feel special. No wonder Vera felt as though she'd lost more than just one of her whores.

## CHAPTER 28

'I don't feel in the mood for prancin' about,' Eddie said.

He waited while Tyrone locked the Mini and stuffed the keys in his trouser pocket. Despite the cold air, girls were huddled around the entrance to Lee Tower in tiny tops and mini skirts and ugly platform shoes. The sound of raucous female laughter reached him, along with the smell of musky perfume and cigarettes.

'You don't 'ave to dance, Eddie, you just 'ave to sample what's on offer.' Tyrone inclined his head towards the girls. They were giggling at them, while pretending not to notice that two full-blooded, good-looking blokes were pushing past to get into the dance hall where the Saturday night disco was in full throttle.

Inside, the flashing lights made Eddie blink until his eyes accustomed themselves to the unreal colours and highlighted white tones. The heady mixture of cheap scent and smoke stung his eyes. He started towards the bar.

'Pint?' he yelled to Tyrone above the noise, and the music of Queen.

He didn't wait for an answer but ordered lager from the dark-haired girl who seemed to appear from nowhere to serve him, despite the disgruntled blokes already waiting.

'One for yourself,' he said with a grin. Then he pushed Tyrone's drink in front of him.

'Can't let you go to a new job without a celebration, can we?'

'I wasn't expectin' to come out...'

'Shut the fuck up and get that down you,' said Eddie.

He stood with his back to the bar, contemplating the heaving mass of people. It wasn't long before he became aware of the sly looks directed towards him from the girls, and the glares from the blokes in their fashionable white suits.

'Lookin' good for tonight,' said Tyrone. Eddie saw him dust an imaginary piece of fluff off the front of his dark suit.

'Leave yourself alone, you bloody great poof,' Eddie laughed, taking a mouthful of his drink then setting it back on the counter. A lot of the blokes were in jackets with the sleeves rolled up. A few wore leather. There were even a couple of blokes gyrating about in brightly coloured enormous flares, complete with white shoes and flowered shirts.

'John Travolta's got a lot to answer for, ain't he?'

The two of them watched the dancers. Him and Ty had been mates for so long they almost

259

knew each other's thoughts.

'So you don't fancy a white suit?'

'Do I fuck!' said Eddie. He looked down at his own dark-blue outfit with a waistcoat and slim-Jim tie. When he'd been younger he'd wanted a suit like Roy Kemp. He'd wanted to wear similar outfits because he admired the man. So what if he couldn't afford Savile Row tailoring? He would one day, he'd promised himself. He also liked to feel the softness of good shirts. Roy had bought him a pure silk one but he hardly wore it, not because he didn't like it but because he liked it so much he didn't want to spoil it. Mind you, he'd seen Roy in his shirtsleeves and jeans doing jobs around the house for his mum and Violet. Then, he looked like a bleeding gyppo. But when he went out, he looked and acted the business.

And now his mum was pregnant by him. Eddie smiled. About bloody time, he thought. Roy had been a sort of father for so long he'd forgotten he wasn't his real dad!

He turned back to the bar to pick up his glass again and that was when he spotted her in the bar's back mirror. Through a gap in the crowd of dancers he could see Summer, slumped at a table in the corner.

'Ty,' he said. 'Am I right in thinkin' that's Summer over there?'

Tyrone didn't make a fuss, just stared in the appropriate direction.

He said, 'I'm thinkin' she's 'ad one too many. She don't usually show that much of her bleedin' knickers. We goin' over?'

'Not straight away. I want to see who she's with.'

He didn't have long to wait. A tall dark-haired bloke wearing John Lennon glasses sat down on the seat next to her. The bloke put his hand on her thigh and rubbed his fingers along her inside leg. Summer didn't seem to mind, but something inside Eddie coiled tight like a spring winding itself up.

Tyrone put his hand on Eddie's arm. 'Wait. She won't thank you for rushin' over there an' causin' a fuckin' scene. If she's got the hots for that bloke it's nothin' to do with you...'

'He's a fuckin' wanker!'

'You don't know that. Maybe he's deciding she's had enough to drink an' is about to take her home.'

'Why is she in that fuckin' state in the first place?' Eddie was breathing heavily and drumming his fingers on the bar top; he looked at Tyrone for reassurance.

'You know what she's like. Summer goes at everything like it ain't gonna be there tomorrow.' The music had changed now to Carly Simon and 'Nobody Does It Better', and slow dancing took over.

'I'm goin' over.' Eddie started forward.

'Wait!' Ty pulled him back. At that exact moment the bloke pulled the girl upright, and enfolding her in his arms, forced her to dance unsteadily with him. Eddie watched intently. Summer wasn't in any fit state to put one foot in front of the other, let alone dance.

'Stupid cow,' he said. 'It's too early for her to be in that state.'

'You might want to be 'er keeper, but you ain't,'

261

Tyrone said.

Eddie watched the bloke leading her around in their small spot of the floor, her shuffling and giggling. He didn't like the way the bloke was touching her, like he owned her.

A couple of slow tunes and the bloke tried to sit her down again. Summer slipped against the wooden seat and struggled to remain upright as the chair slid away from her. When she'd stopped laughing at herself, she took a drink from the tall glass on the table in front of her and grabbed the chair again. Sitting down, she tried to sort her short skirt, pulling it down where it had risen up. The man leant forward and whispered something that sent her into another giggling fit. So hilarious it must have been that her mane of strawberry red hair flew about her face as she swung her head from side to side.

The bloke, Eddie reckoned, was in his early twenties. He looked like some kind of student.

Summer put her elbows on the table and leaned her chin in her hands. Her eyes closed. Her long hair trailed in the puddle of beer. That was when Eddie saw the man put his hand to his breast pocket and take out his wallet. He took something in his fingers and dropped it into the tall glass Summer had been drinking from.

'The fucker,' said Tyrone. 'See what he's doing?'

'I see,' said Eddie and he was away from the bar counter and pushing through the sweat-drenched dancers. His eyes never left the bloke. When he got to their table the man had lifted the glass, and holding Summer by the shoulders helped her to drink from it.

262

Eddie leapt on the bloke, knocking the glass from his hand. It shattered on the floor while Summer slumped over the table. There were dog ends from the ashtray in her beautiful hair.

'What the fuck?'

Eddie didn't let the man get out another word before he grabbed hold of his shoulder and slammed his fist into his face.

'What you given her?' The bloke buckled from the knees and Eddie grabbed him before he fell to the floor. Already a crowd had formed and jeering had started. Gripping the sagging bloke with his left hand, he pulled back his fist and took another shot at him. He heard the man's cheekbone crack. 'What have you given her, scumbag?'

Wild-eyed, the bloke stared crazily at Eddie, with his hand to his face trying to protect himself. Eddie let him have it in the stomach, and this time the bloke creased over the table before sliding down, still trying to cover his mangled face.

'Where's the rest of your stash?'

'Give the bastard a chance to speak, Ed.' Tyrone was trying to pacify him.

The bloke, blood dripping down his shirt, fumbled in his top pocket and handed Eddie a screw of pills.

Eddie poured them into his hand and studied them. He said, bending down to the bloke, 'Open wide.' Frightened, the man obediently opened his mouth and Eddie tipped in the pills. 'Swallow 'em.' The man shook his head, his eyes frantic as he crouched on the floor. Eddie drew back his fist; the man gulped. Then, like a kid, he opened his mouth to show Eddie the pills were gone.

263

'Good boy,' said Eddie, calm now. And never more glad of the darkened interior, flashing lights and deafening music.

Tyrone slipped his hands beneath the bloke's armpits and dragged him away from the table, away from Eddie. He left him propped against a table leg.

'Get out of 'ere before you fuckin' do 'im in,' Ty yelled. 'Get 'er out.'

Eddie hooked his arm around Summer and practically scooped her up. The bloodthirsty crowd was loving it now.

Some woman yelled, ''Ave him!'

'Put the boot in!'

He followed Tyrone's instructions, half walking, half dragging Summer through the baying, sweaty mob. At the exit a couple of beefy blokes in suits and sunglasses stopped Tyrone and asked, 'What's the problem, mate?'

'My mate just 'ad a ruckus with 'is ol' lady. You don't want to know about it. It's sorted now.'

Eddie saw the two bulls look at each other and, for a brief moment, he thought there was going to be another confrontation. Then the shorter of the two grinned knowingly and the bald one said, 'Take it outside.' Eddie pushed past until they were in the open air, where he picked Summer up in his arms and strode towards the parked car.

'Get the fucking door open.' He looked down at the girl in his arms and wished he was holding her under different circumstances. What was in those fucking tablets? Would she be all right?

He gently laid Summer on the back seat of the Mini. She was like a long-legged spider, all arms and legs. Eddie stretched upright outside the car to ease his back and stood looking at her. She was spark out. He closed the door on her, and said to Tyrone, 'I ought to go back in there an' kill 'im.'

'Leave him, he ain't worth it. Anyway, you probably 'ave killed 'im, forcing 'im to swallow his whole stash.'

Eddie thought he'd remember forever the fear in the man's eyes as he swallowed the tablets.

'C'mon,' he said. 'We're finished here.' He opened the car door. 'Jesus Christ, she's thrown up!'

Tyrone looked like the bottom had fallen out of his world when he saw the state of the back seat.

Eddie said, 'That's a bit of a blessing then, ain't it? I was wondering 'ow much salt water I was gonna 'ave to pour into her to get 'er to bring up that shit. Is she awake?'

'Is she, fuck!' said Tyrone.

'I'm sorry, mate. She's gonna have a head to end all heads if she gets over this.' The words flew from Eddie's mouth. What if Summer didn't wake up? His voice was gruff. 'You got any news-paper or something to clean her with?'

'Never mind Summer, I polished inside this car today,' moaned Tyrone. He foraged around in the front and came up with a rag.

Eddie gently wiped Summer's face and tried to get the traces of puke and dog ends from her tangle of hair. The poor girl stank to high heaven.

'Silly bitch,' he said, too softly for Tyrone to hear. 'Don't you know I care about you?' After cleaning as much as he could from her and the car, he threw the rag in the gutter.

'Shame it's so bloody cold, we'll have to drive to my house with the windows open, won't we?' He looked at Ty's glum face. 'Don't worry, ol' mate, I'll clean it for you in the mornin'. Just you drive as if the bleedin' cops is after you. She needs to be looked at fast.'

The house at Western Way, as usual, was lit up like the Blackpool Illuminations. Eddie carried Summer to the front door. He said to Tyrone, 'The key's in me pocket, take it out, will you?'

Ty opened the door and Eddie walked down the hall and into the kitchen with Summer in his arms. As soon as they saw him he thought it was like a load of pigeons descending on bread down on the ferry gardens.

'Can you help her, Vera?' Vera checked Summer's pulse.

'I'll phone for Doctor Dillinger immediately,' she said. 'Put her on the table an' get a blanket an' a pillow.'

'I'll go,' said Daisy, and hurriedly left the kitchen.

'Is she gonna be all right?' He was worried sick. What if she'd taken other drugs? 'What if Doctor Dillinger couldn't help her?

Vera was opening Summer's eyelids and looking into her eyes.

'You know,' Vera said, 'I'm thinking by the state of 'er – 'er bein' all floppy like a big doll – that she's been given that new drug, what's it called, Ro ... Rohypnol. It only came on the market a few years ago but already it's on the streets. An' she won't remember a bleedin' thing about it

266

tomorrow. Poor bitch will be confused, and have a hangover like nobody's business...'

'So there *will* be a tomorrow for her?' Eddie had started walking up and down in the small space between the dresser and the kitchen table.

'Bloody 'ope so. Nothin's certain with all the new manufactured stuff you can get now.'

'Has she been given what they call "Roofies", Vera?' The voice was his mother's. She slipped the pillow beneath Summer's head and gently covered her with the blue blanket.

Vera nodded. 'I reckon,' she said. 'That's one of the street names for it. Too many and you go into a coma.' Eddie didn't want to think about Summer going into a coma, and he pushed thoughts of the bloke at the disco out of his mind.

'She's not comatose!'

'Not yet, she ain't,' Vera said.

A loud rapping at the front door and Daisy said, 'Thank Christ.' Vera left the kitchen and Eddie could hear her talking to Doctor Dillinger in the hall. The man lived not far away but wasn't strictly a doctor any more, having been cast out of the medical association for malpractice. He had a problem. A drink problem. For all that, he was a bloody good doctor and Vera wouldn't have a word said against him. Eddie knew he looked after her girls and did a fine job of it and he was discreet.

And then Jamie came downstairs. 'I can't sleep with all this racket,' he said. 'What's goin' on?' His blond hair was sticking up on end. He took a look at Summer and said, 'What's up with 'er?'

'Nothing that concerns you,' said Eddie. The

267

boy was studying Summer's skimpy top which wasn't covered by the honeycombed blanket and exposed a great deal of her breasts. His mother caught Eddie's glare and said, 'Jamie, why don't you go in the other room and watch television? I don't think it's closed down for the night yet.'

Eddie knew Jamie thought this was a pretty good deal, better than being made to go back to bed.

'Tyrone, you best stay 'ere tonight,' said Daisy. 'Sleepin' bag on Eddie's bedroom floor all right? Go and 'ave a shower, you bleeding look an' smell as though you needs one.'

Eddie watched as Tyrone went upstairs, then he told his mum what had happened, leaving out the bit about the bloke swallowing his own pills. Then, when his conscience got hold of him, he told her about that too.

'He got what he deserved, son.'

He looked at his mother with surprise. She shook her head. 'Your father would have done the same. What goes around, comes around. I'll go and phone her father...'

'Wait until the Doc's seen her, Mum. Won't do to go upsettin' Bri.'

Eddie knew his mother disliked lies but he loved her all the more for agreeing to his suggestion.

Summer was taken upstairs to Susie's room by Eddie, closely followed by Doctor Dillinger. Eddie thought the bloke looked more like a vagrant every time he saw him, with his unkempt grey beard and his long hair. Still, despite that, Eddie knew Summer was in the best hands now.

268

He looked down at himself. Jesus, he was a mess as well. Leaving Vera and the doctor, he went downstairs. Half way down he heard Summer throwing up.

His mother came back into the kitchen.

'Look, I couldn't not phone Bri. If it was *me* I'd want to know if my girl wasn't coming home one night. And she is only a kid. But I played it down, told him she was throwing up bad.'

He nodded, then sighed. 'You put her in Susie's room?'

'Her and Joy 'ave gone away for the weekend.'

'There's some right bastards out there,' said Eddie. 'Nowadays young girls got to be careful who they're drinking with. Ain't no good thinking because a bloke seems all right that he is all right. They got to keep an eye on their drinks at all times. God, I've 'eard some terrible cases.' He sat down on the bench and put his hands to his head, elbows on the table. 'She is going to be all right, isn't she, Mum?'

'Summer's in the best hands.'

Eddie heard Tyrone come out of the bathroom so he went upstairs.

'You know where the bleedin' sleepin' bag is, don't you?'

'Should do by now.' Ty's damp hair had droplets of water clinging to it. There was a towel round his middle. 'I expected to be in a strange bed tonight, mate,' he said, 'but this is takin' our friendship a bit far, me endin' up with you.'

'Piss off,' said Eddie.

# CHAPTER 29

The girl opened her eyes and focussed on Daisy, who didn't let go of her hand.

Summer's brow creased and she struggled to sit up, but immediately fell back again into the white folds of the sheets.

'Stay still,' said Daisy. Summer closed her eyes like the effort had been too much for her.

God, but this girl was like her mother, thought Daisy. Only the vibrant hair showed who her father was. She let go of Summer's hand to tuck a long strand of hair away from her face.

Daisy remembered when Vera had found this child in this very house, shut in a wardrobe while her mother was off her head on drugs.

Daisy and Vera had looked after the baby then taken her to her father, Bri, who'd turned out to be a bleedin' good dad. Summer's nature was such she made herself learn the hard way that the world very often wasn't a nice place. Daisy thought about the relief she'd felt when Vera had come out of Susie's bedroom announcing that Doctor Dillinger had said Summer should be fine.

Daisy had loved her like the daughter she'd never had. Now Summer was finding her feet, rebelling against life. Daisy held her hand over her stomach and prayed she would be able to take good care of the new life growing inside her.

She was aware of Eddie's feelings for the girl.

And if Eddie was truly like his father, he'd make Summer love him, eventually.

She sighed – so young, they were both so young. So much living to do. She shook her head. In Gosport, kids grew up fast, she reminded herself. The town could be a dark battlefield; it wasn't all sunshine and markets and seaside. She'd never leave it though. To her Gosport was like a warm old overcoat.

Summer opened her eyes again.

'Auntie Daisy? Why am I here?' The girl's voice was husky.

'You tell me, sweetheart...'

She could feel Summer struggling to answer her. A little help wouldn't hurt, she thought.

'You were at a disco at Lee Tower.'

'Was I?'

'Yes, and you were given some pills...' A glaze seemed to wash across Summer's eyes. She licked her dry lips.

'Let me get you a drink.' Daisy poured a glass of water from the carafe she'd brought upstairs and helped Summer to drink from it.

'I feel like crap,' Summer said after she'd drunk noisily. Then she looked down at herself in one of Susie's chaste cotton nighties. 'Whatever have I got on?'

'Belongs to Suze. I thought it'd be clean and crisp against your skin; you were sweating a lot.'

The girl seemed to accept it. She lay back on the pillows and closed her eyes again. She sighed. 'My head feels funny, kind of unreal and swimmy.'

'Do you remember the bloke you were with?'

'Bloke? I don't remember nothin', Auntie

Daisy!' Her voice had risen and fear was etched across her face. 'Why don't I remember? What happened? How did I get here?' And now Summer was tossing and turning.

Daisy said, 'First of all, stop all this threshing about. You're safe in my house.'

'You been sitting there all night?'

Daisy nodded and took hold of her hand again. She looked at the clock: it was four in the morning.

'Go back to sleep. I promise you everything's been taken care of.'

'Dad! Dad'll be goin' spare!'

'Shhh! No, he won't, he knows you're with me. Stop worryin' and go to sleep.'

She smoothed the girl's forehead and was amazed to see the worry actually clear from Summer's brow. Within moments the girl was breathing easily and Daisy knew she was asleep again.

Daisy went downstairs, feeling it was safe to leave the girl to sleep for a few minutes. Summer was going to be all right after all. Perhaps her memory would return, but maybe it was better if it didn't.

Eddie was slumped over the table but he looked up at her when she entered. His eyes were red rimmed and his face a stone mask.

'She's goin' to be all right,' Daisy said.

Eddie got up and fell into his mother's arms.

'Thank God,' he cried.

'Vera, you got to trust me, I know what I'm doing.'

Vera sat with her feet in a bowl of hot salty

272

water and Daisy passed her a cup of tea. She'd decided after much heart searching that the only person she could confide in was Vera. Besides, she knew how hurt Vera would be if she was left out of anything.

'If this Italian bloke is a fuckin' killer you're off your 'ead wantin' anything to do with 'im at all. An' you got that baby inside you to consider.'

'I'm pregnant, not bleedin' ill. How much did you love Samantha?'

Vera reached up for the cup but Daisy had already spotted the quick flash of tears just at the mention of Samantha's name.

'Not as much as I care about you.' She paused for a moment then said, 'But I reckon if we got a chance to expose the bloke for what he is, we owe it to Samantha to try an' find out what happened. The fuckin' coppers don't seem to care an' Roy might as well be on another bleedin' planet.' Vera shrugged.

'He's juggling too many balls at once, Vera. There's this bloke Maurice O'Mahoney. He's been spoutin' off about the underworld in London, ain't he?'

'You mean that bloke calls 'imself "King Squealer"?'

Daisy nodded. 'He's a bleedin' armed robber, as violent as they come, but because he's passed on more'n a hundred and fifty names to the coppers all he's got is a pissy five years in Chiswick Police Station of all places, with bleedin' free beer on tap and a bunk-up from his girlfriend any time he likes. I tell you, the bleedin' law 'as gone arse upwards with all these fuckin'

273

informers getting in on the act.'

Vera sighed. 'You want a Bourbon?' Daisy nodded and Vera went over to the cupboard and took out the packet of biscuits. 'Open up these, will you? I don't want to break me nails.'

Vera watched Daisy fiddling with the packet for a while and getting nowhere.

'Your bleedin' nails is too short to do anythin' except scratch your arse,' she said. 'Give us back the packet!'

Munching into the sweetness, Daisy stared around her bright kitchen.

'Once upon a time you could trust the coppers,' she said. 'Roy was telling me about this bloke he knows called Bobby Brown. He's in the nick for killing this woman called Annie Walsh. Roy says he couldn't 'ave done it. He was beat up in the police station, an' this Detective Chief Inspector Butler, or somebody, gathered all this crap against him to convict him of a crime Brown reckons he never did.'

'Well, I never,' said Vera.

'See, Vera, Roy's got to keep on the ball. His worst enemy is Maurie Nelson. Roy reckons even coppers who've been on his payroll for years have got cold feet. Ain't no trust at all anywhere. Can't trust the coppers, can't trust the underworld. Roy's hangin' on by the seat of his pants.'

'Which is why you reckons you can single 'andedly give the legitimate coppers this bloke who might or might not have killed my Samantha.'

'Don't be funny with me, Vera. You said yourself that her ring wasn't with the stuff given back to you before the authorities released her body.'

Vera nodded. 'True,' she admitted.

'Could there be another ring like that one?'

'Dunno. It's possible. You can't make a decision on the basis of a ring that might or might not 'ave belonged to my Samantha.' Vera's expression changed as though she'd suddenly thought of something. 'Wait a minute,' she said. 'Samantha caught her hand in a car door. The ring saved her losing her thumb. But it left a dent in the setting where that green stone is. Now if the ring has a dent in it, then I'll believe it's Samantha's.'

'You'll help me?'

Vera nodded. 'You try and stop me, Daisy. But one thing's definite, you mustn't be alone with that Italian. Not ever, understand? Ain't you scared?'

'Vera, I'm shittin' meself. But as long as I know you won't leave me alone with him, it'll be all right.'

'Why you doin' this, Dais?'

'That's easy, you silly ol' tart. You loved Samantha and I care about you. Plus Samantha needs justice.'

## CHAPTER 30

Daisy drove her MG on to the grass field and parked. This would be the final sale Loving's Farm would be holding until next year. Always the last place to close down for the winter, Loving's was host to a caravan park that was always filled to capacity. There was also a large, inexpensive cafe that catered to the public.

It was going to be a huge sale. Already tables and stalls were set up as far as the eye could see. The weather was cold, and Daisy was glad she'd wrapped up warm. Not so Vera.

Vera pushed herself out of the small car leaving in her wake the smell of perfume.

'Fuckin' cold out here,' she moaned. 'What you got to do to set up?'

Daisy looked at Vera's red wool suit with its short skirt, and her black high heels with the bows on. Beneath the suit was a black frilly blouse that was unbuttoned and wouldn't leave much to any stallholder or customer's imagination.

Daisy sighed. 'I told you to put some decent clothes on. An' why're you wearing high heels? You on a bleeding fashion parade or something? If you don't twist your ankles you'll fall over and break your bleedin' neck on this uneven ground. That's why you was sat in the car first thing this morning, ain't it? So's I wouldn't properly see what you was wearing?'

Vera ignored her. 'Plenty of cold wet ground 'ere, Dais.' God, but she could be exasperating sometimes, thought Daisy.

'What do you expect? I got to get 'ere early. No good arriving when the punters are goin' home, is it?'

Vera looked subdued as Daisy took the folding table from the boot and covered it with a black velvet cloth. Then she ignored Vera and began setting out her jewellery.

After a while, Daisy looked about her. She was

sandwiched between a burger van that was already issuing out smells of bacon, burgers and onions, and a fruit and veg stall. Could be worse pitches, she thought, though if she hadn't had to wait for Vera this morning putting on her pan stick she'd have got the pitch she liked, nearest the entrance. Vera had disappeared until Daisy found her already sat in the car. She glanced again at the burger van. Still, people would come to buy teas and coffees and look at her goods. Daisy peered about. Vera was nowhere in sight, but that was all to the good, wasn't it?

Daisy knew that creep of an Italian, if Vera was glued to her side, wouldn't come within a yard of her. She remembered how he'd disappeared at the auction hall. He doesn't want anyone to re-member him, she thought. Anyway, Vera was enough to frighten anyone off!

She was probably walking up and down the many aisles. That would take her some time, judg-ing by how many sellers there were. From the inside of the car Daisy took out the bag containing the flask.

Because it was the last outdoor sale for the season, Daisy had brought some of her most expensive items.

She'd dressed warmly but carefully. She also had pinned to her lapel the one item of jewellery that never failed to get attention.

She fingered the diamond brooch. It was worth a mint, an absolute mint. And she wore it for a reason.

If the person who killed Samantha was the Italian, he would show more than a passing interest in the brooch. If he *was* marking her out as his next victim, thinking she had money, then she'd show him she could come up with the goods!

She sipped strong brown tea from the flask mug and eyed the steeple of Chichester's cathedral across the strawberry fields, bare now in the winter sun. She enjoyed the laid back atmosphere of Loving's Farm. The burger van bloke gave her a cheery wave and turned up his music so that Abba's annoying voices swept along the aisles of sellers.

Her first customer of the morning was a bleached blonde wearing loads of gold and a green flared coat.

'What can you do me on that bangle?' The woman's tan was almost black. She'd obviously just returned from a holiday abroad. The scent of Evening in Paris wafted across the table. Daisy had a good mark-up on the piece she was holding.

'You bought from me last week at Southsea, didn't you?'

The woman stared at Daisy. 'Fancy you remembering me.'

'I never forget a tan as good as that,' Daisy said. The woman grinned, pleased.

'I've been to Benidorm,' she said, then turned her mind back to the bangle. 'How much?'

'Look, this 'ere is the last sale of the year. I could knock off a tenner.' She saw the woman's green eyes glitter with greed. 'I can't knock off no more. It's Greek gold, see? I'll let it go for twenty quid. To you.' The woman was already foraging in her handbag. Daisy was home and dry on the first sale of the day.

She took the two ten-pound notes and asked, 'Do you want me to wrap it up?' Daisy had some pretty little bags with daisies on them and she liked handing them out.

The woman shook her head. 'I'll wear it,' she said, slipping it over her wrist and turning her arm back and forth to get a good look at it. It jangled with the rest of her bracelets.

'Suits you,' said Daisy. 'Thanks. I hope to see you again.' As the woman wandered off with a satisfied smile, Daisy slipped the money into the pouch at her waist. Twenty pounds for the bracelet was a good price and a bargain.

Daisy hated it when she heard sellers come out with obvious lies to sell an article. They did it to lull the buyer into a false sense of security. How many times had she heard a twenty-stone woman on a clothes stall say to a prospective punter, 'Nice dress that, it was mine an' I don't really like to part with it.' That the dress in question was a size ten had gone right over the buyer's head, and they'd bought it anyway, safe in the knowledge that they knew who'd worn it last! 'It's me dad's, me mother's, my kid's toys...' Daisy knew all the ploys to get the punters to buy.

Daisy looked down at the brooch sparkling away on her coat. If Roy knew she was wearing it to a sale in a field he'd go daft! She'd keep an eye on it, that was for sure. She was proud, too, of her newly acquired knowledge of gold and hallmarks.

When she wasn't absolutely sure about stuff she took the items down to Sol's Gold Shop in the town and he'd soon put her right. If he wasn't in his shop he'd be in The George and Dragon

279

and they'd have a drink there together.

Daisy always charged fair prices. She wasn't out to skin anyone, only to make a living and maybe a bit more besides. Sol was an old customer of Vera's so she knew she could trust him.

Time passed and business was steady. Smells of candyfloss issued from the burger van, and now she was pissed off with Abba songs. Where the hell was Vera?

'How much is this?' The young couple were fidgeting in front of her table and pointing to a gold heartshaped locket on a gold chain. Daisy removed it from the case and handed it to the girl who, after turning it in her fingers, looked expectantly at the young man. They were barely more than kids, thought Daisy.

'Twenty-five pounds.' She took it from the girl and deftly opened the locket. 'It has a place for photographs or locks of hair,' she said and handed it back to the girl. She looked up nervously at the young feller.

'Do you like it?' he asked, stroking his chin as though mulling things over. Daisy noticed the shiny wedding band on the girl's finger. The young man took out his wallet and began rifling through the very small sheaf of notes. Daisy could see he was unsure. Not because he didn't want her to have the pretty object but he wasn't sure they could afford it.

'How long you been married?' Daisy asked. The girl looked up as though she couldn't believe it showed all over her face that she was a newly wed.

'We're on our honeymoon,' the man said. He looked at the girl as though she was more precious than any piece of gold. Daisy understood the problem immediately. He wanted his wife to have it but money was tight.

'Did I say twenty-five pounds? I meant eighteen!'

The looks that passed between them filled Daisy's heart with pure joy. The world wasn't such a bad place after all, she thought. The piece had come from a house clearance so Daisy would make a profit. And the locket was well worth eighteen pounds.

'I'll take it,' said the man. The girl looked as if she'd never stop smiling and the relief on his face sent a warm feeling to Daisy's heart. She slipped it in one of her special bags and exchanged the locket for the money. As they walked away, Daisy heard him say, giving the girl the bag, 'I hand you my heart.'

Tears rose to Daisy's eyes, and she turned away fumbling inside the car for a tissue.

'That was a really nice thing you do for that pretty girl.'

Daisy whirled at the sound of Bruno's voice. He was lounging against the wing of her car. Her heart dropped. He was invading her space. Buyers didn't come this side of the table. Okay, so he wasn't a buyer but it showed her he had a high opinion of himself.

'Jesus, fuckin' 'ell, you startled me,' she said. Her hand went to her brooch. She kept her fingers there and forced herself to smile at him, all the time watching as he registered the diamond brooch.

'I wouldn't like to frighten you, Daisy,' he said.

He was smartly dressed in a grey suit and the mac was slung over his shoulder.

'Do you have a pitch here?' It was obvious he didn't, else why would he be wandering around? She had to appear naïve though, didn't she? To her surprise he replied, 'I come because I think to myself Daisy will be here today. There's much money to be made. Daisy will not miss this last sale.'

'Then you thought right and today's been a good day.' She looked at her watch. Where the hell was Vera? For an ally against this man her friend was rubbish. 'Oh, dear,' she said. 'I'd 'ave liked to offer you a cuppa but I've drunk the last of my tea.'

'Perhaps when you finish we could go to the cafe and sit in the warm?'

'I'd like that,' she said, relieved he'd taken the bait. She saw his eyes fall to her brooch again. She picked up his hand. 'That's a nice ring you have.' She studied the silver piece. He wore it on the third finger of his right hand. The green stone glinted in the sun. 'If ever you want to sell it, I'll give you a good price.' She held his hand firmly, hoping he'd think she was flirting with him. And all the while her eyes were scanning, looking for the tell-tale dent where Samantha had caught her hand in the car door.

Her blood suddenly ran cold.

There it was!

'I couldn't possibly get rid of it,' he said. 'It belonged to my father. I don't think there's another like it; it came from the old country.'

Fuckin' liar, she thought. You greasy little prick! She also realised she might have made him suspicious so she grinned and said, 'I've been thinking about selling silver as well. It's in vogue at present. That'd make a fine start for me. Think about it anyway. I'd give you a hundred for it.'

His eyes widened. He hadn't expected that.

'A lot of money,' he said.

'I'm guessing it's hand crafted?' He nodded. The prick didn't know hand crafted from a hand job, Daisy thought. 'I've always got cash on me.'

He nodded thoughtfully. He really was a good-looking bastard, she thought. What a pity that handsome face masked an evil heart.

She thought about Vera. 'How long have you been here today?'

'Not too long,' he said. Then he didn't know Vera was with her. Though she might well have been on her own for all the company she'd had from her supposed best mate!

The crowd had thinned now.

She patted her money belt and felt his eyes on her. Jesus, I'm so obvious, she thought.

His dark brown eyes were gazing into hers; he was so fucking cocksure of himself.

'I could meet you in, what? Say, forty minutes in the cafe?'

He nodded, picked up her hand, and kissed the back of it.

'Until then, Daisy.' As soon as his back was turned she wiped her hand on the velvet cloth and shivered. She was suddenly aware of the woman from the secondhand clothes stall opposite smirking at her.

'Got yourself a pretty bloke there,' she said. Daisy laughed and raised her eyes heavenwards.

283

The wind had started up now, cutting across the field. Already the burger bloke was fastening down his shutters. Earlier the fruit and veg man had sold out by lowering his prices and selling off the produce in baskets for twenty-five pence each.

'Is that 'im? He's a fuckin' slimeball!'

From behind the MG Vera appeared in a red belted coat and a cloud of freshly splashed on Californian Poppy.

'Where the fuckin' 'ell you been an' where did you get that coat?'

'One question at a time, girly. I stayed away because I spotted 'im arriving about an hour ago. Can't mistake 'im from the description you gave me; even 'ad the same belted mac, didn't he? I saw 'im take it off an' sling it over his shoulder like he was some bloody film star!'

'So?'

'So I been shelterin' from this fuckin' cold in Dave's van. Dave used to be a client of mine...'

'Don't you start telling me about Dave, I'm asking about you. You're supposed to be lookin' out for me!'

'I been at the end of this row. See the market bloke stowing the new clothes away? That's where I been. I was bein' *unobtrusive!*'

'You don't even know what that means!' Vera looked pained and Daisy's heart went out to her.

'You can be very cruel sometimes, Daisy. I been keeping a *low profile*. You wasn't out of me sight for a minute!'

'Fair enough,' said Daisy, relenting. Then, 'Where did you get this coat?' She fingered the warm woollen material. Actually, she thought, it looked a treat on Vera.

'Me and Dave started talking about ol' times, Daisy, an' I 'appened to say I was cold now, an' he says we can't 'ave you cold, can we, girl, you was never cold to me. Then he says, pick yourself a coat, Vera, any one you like. So, do you like it, Daisy?' She did a twirl. Then she stood and faced Daisy, her hands on her hips. 'Let me tell you, missy, I really ain't 'ad my eyes off you for one second!' Now she stood waiting defiantly as Daisy packed her goods away. 'Was he wearing the ring?'

Daisy spun round after stowing the glass-topped case in the boot. 'It's Samantha's all right.'

'What 'appens now, Dais?'

'I led 'im on. He's copped an eyeful of my brooch, an' he's got to be bloody thick if he doesn't see how much it's worth. Anyway, I'm going to have a cup of coffee with him in the caff, so I need you to make yourself scarce again.'

Vera nodded, looked down to where the clothes man was still packing away and said, 'I'll hang around with Dave. He'll appreciate a bit of a chat in his warm van. You make sure you don't go off with that Eyetie. I can't see the caff from 'ere, but there'll be people about.'

'I'm going to set up something,' said Daisy.

'Just you make sure you're not alone with 'im.'

With everything packed away in the car, Daisy dropped Vera off at Dave's vehicle. He was a jolly feller and gave Vera a push up into the back of his van. Daisy wound down the window to wave Vera goodbye, but already girly giggles were coming out of the big van. Somehow it eased the tension Daisy was feeling.

She parked on the gravel outside the cafe and opened the door. The heat hit her and immediately she felt her fingers and toes begin to thaw out. She thought of Vera in her younger days, outside in all weathers waiting for punters. No wonder Vera was such a hardy woman.

He waved to her. He must have been watching the door. She grinned and walked over to the table in the corner.

'What do you want to drink?' He motioned to the waitress and before the elderly woman reached the table he'd taken out his wallet.

'No,' said Daisy, putting her hand out to stop him opening it. 'I've had a really good day, I insist on paying. A good strong cuppa for me, please. What you want, Bruno?'

'The same,' he said.

She sat back in the chair, watching the woman walking away in her plimsoles that looked too large for her. Daisy was aware of him watching her.

She made eye contact with him and smiled. She had to be very careful. Prove to herself that he'd known Samantha without him becoming suspicious – and possibly find out if he'd recently come from Hayling Island. Daisy knew, she just knew, call it a sixth sense, that the man sitting opposite her was a murderer.

'It's good,' she said. 'This tea hits the spot, certainly warms me up. I shall be glad to get home though.'

He put his hand across the table and touched her wrist.

'Daisy, I talk plain. You must know I like you?'

She nodded, though feeling his hand on her

286

made her want to be sick, and said, 'With your looks you could have anyone you wanted. I'm only a woman who works hard for a living because I have responsibilities.'

'I know you work hard for your family...'

She'd never told him about her family. How did he know she had a family? Had he been spying on her?

She had to think carefully about how much information she let slip. Enough to let him fall into a trap perhaps?

'Do you have a family?'

'No, not now,' he said. 'I had brothers.' Furrows appeared in his forehead, like it pained him to think about them. 'They are dead now.'

'I'm sorry,' she said. He didn't attempt to add anything. 'I live in Gosport,' she added. 'A large house that takes a lot of upkeep.'

'A good house.' It wasn't a question; it was a statement. 'And you used to work in the club by the ferry owned by the gangster, Roy Kemp.'

Fuck me, thought Daisy. Except he wasn't right, was he? *She'd* owned the club.

'You sound as though you don't like gangsters.'

'No, I don't,' he said. 'It was a gangster who killed my brothers.'

'Oh, I'm sorry,' she said. She licked her lips and took a sip of her tea. It was possible he was talking about Roy. Was this the man who'd burned down Daisychains?

She flinched as he reached across the table but it was the brooch he was interested in.

'You are not frightened you will lose it?'

She shook his hand away; he was a little too

close for her comfort and his cologne was too sickly.

'It's meant to be worn.'

He nodded thoughtfully. He's hooked on the diamond, she thought, really hooked. 'Look, I 'ave to go.' She looked at her watch and a thought suddenly struck her. If he had been watching her, watching the house, he would know the occupants. He wasn't stupid; he might also have recognised Vera at some time during this morning. He'd expect Vera to have arrived with her and to leave with her. If she pretended Vera wasn't here it would look suspicious.

'I must go. I came with a friend and I have to collect her.'

He sat back on the wooden chair as though he was very comfortable and pleased with himself.

'Can we meet again, without your friend?'

'I'd like that,' she said. 'Only it can't be for a while. The family, you see, I've got a belated birthday to celebrate.' He nodded. They discussed dates and Daisy ended by saying, 'Okay, seven o'clock then. It's a date.'

She leaned across the table top and kissed him on the forehead, then left after giving him the widest of smiles. But her heart was heavy. If either Roy or Vinnie knew what she was about to do, they'd fucking kill her.

288

# CHAPTER 31

As the Italian pushed open the side door of the Black Bear where he was renting a room, he smiled to himself.

Why were women so gullible? He only had to pretend he couldn't speak good English and the bitches fell for it every time. They loved his put-on pidgin English and his Italian phrases. Stupid cows.

He placed his raincoat over the back of a chair. It was good to get away from the smell of beer and fags that permeated the lower floors from the bar directly beneath. He threw himself on the bed, trying to ignore the sound of the juke box pounding out Leo Sayer. He knew the music, laughter, loud voices and probable arguments wouldn't stop until the pub was shut.

He thought about Daisy Lane. Once again he'd used his looks to get what he wanted. The silly cow had been flattered that he'd made it his business to find out about her. If only she knew he was simply checking that she *was* Daisy Lane, the only woman Roy Kemp valued besides his mother. She might be attractive in a pale blonde sort of way but she was too skinny for his taste.

He admired the way she worked hard, though. Italian women worked hard. His mother had worked hard when she'd first come to England bringing his three brothers with her.

She'd cleaned houses for the rich and offices for businessmen, and every penny she'd earned had gone to clothing and feeding his brothers and paying the rent on that dingy London flat.

He'd been in Italy, waiting for their father to die. Families stuck together, even if the head of the family was a fucking waster who'd gambled everything except the grandmother's house. With their own home gone they'd been forced to live like cattle, herded together in the tiny rooms.

When his father finally died, helped by a pillow – Bruno laughed to himself, remembering the surprise on the old man's face – he'd taken what money remained, and a work permit from a re-staurant owner allowed him to have a legitimate job in London.

The scenes in his head ran like a continuous film, never letting him forget how much he hated Roy Kemp and how he needed to destroy the gangster.

He'd been at work that night, in the sixties, when Roy Kemp had come looking for his young brothers.

Roy Kemp paid a visit to the flat, found his brother in and left him with his hand skewered to the table with a meat fork. At fifteen, his other younger brother had died from a gunshot wound. The innocent boy had been caught in the crossfire from a bullet fired by one of Roy's men.

And himself? He'd been doing well until a few years back, making and selling porno and snuff films until one of the women turned out to be Roy Kemp's mate's missus. Then that fuckin' clever DCI Endersby had found the bodies of the women he'd conned into performing in the films. The whole profitable game had blown up in Bruno's face.

When he'd got out of prison early for good behaviour the world had moved on. Not for Roy Kemp, though. He was still cock of the walk.

Changing his name from Gaetano Maxi to Bruno Pace meant Roy Kemp couldn't keep track of him.

Whatever else had gone wrong, his mate Maurie Nelson had believed in him.

'Pay me a wedge and you can join me, Bruno,' Nelson had promised. 'Together we'll topple Roy Kemp and take over his manor.' And with Nelson hand in hand with the coppers it all seemed possible.

Bruno opened his wallet and took out the photograph of his grandmother and kissed it. Behind it was the photograph of his mother who had died of cancer. Next came his photograph of the Pope and a small snapshot of himself. He smiled at his image. He used his looks to get what he wanted and he was proud of it. And he'd be prouder still when he could return to London to live. If Roy Kemp had a sniff that he was out of prison before he'd accomplished his deal with Nelson, things would become difficult. By the time that happened, if it happened, Daisy Lane would already be done for.

Women were so fucking stupid and gullible, even Daisy Lane.

He didn't want the skinny bitch, but he'd take her money and he'd sure as hell have that diamond the size of his fucking knuckle. He looked at his hand, noticed the ring. She'd liked that bit of silver, hadn't she? Let her pay good money for that as well, he thought.

He laughed, thinking of how he was getting back at Roy Kemp.

The club had gone up a treat, hadn't it? Petrol through the letter box, easy as pie. Must have set Roy Kemp back a bit, losing money like that. And now it looked as though someone else was using the site to rebuild. Not so Kemp's other burned-out places though. They looked like bombsites.

Roy Kemp's days were certainly numbered and the Krays were gone. The judges, helped by narks, had put Reg and Ronnie away for thirty years. They'd be old men when they got out.

'Happy Birthday, Dear Eddie, Happy Birthday to you!' Their voices rang out, filling the kitchen with sounds of happiness.

'I don't like bein' made a fuss of.' But anyone could see he did, thought Daisy.

Her eldest boy sat at the lunch table, wrapping paper all around him, sandwiched between Lol and Vera. In his hand, and he seemed loath to let go of it, was a card from Summer. Daisy had managed a peek and the simple message read, Happy Birthday, Thank you, love from Summer, and there was a solitary kiss. Daisy guessed that would be the card he would cherish.

What with everything that had happened – Samantha's death, Tyrone's exit from Eddie's business, Daisy's pregnancy and Daisy trying to be in ten places at once to earn money – Eddie's birthday had been a very low-key affair this year, with a lunch celebration held in his honour.

She tried to push away her fears. She wanted to stuff them in a box and throw away the key, if only for today at any rate. But thoughts of the Italian and what he'd done to Samantha, and to the other women he'd murdered, only made her realise how careful she had to be.

Her thoughts were interrupted by the sound of her sons bickering.

'It's my birthday, so it ain't you getting any presents. Put my dad's fuckin' knife back in my room, all right?'

Jamie nodded and scowled.

'Stop arguing,' she said, then watched as Eddie peeked at Summer's card again with a grin on his face. He had a soft heart, that one.

Eddie pretended not to know that Susie had made a chocolate cake, his favourite, and Joy had decorated it and put candles on the top. Susie was at this moment using her body as a shield so he wouldn't see her light them.

Susie turned round holding the cake high and Joy shouted, 'Can I help blow them out?'

'Course you can,' Eddie said, and Joy clambered on to his lap. As soon as the cake was set before him they both puffed out their cheeks. Daisy noticed Eddie let go his breath so it was Joy who blew out nearly all the candles.

'Make a wish,' he said to her. She giggled. Daisy thought she looked very pretty in a new frilly white dress, but she didn't reckon much to the dress's chances with the chocolate cake.

'It's your birthday, you should wish,' said Vera.

'Close your eyes, Joy, and wish with me. But

don't tell anyone what you've wished for or else it won't come true.' They both shut their eyes tight and Daisy thought how nice it was to have her family around her. Joy was giggling again, making her red curls bounce around her face.

A great sadness suddenly overtook Daisy. Eddie Lane, Eddie's father, had been the love of her life and oh, how she wished he could be here today. For one moment she could remember the feel of his arms around her, the touch of his lips on her skin–

And then the noise of the family suddenly hushed as a knock on the front door intruded.

Susie dropped a spoon and became flustered. Her voice wavered as she spoke, with her face as red as a cherry.

'I know who's at the door.' She paused.

'Let 'em in, then,' said Vera, 'It's so cold out there it would freeze the balls off a bleedin' brass monkey.'

Susie took a deep breath. 'I've met someone.'

As Daisy took in her words, she realised the significance. 'You mean someone very special, Suze? And that someone's at the door?'

Gratefully, Susie nodded. 'I 'ope you don't mind, but I invited him to meet you all an' we're not always all in the house at the same time. I don't want to spoil your special day, Eddie, I just want to add to it. I have some news for you. I'm getting married!'

The hush that followed could be cut with a knife.

Until Joy piped up, 'He's ever so nice.' Then the babble began again, heightened with stares of amazement at each other and at Susie.

Daisy got up from the table. 'Better bloody let 'im in then, or he'll die of the cold out there on me bleedin' porch an Suze won't want to marry a bleedin' corpse.' She took a step towards Susie and said, 'C'mon, girl, let the dogs see the rabbit.'

Daisy gave Vera a broad wink and turned to leave the kitchen.

'Why didn't you tell anyone?' Lol asked.

'I never felt anyone could love me the way Si did,' said Susie. 'So I thought I'd wait until I knew he was very special to me...'

Daisy stopped walking and threw her arms around Susie.

'Oh, sweetheart! He must be a lovely man if he's stolen your heart.'

Susie's hand was on the latch. Daisy saw her take a deep breath before opening the door and throwing herself into the arms of a happy-faced man, who was as tall as he was round and clutching a huge bunch of flowers.

'Get him inside, Suze.'

Daisy made herself very small against the hall wall as Susie pulled her man inside. Well, this really was a turn up for the books, thought Daisy. He was nothing like the spare-framed Si that Susie had adored and married. This man filled the hall. His rosy cheeks and large moustache made her think of a figure in a child's story book.

Daisy clicked the door shut, saying, 'Welcome to my home, let's shut all that cold out.'

'These are for you, Daisy. That's if I might call you Daisy? My name's Bill Boswell.' He handed her the flowers and already their hothouse scent was filling the hallway.

'Thank you, they're beautiful.' She pushed her nose into the blooms after taking them from him. They were sweet and musky. It was nice to receive flowers, she thought, but she could see he was very, very nervous. After foraging around in his overcoat's vast inside pocket he produced a bottle.

Champagne!

'I thought we could toast your son's birthday?'

'How lovely,' said Daisy. 'C'mon, take off your coat. I'll hang it over the banister.' He shrugged himself out of his coat and passed it to her. Susie was back in his arms again and gazing at him with adoring eyes. 'You'd better go in and show him off,' said Daisy. 'They're all waiting in the kitchen with bated breath.' Big as the bloke was, he was shaking. 'They won't bleedin' bite you,' she said. 'On second thoughts, Vera might!'

Daisy pushed the couple towards the kitchen and followed after laying the flowers on the hall table. She'd sort them out later. For now she didn't want to miss any of the action. There wasn't a sound coming from the kitchen. She could imagine them all craning their necks, waiting to see Susie's man.

His bulk almost blotted out the light from the doorway.

The day had already begun to darken. Daisy shivered; she hated the dull winter days.

'Here he is,' said Susie. Daisy heard the shyness in her voice and began clapping so that they'd all follow her example and ease the tension.

Vera was the first to speak. 'I bloody know you!'

Daisy's heart dropped. The man was a good few

years older than Susie; surely, he and Vera hadn't...

'You're Bill, the butcher from the market, ain't you!' Daisy's heart almost exploded with happiness; thank God this man wasn't another ex client of Vera's!

'I am that,' said the man, leaning forward to shake Vera's hand. By now she'd risen from her chair and was standing, hands on hips, waiting to assess him. Very protective of our Susie was Vera, thought Daisy. He had a deep voice, must be all that shouting out to customers. She could see in her mind's eye his large red and white van, always parked on the corner of South Street. He had several people working for him and they all seemed a jolly crowd.

'No wonder we've been 'aving some really good chops just lately,' said Eddie. 'What a clever girl to bring a butcher into the family!' Vera laughed at Eddie's wit but she pushed away Bill's outstretched hand and instead gave him a cuddle.

And then the room was filled with laughter and chatter, and Daisy moved forward and said to him, 'You're very welcome to join us. Jamie, go an' get another chair out of the living room. You can sit down then, Bill.'

Jamie, grumbling, got up. 'Don't take any notice of 'im.' Daisy put her face to the big man's ear and whispered, 'He's goin' through an awkward stage.'

'It's lasted his whole bleedin' life so far,' chimed in Eddie.

'See,' said Susie, 'I told you they're a bit special, my family.'

Jamie came back with the chair and set it at the table between Susie and Lol, who were all smiles.

Immediately the big man sat down, Joy came over and clambered on his lap. Daisy knew then that her Susie and her Joy were safe.

This man *would* look after them.

Again, everyone was chattering at once, introducing themselves and asking questions, and Daisy slipped back into the hall and picked up the champagne.

Back in the kitchen she pointed to the bottle and Vera got up and started rummaging in the dresser for glasses that were passed around the table. When Vera signalled to ask whether Jamie should be included, Daisy nodded. Going over to Eddie, she put the bottle on the table in front of him and whispered in his ear.

'You're the man of the house, you should propose a toast.'

He looked up at her and grinned. Daisy glanced over toward Jamie and picked up a glass, nodding to show he was going to be allowed a taste of champagne. His eyes stared back at her, cold and calculating. A shiver ran through her but then he smiled and all was right with her world. She shouldn't read too much into her imaginings, she told herself.

Eddie stood up and tapped on his glass with his knife that was still coated with remnants of chocolate cake.

'I'd like to say a few words,' he said. Daisy thought her heart was going to burst with pride.

'First of all I'd like to say thank you to my Auntie Susie for making this brilliant birthday lunch. Let's give her a clap.' Everyone did as he asked, then he had to quieten them down again.

'Then I want to say thank you for your kind wishes...' Again the noise erupted and he had to tap the glass once again. 'But most of all I'd like to propose a toast to Auntie Susie and Bill. I guess in due course we'll find out when and where the wedding'll be. To Susie and Bill.'

And then there was silence until Vera said, 'It would 'elp us to toast the bleedin' 'appy couple if the bleedin' bottle was opened and we 'ad somethin' to toast them with!'

## CHAPTER 32

Eddie had an hour to get showered and changed before Tyrone came. They were going to Joanna's nightclub at Southsea. He smiled to himself: for once it was a club that had nothing to do with Roy.

Susie, Bill and Joy had gone to the pictures to see *Saturday Night Fever.* Joy had just started a small tap and ballet class held on a Saturday morning and she'd been told it was a film with lots of dancing in. He sighed with happiness; it had been a great day and there was more to come.

He thought about Bill. He was a nice guy, an even-tempered bloke who'd taken with a pinch of salt all the ribbing he'd got this afternoon. And he adored Susie.

Daisy was having a shower and Vera was sitting at the table sorting her eyelashes out. Peeling them off and cleaning off the glue and putting them back in their funny little box ready to go on again tomorrow.

Eddie bounced open the bedroom door and smiled at Kibbles on the end of his bed. He went straight over to pat him.

Eddie's heart stood still.

Kibbles' eyes were open, like dull jewels but seeing nothing.

He pushed his hand into the cat's furry stomach. No warmth and no purring greeting.

'Hello, boy,' he said quietly. Eddie's heart was filled with sadness. He knew but didn't want to believe it.

Kibbles was dead.

His lifelong friend had gone from him.

Eddie picked up the cat and rocked him in his arms.

'No, oh, no, oh, no!' Tears were falling on the animal's fur and onto Kibbles' face. The cat's mouth was open, showing his still strong teeth, which only made Eddie cry out more. He thought of all the times he'd held the fat, heavy cat in just such a way, his legs and tummy uppermost.

And now Eddie carried the animal, light as a feather with age, downstairs to the kitchen.

Vera looked up as he entered. 'I got sardines for–' Her mouth stopped moving and she looked from Eddie to the cat and back again to Eddie.

'He's gone, 'asn't he? My boy's gone...'

Eddie nodded. Fresh tears stung his eyes.

'Give 'im 'ere,' Vera said.

She put out her hands and Eddie tenderly passed the cat into her waiting arms. She put her face into the mackerel-coloured fur and cried as though her heart would break, and Eddie stood by her side, his arm across her slight shoulders, and cried with her.

It was ridiculous how empty he felt inside.

Like a part of him had gone. Which, of course, it had.

The telephone rang and his mother shouted from upstairs, 'Don't worry, I'll get it.' Eddie heard her run down the stairs and pick up the receiver from the hall table. He knew it would be Tyrone. He squeezed Vera's shoulder, then wiped his running nose as he walked into the hallway.

'Tell 'im to forget about tonight...'

'Whatever's the matter?' Daisy said. Her face was scrubbed but worry suddenly etched itself across it. She was holding out the receiver to him.

'I can't talk... Tell Tyrone I'm not coming. Tell him I'll catch him later. Tell him... Tell him whatever you like.'

He turned away, knowing she'd do as he asked. He went back in to Vera who hadn't moved from the spot she stood in and still had her boy gathered in her arms.

'What's wrong?' Daisy bustled into the kitchen and stopped when she saw Vera holding the cat. 'Oh, my Lord,' was all she said.

Vera's face was a mask of pain. 'My boy's gone, Dais.' Daisy didn't, or couldn't, speak, but Eddie knew exactly how much she was hurting inside for Vera.

'Shall I make a nice cup of tea?' he asked. Eddie wondered why it was always a *nice* cup of tea that was supposed to work miracles. No amount of miracles was going to bring his mate back. The tears rose to the surface again but he forced

301

himself to be busy, to plug in the kettle.

'I don't want no fuckin' tea. I wants him buried *now*, in the garden.'

He turned and looked at Vera. She nodded at him. He looked at his mother for reassurance. In her damp eyes was the permission that he should do whatever Vera wanted.

'He don't want to be left goin' all stiff an' 'orrible...'

'All right, whatever you want, sweetheart,' said his mother. 'But don't you want to wait for Susie to be here?'

'He wasn't Susie's cat. He was *mine*.'

Vera was crying so much that her running nose, tears and spittle were all mixed up but her arms were like chain links around Kibbles' body. Then she asked, 'Can you bear to bury him, Eddie?'

He swallowed and nodded, then switched on the outside light and went out of the back door. A shaft of cold air passed him and crept into the kitchen. He looked up towards the windows and thought he saw a light flicker in Jamie's room. If the boy was awake maybe it would be better to tell him about Kibbles immediately. He looked at the window and made a split second decision that Jamie couldn't possibly be awake. If he was, surely he'd have shown his face before now with all the noise that had gone on. Why wake up the poor little sod to make him miserable? Though he doubted Jamie would shed a tear. He'd never ever seen him make a fuss of Vera's beloved pet.

In the shed he found the fork and spade and went down to a large tree that in summer blossomed with yellow flowers. He didn't know what the tree was called, only that he'd often found Kibbles asleep beneath its shady branches.

He allowed himself to cry while digging. There was no one to see or hear him, and even if there had been he wouldn't have cared. He knew when Vera brought out her 'boy' he'd have to be the strong one. Vera would need all the love his mother and he could give her.

When he judged the hole was plenty deep enough, bearing in mind that there might be predators who would dig up the body, he put down the tools. He stood for a moment smelling the fresh evening air and the peaty soil. It was bitterly cold but his exertions had made him sweat.

He didn't need to go back into the kitchen, for a sad little procession was coming towards him. Vera was still carrying the body but now he saw Kibbles had been swathed in the baby shawl he himself had worn as a child.

'You don't mind, do you, Eddie?' she asked.

'I'm honoured,' he said. He couldn't add any more because his heart was crying.

Vera knelt down on the grass and laid Kibbles in the hole.

'I couldn't close his eyes,' she said. She stared at the white bundle then up at Eddie. 'Cover him up,' she said.

Daisy helped her to her feet and Eddie began shovelling the dirt. It tore him in two watching the white shawl disappear beneath the soil.

When the hole was filled he stepped back and looked at his mother with her arm around Vera's shoulder. She nodded to him and they stood as though in prayer until Eddie felt the cold wind ruffle against his face and he saw that Vera was only wearing a thin silk blouse.

'Take her indoors, Mum.' Vera allowed herself to be led away. Eddie looked at the small mound of earth, wiped his nose and eyes with the back of his hand, and returned the tools to the shed.

In the kitchen he was surprised at how warm it was. He washed at the sink and dried himself on a tea towel. His mother had made Vera a very large gin and tonic and was forcing it down her.

Vera said, 'You want to go out with your mate? It's not that late, Eddie.' He shook his head.

'I feel like I've aged ten years.'

His mother turned to face him.

'Well you don't 'ave much of a choice about goin' out this evenin'. I phoned Tyrone. He felt same as I did that you need to get out of this 'ouse.' She looked at her watch. 'He'll be 'ere soon.'

'I don't feel...'

'An' that's precisely why you should go.'

There wasn't any use arguing. He went upstairs and before he opened the bathroom door he thought he heard movement from Jamie's room. He listened for a while but only silence rewarded him.

His mum was right: nothing would be gained by joining the two women downstairs. Vera needed to grieve and she'd do that better with his mother's help. He wasn't looking forward to going out with Tyrone but perhaps a bit of his mate's mindless chatter and a couple of pints might help him put the death of Kibbles into perspective.

304

The house was in darkness when Eddie arrived home. He let himself in and went through to the kitchen. Empty glasses had been left in the sink and a brandy bottle and gin bottle were on the table. Both looked as though they'd taken a hammering.

He'd had a couple of pints with Tyrone but then he'd stopped drinking. Eddie liked his head clear. There'd always been alcohol in the house and his mother had never kept him away from it. He just didn't like the out-of-control feeling it gave him. The thought of Kibbles' death was heavy in his heart but getting drunk wouldn't solve a thing, he knew that.

He climbed the stairs, peed in the toilet, and then went into his own room, switching on the bedside lamp.

He saw the screw of paper on his pillow alongside his father's flick knife. His brain noted the strangeness of it. He shrugged as he sprung the catch on the knife. The blade was dirty. He set it down on the bedside table.

The screw of paper was damp. His fingers picked it open. It took precious moments for the contents to register.

Two small milky white tendon-covered balls nestled in his palm.

His hand closed over them, his nails digging into his skin so hard he welcomed the pain. His heart and brain were appalled by the horror.

He reached the toilet and threw up.

The dismay, the revulsion of his discovery would never ever leave him. He gripped the sides of the bowl, his heart turned inside out. His head was like a volcano about to erupt as he knelt on the lino.

As soon as he felt able, Eddie rose and flushed the contents of his stomach away. He walked slowly to Jamie's room and opened the door, closing it softly behind him.

Moonlight streamed through the thin curtains.

Eddie sat down heavily on the bed and pulled his brother to a sitting position. There was no question the younger boy had been waiting for him. What surprised him momentarily was that Jamie didn't struggle but was staring fixedly at him with a grin on his face. Eddie put his hand across the boy's mouth then bent close. In his other hand, in front of Jamie's face, he held the crumpled paper.

'Doing this sick thing has hurt me more than you could ever imagine. But I'm telling you, ever breathe a word of this to Vera and *I will kill you.* And from this time on there is nothing between us. *Fucking nothing,*' he repeated.

Then he got up, and without a backward glance quietly left the room, went back into the bathroom and flushed Kibbles' eyes down the lavatory.

## CHAPTER 33

'Bloody big difference between this place and your club we've just had a meal in,' said Daisy. She looked around the Fulham bar. 'The Thames Club don't exactly live up to its posh name of club, does it? I swear since I was 'ere last they ain't even emptied the bleedin' ashtrays.'

She eased herself down on the stained red velvet stool, thinking it was a good job she was wearing a black dress; at least it wouldn't show the dirt. She set her velvet clutch bag on the table, careful to avoid a damp beer stain.

'A couple of drinks while I do a bit of business, Dais, then the three of us'll go on to somewhere a bit prettier. Come with me, Eddie.'

She nodded, and watched as her son, nearly as tall and broad as Roy, swaggered with him towards the bar. Roy shook the hand of the man Daisy knew as Maurie Nelson. Roy was always respectful, even to his enemies. Roy and her Eddie made a handsome pair, she thought, both suited and booted for London town.

At first she'd wondered where Roy was taking her and Eddie when they left the security of his Rolls Royce to walk down the badly lit, rubbish-strewn passage to the dreary frontage that was the entrance to the club. The light seemed to fade so quickly these winter afternoons. She was even more surprised to find the place heaving with cigarette smoke, beer fumes and mostly male customers.

Almost before she'd had a chance to have a good look around, a barmaid arrived with a large brandy on a tray for her, then slipped back into the crowd before Daisy could thank her.

Instead, she raised her glass to Roy who nodded back at her from the bar where the customers were knee deep trying to get served. Roy got preferential treatment wherever he went. Daisy had never known him wait in line for anything.

Suddenly screaming and shouting filled the air. Daisy rose to peer through the heaving mass of bodies and saw the barmaid who'd just brought her drink fighting with another woman.

'You fuckin' slag! What fuckin' right you got to take 'im away from me...' Daisy heard the words and sat down again. She'd no wish to get into a slanging match between two women over some bloke unable to keep his dick in his trousers. As she sat down she caught sight of Teddy Baird, who said something to the man beside him then began making his way to the gents'. Maurie Nelson was watching him.

Daisy hadn't really wanted to come up to London but Roy had said, 'You need some time away from Vera and her sadness. Come up with Eddie.'

'I need to be with Vera,' she replied. And as a cloud of foul-smelling smoke from some bloke's cigar washed over her, she wished she *was* home. But Roy was right, she thought. Daisy had never seen her smart friend slouching around the house, without make-up and just drinking more tea than she'd ever drunk before. The one saving grace was that it wasn't the gin Vera was on. At least she wasn't going down the alcohol road to ease her grief, though she was taking a sleeping tablet nightly from the pack Doctor Dillinger had given her. And thank God for that, thought Daisy.

Daisy had arranged to meet Bruno, and she needed Vera there in a sensible frame of mind. She didn't want to think about her fear, didn't want to think about how she really had very little control over her own life and the lives of her loved ones.

Still, with Vera looking out for her, everything should go according to plan. Samantha's killer *had* to be brought to justice. Daisy was sure her plan would work, but she couldn't do it without Vera's help. She put a hand over her stomach and whispered, *'Don't worry, little one. No harm will come to you.'*

Eddie had driven her MG up to London and Daisy would be returning alone. And now she looked about her and sipped her brandy and watched the two best-looking blokes in the club chatting at the bar. She was also aware of the women's eyes on them. It was easy to see what was going through their minds!

'Hello, Daisy!'

Her eyes were drawn to the man who'd called her name.

'Hi, Teddy,' she called back. Teddy Baird was a lovely bloke but a bit too volatile for her tastes. He'd emerged from the toilet just in time to witness another scuffle start.

This time it was the blokes' turn.

Baird charged up to the other end of the bar, elbowing drinkers out of the way to get a look at what was going on.

Maurie Nelson suddenly drew a knife and drove it at the man who'd come into the Thames Club with Baird. A woman screamed, then all hell was let loose. Nelson was stabbing the man repeatedly in the back then began slashing at his face and neck.

Arms and fists were everywhere. Blood was spurting about like burst water pipes. Daisy saw

Teddy Baird try to get the knife away from Nelson and then she gasped as a flash of steel went into Baird's back and was withdrawn. He was sinking to the floor, with Nelson leaning over him, and then the knife was plunged into his chest. The smell of sweat and the metallic tang of blood mixed with the stench of fearful excitement filling the place. Daisy saw her son move towards the fray but Roy held him back. He said something to her boy and Eddie's body seemed to lose its tenseness. Roy looked angry as he stepped back and into the alcove away from the brawl in front of him. He stood watching, his face as black as thunder.

Daisy watched too, mesmerised as she heard Teddy Baird begging for his life.

He managed to roll away and tried to rise. Then it was as if some inner force filled him, and he began striking out with his knife again.

Daisy saw he'd now got out of Nelson's clutches, but that his neck was pouring with blood where Nelson had gone for his throat.

She was terrified that Roy or Eddie would get hurt. Around her the noise was deafening. She moved to get them in her sights again and had to duck as a bottle narrowly missed her on its way to smash against the wall. There was no way she could reach Eddie and Roy without them becoming involved in the fighting, and there was no way they could get to her, either.

From her vantage point away from the fray she could at last see Roy watching her. He was calm, his slate-grey eyes not missing a move. She could sense he had no intention of getting involved and every intention of persuading Eddie that it had nothing to do with either of them.

She could see Teddy Baird and Maurie Nelson amongst the dog ends on the floor, knives flashing as they found flesh time and time again.

And then fresh screams rent the air as a machete-wielding feller heaved the weapon in an arc until it stopped, embedded in Maurie Nelson's back.

Nelson fell.

Blood was everywhere; the sight and smell made Daisy feel sick. And then suddenly the men seemed to be moving about. Maurie Nelson was being carried out of the door by a couple of men and Teddy Baird was half kneeling, half lying, well and truly injured on the floor of the club in a huge pool of blood.

Roy's voice rang out. 'For fuck's sake get him out of 'ere and get him some help!'

Teddy Baird was dragged to his feet by some of the men.

Eddie finally pushed through the mass of people to Daisy.

'We got to go before the coppers come, Mum.'

Daisy was on her feet in a flash. 'What about Roy?'

'Forget him. He'll be along later. Nelson's had it.'

It took her a few seconds to register that he meant Nelson was dying, or possibly even dead.

Daisy felt herself being propelled along the alleyway behind Teddy Baird and his mates who were half dragging, half carrying him towards a waiting car.

'Where'll Baird go?'

'Don't worry about that,' Eddie said. 'My job's to see you get to Roy's club safe and sound.'

When Daisy saw Roy's car she breathed a sigh of relief.

She asked again, 'What about Roy?'

'He'll sort it,' Eddie said. He started up the car and within minutes the Thames Club was behind them.

'I don't want to go to a club, I want to go to his mother's house,' Daisy said. She knew her voice was shrill. She was shaking and sweating at the same time. She'd just witnessed a murder, possibly two. 'I don't see 'ow Baird'll survive, he's bleeding like a stuck pig. He's cut about everywhere,' she said.

Eddie let go the steering wheel and touched his mother's hand. Daisy realised she'd been turning her velvet clutch bag over and over in her fingers without thinking.

'Stop that,' he said. 'It'll be all right.'

When they reached the street and Daisy saw the light shining through the curtains and on to the pavement from the terraced house, she almost cried with happiness.

The sound of Eddie's key in the door brought Violet scurrying into the hallway.

'Whatever's the matter...'

Violet got no further for Daisy threw herself into Roy's mother's arms, and drew comfort from the motherly roundness of the woman. For a few seconds neither of them moved, until Eddie urged them into the kitchen, shutting the door behind him.

Violet extricated herself and drew Daisy towards the kitchen table, sitting her down on a chair. Daisy could hear Violet and Eddie talking but their words were like bees buzzing around in her head until she heard Violet say to Eddie, 'Get the kettle on.'

Daisy sat with her elbows on the table and her head in her hands. In her mind she was exchanging the knifed figures for her Eddie, or even Roy. It could so easily have been them lying in the pools of blood. That was what was going through her brain until she heard Violet ask, 'Is it done, then?'

'Baird's got to be taken somewhere safe.' Eddie was clattering cups and Daisy heard the tap running.

'So Nelson's sorted?'

Daisy raised her head and looked at Violet, who was busy cutting scones.

'Did you know this was going to 'appen? Violet?'

Violet said, 'These scones are so warm they're crumbling as I cut into them.'

'Violet, you knew! You fuckin' knew that Maurie Nelson was goin' to cop it, didn't you?' Violet went on buttering the soft floury rounds. Daisy looked at Eddie; she could tell he was keeping something from her from the way he refused to meet her eyes. She got up and went over to him.

'Look at me! Did you know today that bloke was gonna get fuckin' knifed?'

Eddie gave a long drawn out sigh. She got hold of his arm and twisted him around so he was facing her. She felt small and insignificant glaring

313

up at him.

'Did you fuckin' know?'

Violet said, 'Come on, love. There's no need to get uptight about this. Sooner or later someone was gonna put an end to Maurie Nelson. The man was destroying Roy, you could see that...'

Daisy collapsed back down on the chair.

'Was this planned for today?'

Eddie fell on one knee in front of the chair. 'No, no, NO! You mustn't think we were in that place this afternoon to view a fuckin' murder!'

'I don't understand...'

'You don't need to,' Violet soothed. 'It's been on the cards that Nelson had come to the end of his little spree. Roy couldn't take another of his clubs bein' burned down. And to hear that the coppers had paid Nelson more'n a thousand quid for information received was like a red rag to a bull...'

'Roy never 'ad nothin' to do with this, did he? Tell me he didn't?'

'Let's just say Nelson had it coming to him–'

Daisy didn't let him finish. 'But Roy took us to that place. You could 'ave got killed, Eddie!'

'Mum, stop it! That's the last thing Roy'd do, to involve me or you in anything where we'd get hurt. You must know that!'

Of course she did, didn't she? Calm down, she told herself. Roy loved Eddie like he was his own son. Hadn't she seen him hold Eddie back when the fighting started? He'd also made Eddie get her out pretty sharpish before the cops came around, so that showed how little he wanted her and Eddie involved.

It was then she remembered the pub near Baird's place and the conversation Roy and Baird had had. Ten thousand pounds being the sum mentioned.

'Roy has to protect his empire, you know that, Daisy,' said Violet in a soft voice. 'Nelson fancied himself as the next empire builder. The bloke had a nasty habit of sitting on both sides of the fence and villains don't like other villains grassin' them up. Coppers are paying hefty sums to put the likes of Roy away.' Violet looked over towards Eddie and smiled as she put a plate of buttered scones and a pot of home-made raspberry jam on the table. 'Take one of these, Daisy, and get it down you. Think of that lovely baby growing inside you. You really need fattening up, love. You should be eating for two now. Eddie, you done fiddling with that tea yet?'

Daisy turned as she heard the sound of the front door opening.

Roy couldn't get his key in the lock fast enough and as soon as he was inside and the door had slammed behind him, he strode into the kitchen and squared up to Eddie.

'Why didn't you go to the club like I told you?' He could feel the nerve at the corner of his lip flickering.

He wasn't prepared for Eddie's reply, but just seeing him and Daisy safe in his mother's kitchen took the wind out of his sails. He let out a great sigh as Eddie said, 'Mum wanted to come 'ere. Nothin' wrong with that, is there?'

Turning from Eddie, Roy pulled Daisy up from

the kitchen chair and into his arms.

'I didn't know where you were,' he said. He could feel her shaking. 'I been imagining all sorts of stuff an' none of it nice.' He could smell her scent. He buried his face in her neck. 'I wish to God I'd never taken you with me this afternoon.' But she was safe, that was all that mattered, he thought.

'There's going to be a lot of fall out from this murder...' He released Daisy and looked over to Eddie. 'Just obey my rules in future, lad.'


# CHAPTER 34

Vinnie Endersby wondered how many more times he'd knock on the door of this terraced house before the place was pulled down in the name of progress. So many of these cosy little houses had given way to high-rise flats. He had the feeling that the flat-dwellers would present their own problems sooner or later. He smiled at the shiny brass door knocker and wondered if Violet had been baking.

As she opened the door the lemony smell enveloped him.

'You knew I'd just pulled a lemon cake from the oven, didn't you, love?' She turned and walked back down to the kitchen and he followed her. At the dresser she began taking down china cups and saucers. 'He's in the garden. Them leaves from that ol' willow make it fair slippy for me when I'm putting out the washing.'

'Is it all right if I just go on out?'

Violet turned her deep violet eyes towards him. 'Course it is,' she said.

'That's a nice pile of leaves you got there, mate,' said Vinnie. Roy, dressed in jeans and a dark pullover, stopped sweeping and leaned on the sturdy brush. He didn't look at all surprised to see him, Vinnie thought.

'What are you doing in this bleedin' neck of the woods, copper?'

Vinnie could see why the women went for Roy Kemp. They'd undress him with their eyes even if he didn't have money and power. Despite the rough clothes his muscular frame hadn't an ounce of fat.

'Still go to the gym, Roy?'

Roy's laugh was like a rumble coming from deep down inside him.

'You didn't come all this way to ask me that?'

'No, I was in the neighbourhood and decided to look up an old mate.'

Again Roy laughed. 'We've never been mates, Vinnie. We use each other, that's all, except for the connection we both got to Daisy Lane.'

Vinnie shivered. It was bloody cold out here, he thought. The heatwave they'd had in the summer only made it worse.

'C'mon, copper,' Roy said. 'I can see you got no stomach for a bit of fresh air. Let's go inside.'

Vinnie followed him back into the house and the heat hit him as soon as he entered. Roy washed his hands at the butler sink and wiped them on a tea towel while Vinnie pulled out a kitchen chair and sat at the table. Violet looked at him and smiled, her blue-rinsed permed hair making her look like a small dumpy doll.

She asked, 'Lemon or fruit?' He must have looked perplexed for she said, 'Cake.'

Vinnie said, 'Lemon, please.'

Roy hooked a long leg over a chair and slid it to the table, opposite Vinnie. Then he looked as though he'd suddenly forgotten something and said, 'You need any help, Ma?'

'Since when have I needed help to feed your friends?'

Roy treated her to a smile, then turned to Vinnie and asked, 'What you got a bee in your bonnet about this time?'

'The murder of Maurie Nelson at the Thames Club—'

Roy broke in with, 'I 'eard about that. Must 'ave been some scary do.'

Vinnie said, 'You're telling me you weren't any-where near the place?'

Roy shook his head. 'I 'ad Daisy an' her boy Eddie up here. We had a nice lunch, salmon, in my Rainbow Club. The fish must 'ave upset Dais because she felt bad; well you know what these pregnant women are like...'

Vinnie had taken a long time to reconcile him-self to Daisy and Roy producing a child. His heart was beating fast but he nodded his head know-ingly at the vague illnesses of pregnant women.

'So we came back here. Luckily Mum was home, so she took Daisy under her wing an' me an' Eddie an' Charles played cards 'till the early hours.'

Vinnie didn't look at Violet as she set a cup of tea and a big slice of fragrant lemon cake in front of him. He knew she'd back up Roy.

'I hadn't got around to asking you where you were, but thanks for jumping the gun and telling me anyway. This is only a social visit.' Vinnie knew Roy was lying, but what could he do about it? The alibi fitted neatly together, like pieces of a jigsaw puzzle.

'You got Detective Chief Superintendent George Mould on this, ain't you? Good bloke, he was in on the Hanratty case and the Christine Keeler fiasco.' Roy nodded his head. 'Good bloke,' he said again. Then, 'When I heard about Maurie Nelson the next morning I thought, what a waste of a good informer.'

'Give us a break, Roy. You going to tell me what you done with Baird?' Roy took a drawn out swig of his tea as though considering the pros and cons.

'Sure. Ireland,' he said. 'He's cut up bad. Thought he was going to pop his clogs.'

'You'd better get him back to London. If he stays away they'll crucify him and he'll be found guilty. Much better he comes back here of his own accord.'

'Baird can't do fuck all at present – except die if he ain't cared for properly. He's got porridge for a face. His good looks'll return if he's allowed to get better in peace.' Roy picked up his slice of cake and bit into it. 'Good, this is, Ma,' he said. At the sink up to her elbows in suds, Violet preened at the compliment.

Vinnie said, 'I don't have to tell you how the law works.'

319

'No, my old cocker, you don't,' Roy said. He pushed his cup to the middle of the table and shook his head at Violet's enquiring look. Vinnie did the same but said, 'Lovely bit of cake that, Violet. Filled the spot.'

'You been down the Thames Club, I take it?'

'Might as well not have bothered, Roy. We got to keep the information under wraps for a while. Not that we got anything from the club. It was cleaned through and through before the coppers got there yesterday and nobody saw nothin'.'

'Well, well, well, who'd 'ave thought it, Vinnie?'

'I think Maurie Nelson's death is a bonus for you, Roy. You can breathe again now that he's gone.'

Roy nodded his head. 'You're right, I can. And you know as well as I do that you'll make Baird your number one suspect. You'll also let him go after a costly trial. Nelson was bleedin' trouble for me – and for you. I got a feelin' you're glad he's gone an' all. The last thing you coppers need coming out is all the dirt on the money you lot paid him for services rendered over the years. He was a fuckin' grass, an' good fuckin' riddance, I say.'

Roy gave a sigh that seemed to come from deep inside him. He stared at Vinnie then said quietly, 'Now, talking of deaths and murders. You any further in finding out who killed Vera's Samantha?'

Vinnie shook his head. To be honest, he was hoping Roy Kemp had put out feelers and come up with something. Obviously he hadn't.

'We think he's foreign. Nice looking by all accounts. Nobody seems to know much and it

320

feels like we're banging our heads against a bloody brick wall. The bloke's clever, I'll give him that. I don't believe he's a genuine nine-carat mass murderer...'

'How come, Vinnie?'

'He's got this thing with the stick going, but he slits throats as well as strangling. Bit extreme, some of the stuff he's done.'

'So he's not true to type?'

Vinnie shook his head. 'I think he wants us to believe it to disguise his real motivation...'

'Getting a bit fuckin' deep for me, Vinnie boy. Now, let's talk about lighter stuff. I'm issuing you with an invite to Gosport on Friday night. I'm setting Eddie up with his own business.'

## CHAPTER 35

Daisy dressed with care, a plain black outfit, black high heels, and the diamond brooch. She studied the gold setting and, for perhaps the first time, saw what a marvellous piece of workmanship it was. She remembered Violet pinning it to her breast all those years ago and telling her that was all she needed on a black knitted dress. Violet said she had class, with or without the brooch. Daisy's gold bangle caught the light and she smiled. She cared next to nothing for the diamond, but the plain gold bracelet that Eddie Lane had given to her so many years ago was treasured.

She brushed her hair until it shone, framing her

face in a long bob. She stood away from the mirror and decided she was pleased with her reflection. She was beginning to show now, the baby inside her giving her slim body roundness. She stood, her hands to her belly, looking with aching wonder at what she knew was her child within.

'Where you meetin' the bastard?'

Vera seemed to have appeared from nowhere and was standing in the bedroom doorway watching her. Daisy turned and smiled at her. Vera had lost weight and her eyes seemed to have sunk back in her head. Even her false eyelashes looked wrong, somehow – probably for the first time in her life Vera had got them on straight.

Earlier on Daisy had watched through the kitchen window as Vera sprinkled the thin petals of Michaelmas daisies, the last vestige of colour in the garden, over the grave of Kibbles.

'Ferry Gardens, the Victory pub,' said Daisy. Butterflies had started fluttering in her stomach. What if anything went wrong? She pushed the negative thoughts away. She couldn't afford to think Bruno might hurt her.

'Well I 'ope you're puttin' a bleedin' coat on, it's taters out there.'

Daisy picked up the black belted coat off the bed.

'See?'

'That's all right, then,' said Vera. 'You nearly ready?'

Daisy nodded. Earlier, she'd waved goodbye to Roy, Eddie, Jamie and Vinnie. They'd gone down to the pool hall to admire the place.

Apart from Roy, no one had set foot in there

except the builders and decorators, and herself and Vera who'd had a preview before tonight's get together.

Daisy asked, 'What did you reckon to the pool hall?'

'Not too big, not too small. It can easily be run by one person, especially with the bouncers that Roy's providing. Young Eddie'll have nothing to do except go in there and make his mark on the place.'

'I wouldn't mind it,' said Daisy.

'You could 'ave anything you wanted, you stupid cow, if only you'd give Roy the nod.'

Daisy sighed. It seemed whatever she said Vera wanted to have a go at her. Still, Vinnie had arrived as promised to celebrate the handing over of the keys. She and Vera said they'd get there an hour later. When the boys had finished playing with the balls and cues, Daisy had said.

'I'm a bit peeved Susie ain't gonna show 'er face,' Daisy said.

'She'd 'ave a bloody 'ard job, bein' as she an' Joy's in Benidorm with her butcher,' said Vera.

'She deserves a bit of 'appiness...'

'Don't we all, Dais? You more'n most.'

'I'm all right,' said Daisy. 'Least, I will be when we got that bugger confessing to what he did to our Samantha.'

Vera said, very seriously, 'You know what I did today, Dais?' Daisy shook her head. 'I went into the fishmonger's and bought a nice bit of cod for Kibbles' tea. It wasn't until I was on the bus that I remembered...'

Daisy went and put her arms around her.

'You didn't bring it home. What did you do with it?'

'Left it on the bus seat when I got off, Dais.'

Daisy laughed and Vera joined her.

'That's better,' said Daisy. 'I been missing hearing you laugh.'

'Silly bitch,' said Vera. She looked at her watch. 'We better get it over with. It's time.'

'I'm going to park round the back of Heavenly Bodies an' walk down the High Street,' said Daisy. 'I want you to get on the other side of the road, and watch me like a fuckin' hawk! He mustn't know you're followin' me else he'll smell a rat.'

'He's the fuckin' rat,' said Vera.

'I know, but I got to make out I'm there just for him. As soon as I got 'im in the pub I need you to watch while we chat for a while. You got to stay out of sight, Vera. We can't do any fuckin' thing without proof. He'll 'ang around me as long as he thinks he can get his hands on me wad of notes and this little beauty.'

She ran her fingers over the smooth surface of the large diamond.

'Keep your eyes on me until I get up and leave him to go to the toilet. When I come back an' sits down, I'll 'ave to play it cool but I'll give you a sign. Then run like fuck round to the pool hall and get them buggers out of there pretty sharpish an' over to the Victory.'

'Bloody good job the pool hall's right opposite the Victory then, ain't it? If it was any further away I might break me neck runnin' in me 'igh 'eels!'

'For fuck's sake, can't you wear flat shoes just

324

for once?'

Vera gave her a look that might have turned the milk sour if it hadn't been tucked away in the fridge.

'I don't wear *flat shoes!* Supposin' one of me old clients sees me, they'll think I've let meself go!'

Daisy looked at Vera's grief-ravaged face and thought, thank God she's on the road to recovery. Vera hadn't had an outburst like that since before Kibbles had died. Again she put her arms around the small woman.

'Please, please make sure you get them into the bar, *after* I've been to the lavatory but before he tries to get me outside. He'll not want me to look in my bag. And once we're outside, he'll 'ave me up an alleyway quicker than that.'

Daisy looked down at the brooch. The enormity of what she was doing filled her with fear. She thought about Samantha and what the Italian had done to her, and shivered. Then she shook her hair from her eyes and stood very straight. 'It might not be him, but if it is I'm going to nail the bastard. He'll never hurt another woman!'

Daisy parked the car round the back of Bemister's Lane. The lamplight cast shadows in the darkness.

'Get out, then,' she said to Vera.

'I can't let you do this!'

'Don't you start going all dramatic like a bleedin' Joan Crawford and John Garfield movie.' Daisy was cross. 'I've planned this, an' if you mess it up, I'll bleedin' swing for you.'

'That's just what I don't want, you 'anging

anywhere. Oh, Daisy!'

'Get out of this bloody car!' Daisy leaned across her and pulled up the chrome lever and pushed Vera from the two-seater. She saw Vera had a brown paper bag in her hands. 'What you got in there?'

'A pair of flat shoes, Daisy.'

A lump rose in Daisy's throat. That Vera had brought flatties to run in touched her deeply. She could smell her perfume. In a funny sort of way it comforted her and gave her courage.

'When we get to the bottom of Bemister's I'll go on ahead in case he's not inside as planned, but outside the pub.'

Vera didn't answer her and Daisy strode off before she took the easy way out and forgot the whole thing.

Daisy walked swiftly down the High Street, past Woolworth's and Littlewoods and the Porthole fish and chip restaurant. A fine mist had come in off the sea. It would rain later, she thought. She stopped for a while, breathing in the crispy batter smell, and looked about her. There were very few people about in the cold, certainly no one waiting outside the Victory.

With her heart thudding against her ribs, she pushed against the heavy door of the pub and stepped into the warmth and stink of beer and fags. She looked around but couldn't see him for the mass of people in the bar; then she spotted him at the end of the room, where he was sitting in an alcove. The jukebox was loud and it seemed as if Elvis was running through her veins as she made her way to the counter.

'Orange juice, please,' she said. The barman scowled at her. She knew he didn't like serving unaccompanied women so she said, 'I'm meeting that bloke over there.' She waved at Bruno, who waved back. Daisy hadn't expected him to get up and come across to greet her. If he had he'd have lost the tenure to the alcove seats.

Daisy wound her way towards him through the crowd of sailors and girls.

'I am so glad you come,' he said in his broken English accent.

'I nearly didn't,' Daisy said. 'I've been on my feet all day today. Still, that's what it's all about, isn't it, making money?'

He nodded and a big smile split his face. Daisy put her drink on the table and took off her coat.

'Oh, bugger,' she said. She unfastened the brooch and slipped it in her bag. Then she slid onto the seat beside him, putting her handbag in between them.

He was looking at her with creases in his forehead. 'What's the matter?'

'The clasp is faulty on my brooch. Better to leave it in my bag in case I lose it.' Then she took a sip of her drink and said, 'I hope you haven't been waiting long?'

'I would wait all day for you,' he said.

'Oh, that's a lovely thing to say,' she said, pulling out her bag again. 'Excuse me,' she said. 'Now I think I've let my brooch slide in between the money. I don't want to pull it out by mistake when I get my round of drinks.' She fished out the brooch and put it in the pocket of the bag, making sure he could see the large roll of banknotes she had. Then the bag went back on the seat but with the clasp open. She was chattering away and looking at him the whole time. She hoped it all seemed natural. The last thing she needed was for him to suss her out.

He was wearing some kind of sickly cologne and his hair was greased. Brylcreem? she wondered. She realised she was going to have to pretend she liked him otherwise he'd discover her deception. Questions ... she should ask him questions.

'Where in Italy do you come from?' She barely heard his reply for her eyes were scouring the front window, over his left shoulder, for the unobtrusive Vera.

Bruno picked up her hand. She forced herself to look into his eyes. She felt the ring digging into her skin.

'It belonged to my mother,' he said. 'It was made especially for her by my father.' Daisy traced her finger around the dent where Samantha had caught it in a car door, and thought about the out and out lie he was telling her. Last time she'd asked about it, it had been his father's ring, handed down to him. He wasn't a very good liar!

'I don't think I've ever met anyone quite like you before,' she said. Catching sight of Vera peeping through the door as it opened to allow some drunken young men to enter, Daisy said, 'Will you excuse me? I must go to the toilet.'

'*Non ti scordar di me*, Daisy.'

'What does that mean?'

'Forget me not,' he said.

'Oh, how lovely,' replied Daisy. What a slimy

git, she thought. She got up, leaving her handbag on the seat. She could feel Vera watching her. In the toilet she stood with the door closed and laid her head against the cubicle's tiled walls.

She'd suggested the Victory because the manager usually closed his eyes to the slags touting for business with the sailors, and the scuffles that frequently occurred, unless it was absolutely necessary that the police should put in an appearance. Both she and Bruno would be practically invisible there. She suspected he knew this, otherwise he'd never have agreed to meet her in a public place. And no one would cause a fuss if they happened to see him rifling through her handbag.

When Vera returned with Roy and Vinnie, the evidence of the ring and her stolen articles on his person would confirm he wasn't all he pretended to be. If Bruno was the killer, Roy and Vinnie would soon get it out of him.

Then she thought about Vera. Her business had picked up with Lol's popularity, and Lol was very chirpy, thinking about the surgery she would eventually have.

Susie was happy and her future was assured.

Roy had not only given Eddie the key to a super business he could run single-handedly, but her son would be kept an eye on. And Jamie ... well, he had Vinnie, who might even knock a bit of sense into him.

What more could she ask for if anything happened to her?

Daisy pulled the chain. She'd given Bruno time enough to look through her bag.

She smiled as she sat down next to him and

took hold of his hand again.

'Where were we?' She glanced at her bag, picked it up and put it on the table. She could tell by its lightness that he *had* taken her large roll of money. Daisy pulled his head towards her and kissed him lightly on the lips.

'I did not expect that but it was very nice,' he said.

Daisy kissed him again. He had his back to the window that looked out over Gosport High Street. Vera was still peeping in. Daisy caught Vera's eye and winked. Please go, she thought. *Please, Vera, go and get Roy.*

It cost her three more nauseating kisses with his repulsive tongue in her mouth before the pub door flew open and Roy, closely followed by Vinnie and Eddie, burst in. Vera was panting heavily and leaning on Jamie for support which he didn't seem to like one bit.

'Oh, Vera,' Daisy said, standing up, 'I'm so glad you're 'ere.'

For a moment it seemed as if nothing was happening. Roy and Vinnie approached the table. Their faces were grim.

Then Bruno suddenly seemed to come to life, almost as if a switch had been turned on inside him. He jumped to his feet, but Daisy held fast on to him. He mustn't get away, she thought, not now. People parted like a hot knife through butter as Roy swept towards them both.

'Fuckin' hell!' Bruno said, then started swearing at Daisy in a torrent of Italian.

'Well, well, Gaetano Maxi,' said Roy. 'I believe you've taken Daisy's money and her brooch.'

'Gaetano?' Daisy said. 'He said his name was Bruno Pace.' She was surprised Roy had called him by a different name.

'You fuckin' cunt, you planned this, you bitch!'

'He speaks bleedin' good English now, Vera,' said Daisy. 'The pretty talk is only put on to win the women over.'

Bruno stood in front of Roy, his eyes darting for an escape route, but he was hemmed in by Roy, Vinnie and Eddie. Now Daisy was at Roy's side, her heart thumping, but she knew she had nothing to fear now.

Customers gathered around them, shouting and jeering as soon as they heard the Italian had stolen something. Daisy could smell the fear coming from him.

'Fuckin' Eyetie. Bleedin' wop.'

'Turn your pockets out,' said Vinnie. Bruno ignored him.

'Turn your fuckin' pockets out,' repeated Roy. He made a move towards the Italian who immediately shoved his hand in his trouser pocket and came out with Daisy's brooch and her money. He threw them on the table.

Vinnie said, 'Take off that ring.'

Bruno stared at him as though his words were difficult to understand, then he twisted the ring from his finger and put it down on the table with the other stuff. Daisy stared at it.

'That's Samantha's ring, isn't it?' she said.

Vera grabbed at the ring and squinted at it, turning it round in her fingers.

'It is an' all, Daisy.' She shoved it towards Bruno's face. 'How did you get this?'

331

He didn't answer.

Roy said, 'I'm thinkin' you're using a different name so I wouldn't guess you were out of the nick.'

Bruno didn't bat an eyelid.

Vinnie said, 'You might as well come clean. You'll be going along to Gosport Police Station and they're very persuasive round there.' Vinnie looked at Daisy. Their eyes met. Daisy shivered, realising that whatever there was in the past between her and Vinnie had now gone. Vinnie frowned as he returned his gaze to Bruno.

The Italian seemed to be weighing up his chances. Daisy was surprised when he said, 'I'm ... I'm going into business with Maurie Nelson. I need money...'

Daisy opened her mouth to speak but Roy shook his head and she clammed up.

Vinnie said, 'You tricked the women out of their money and jewellery and–'

Bruno broke in with, 'Stupid slags, they deserved everything they got.'

Vera couldn't control herself. She shouted, 'Maurie Nelson's dead, you bastard. He can't 'elp you now.'

Daisy saw Bruno's face, saw the amazement in his eyes. He hasn't heard, she thought. He doesn't know about Baird offing Nelson in the Thames Club.

But then, how could he have known, when the newspapers hadn't got hold of the full story yet?

'So I don't think you'll be takin' over my manor just yet,' said Roy.

Bruno moved swiftly. 'Perhaps not,' he said,

taking from his pocket a length of piano wire. It was around Daisy's neck before she knew what was happening. She could feel it digging into her flesh. He was pulling it tighter and tighter and the customers were screaming and it seemed to Daisy as though this couldn't possibly be happening. But the pain told her it was. It was hard for her to breathe now.

'I've called the law,' shouted the barman.

'I *am* the fuckin' law,' shouted Vinnie, then to Bruno, 'You bastard, let her go.'

'Be calm,' said Roy to Bruno. 'This ain't gonna help none.'

'Get away from me, all of you,' warned Bruno.

Daisy could see the colours blending together behind her closed eyes. She felt herself growing heavy, but she knew if she let the wire take her weight she would hang. She mustn't struggle. Movement would make the wire cut into her flesh all the quicker. She didn't want to die. She didn't want her baby inside her to die.

Vera cried out, 'For fuck's sake do something, someone.'

Daisy opened her eyes and it seemed as though everything began to happen in slow motion.

'Eddie, catch!' she heard Jamie shout.

She saw Jamie throw the closed flick knife to Eddie who, in one fluid movement, caught it, pressed the button locking it in the open position and threw it. It flew threw the air and at first Daisy thought it was coming straight at her but it skimmed past her cheek and embedded itself. From the corner of her eye she could see and feel the handle quivering.

She felt the splatter of something wet against the side of her face, then the tightness left her throat. There was a gurgling sound. Daisy put her hands to her neck and pulled away the wire. The slipperiness of her skin confused her. Was she cut?

She was pulled roughly away from the Italian by hands that were strong and into arms that she recognised. She knew Roy's smell, knew she was safe. She put up her fingers and felt for her wounds. Then she realised the blood covering her face wasn't hers. The crowd was yelling and screaming and jostling, pushing against her.

'It'll be all right now,' Roy said. She saw how grey his skin was, how worry had aged him.

Daisy's head cleared. She looked below her and saw Bruno Pace who was really Gaetano Maxi lying on the floor. His body was writhing and his neck was pumping blood that was fast flowing over the dirty floorboards.

Eddie's knife was embedded in the Italian's throat.

Her son had saved her life.

Then she saw the police bearing down on them. Voices, lots of voices all speaking at once. Statements, they wanted statements. She saw the crowd melt. No one ever wanted to get involved. She saw Eddie across the room and the hand-cuffs slipped onto his wrists. She saw Vera begging for him to be set free.

'It wasn't his fault, he saved her life. It wasn't his fault, he saved her life...' Vera's voice was a never-ending plea.

Daisy tried to push through the crush of

people, who were more confident now and trying to get a look at the dying man.

'I'll go with him,' she heard Vinnie say.

'Can't you sort this?' Roy was asking. Daisy realised it was the first time she'd ever heard fear in Roy's voice.

'This isn't something between me and you, Roy,' came Vinnie's soft reply. 'That fuckin' nutcase behind the bar called South Street nick. These coppers won't let this go away, Roy.'

And she still couldn't get near to her boy. She was being pushed back all the time to where uniformed men were kneeling over Bruno Pace, trying to staunch the blood. There wasn't anything anyone could do.

And she didn't care.

'He killed those women,' she said to nobody in particular.

The handcuffs on Eddie registered in Daisy's brain. Again she began battling through the people.

Her son had saved her life.

'Wait!' The strangled sound came from her throat. Eddie was being led towards the door, the mob pushed unceremoniously aside to allow the police easy exit.

She fought her way towards them and grabbed a blue-coated arm. 'Let me talk to my boy,' she said to the officer. The policeman paused and she threw herself at Eddie, her arms going around him. She never wanted to let her boy go.

'It'll be all okay, Mum. Are you all right?' He was very calm. She nodded.

'We'll get you out. You won't go to prison...'

'Mum,' he interrupted. She looked up into his green eyes. 'Roy and Vinnie can't fix everything. A whole pub full of people saw me throw the knife...' He tried for a smile but she saw the glitter of tears. 'Pretty good shot, eh? You reckon my dad would have been proud...' He couldn't finish the sentence or the act he was putting on for her benefit.

'Come along, lad, can't hang around here all day.'

The copper was pulling him towards the door, away from her. She could see a police van outside.

'Eddie...'

'I killed a man, Mum,' he said. 'I killed a man and now I have to pay for it.'